MW01710207

# Other Books
# By
# Helen Macie Osterman

Song of the Rails

Notes in A Mirror

# Emma Winberry
# and
# The Evil Eye

# A Prequel

Helen Macie Osterman

# Emma Winberry and The Evil Eye

## A Prequel

Helen Macie Osterman

Weaving Dreams Publishing
Watseka, IL

Weaving Dreams Publishing



ISBN # 978-1-937148-14-0

Library of Congress Control Number
2012908102



Cover Art by
Robyn Hyzy

Printed in the United States of America
10 9 8 7 6 5 4 3 2

# Dedication

To the supernumeraries of the opera world.

# Acknowledgements

I am grateful to the members of my writers group, The Southland Scribes, for their input while writing this book; and to John Morton, my first reader.

Thanks to Bill Schendel, former supernumerary for the Florentine Opera in Milwaukee, for sharing his anecdotes while performing onstage.

And thanks to Weaving Dreams Publishing for bringing the prequel to the Emma Winberry series to the printed page. Many fans have asked for it.

# Prologue
# Murano, Italy 14th Century

The old artisan bent over his table molding a glass object with extreme care. Behind him, the oven glowed red hot. He reheated the fragile instrument from time to time to reshape it to the exact proportions he wanted.

An acrid smell rose from the molten glass; he had added a special ingredient known only to a select few. He coughed violently as the fumes irritated his throat, and he spat a glob of green mucous streaked with blood onto the dirt floor.

"Soon I shall be able to leave this hell-hole," he said aloud. He looked down at the festering burn on his arm. He was growing careless.

Finally, he fashioned the last of the objects, set them aside to cool, and gave a sigh of relief. The *Patrono,*_would come soon, and then, with the fat purse of gold, he would leave this place forever.

Finished. Carefully, he packed the objects in a box cradled in straw.

He heard the clop-clop of horses outside. They were here.

Two men in long cloaks entered, their faces set in a grim frown. "Is the order finished?" one of them asked.

*"Si Signore,* ready and secure in this box."

The larger man carefully pulled back the straw, raised one of the objects in his hand and held it up to the light. The spectral colors broke through the fragile glass casting a rainbow of colors on the wall.

"You have done well, glassmaker."

*"Grazie."* The little man stood posturing and rubbing his hands together, anticipating the feel of the heavy purse.

"Now, here is your payment." The man drew his sword from its scabbard and plunged it into the glassmaker's belly.

The man's eyes widened in disbelief as he grabbed himself, felt the burning pain. The blood flowed through his fingers as his eyes grew dim. The last thing he saw was the gates of hell opening to receive him.

# Chapter 1
# 21st Century
# Brookfield, Illinois

Oh God! What a strange dream. I felt like I was in hell. Emma Winberry carefully swung her thin legs over the side of the bed and sat for a moment, her heart pounding, and her breath coming in gasps. She shook her head, and then headed for the bathroom and a reviving shower.

"These dreams," she muttered, "I wish they would stop. First it's shiny glass objects that I can't identify and now the flames of hell." She shivered as she turned on the water and stood for a long time letting the heat and steam wash away the dream. She wrapped her slim, shapeless body in a large bath towel and went down to the kitchen to put on a pot of coffee. Finally she had returned to her own world. She glanced around her comfortable house. It was much too large for one person, but Emma was content to stay in the two story home as long as she could.

Emma hurried through breakfast and waited anxiously for the limo to take her to the airport. She tried to curb her excitement, but she felt like a schoolgirl.

She was on her way to New York to meet her best friend, Gladys Foster. From there they would fly to Naples, for a tour of southern Italy.

The women had grown up together in a suburb of Chicago. When Gladys married Cornell Foster, she had moved to Long Island. Emma married and stayed in her native Brookfield. But through the years, the women had remained fast friends.

She checked the house one more time; the gas on the stove was off; she had turned down the hot water heater. Everything seemed to be in place. As she looked out the window, the limo was just turning into her driveway.

As Emma locked her door, she saw her neighbor, motherly Marie Russo, standing on her porch and waving.

"Don't worry, I watch the house, and have a good time."

"I will," Emma answered as she climbed into the limousine.

When Emma and Gladys saw each other at O'Hare Airport, they were all giggles, like a couple of teenagers.

"Can you believe we're actually doing this?" Gladys asked.

"I've been pinching myself since the limo picked me up," Emma said. "Look at all these people! I wonder where they're going?"

"All over the world, my friend," Gladys said. "It's the only way to travel."

After the trek through security they made it to the gate. The flight to Italy would be a long one, but it gave them time to catch up on each others' families. Then they settled back and tried to read. Lulled by the drone of the plane, Emma was soon fast asleep.

In the Naples airport, they trudged through long lines of security before the long wait at customs.

"If I had known it would be like this, I might have given this trip a second thought," Gladys said. Her round cheeks reddened from the effort.

"Are you all; right?" Emma asked.

"As soon as I lose twenty pounds, I'll be fine. The doctor is after me and, after this trip, I'm on a serious diet."

Emma never had to worry about weight. She had always been thin and, no matter what she ate, never gained a pound.

They reached their hotel, hot and tired. The lobby was fairly modern but retained its Mediterranean flavor. Emma nodded at the rounded arches and colorful mosaics hanging on the walls.

In their small, but comfortable room, Emma plopped on one of the beds. The mattress was not exactly a posturepedic, but, at the moment, she didn't care. Gladys did the same and soon, they were both sound asleep.

After two weeks of getting on and off tour buses, walking up and down hills, in and out of churches, listening to the chatter of various dialects, each unique to the province, Emma and Gladys sat in their hotel room in Palermo, thoroughly exhausted.

"I think I'm about saturated with Italy," Gladys said. The temperature soared while the management apologized profusely for the failure of the air conditioner. The women fanned themselves with no relief. They had traveled from Naples to Pompei and Herculaneum, through the Puglia region and finally, to Sicily.

"Shall we take that side trip to San Guiliermo?" Emma asked. "There isn't much else to do and the famous tenor, Marcantonio Speranza, is going to put in an appearance."

"Ugh," Gladys responded, "ask me later. I can't make any decisions now. I'm wiped out." She resettled her generous frame in the lumpy chair and wiped her face with a wet towel.

The following day the temperature dropped a few degrees and the women decided to take the side tour to the small town where the famous Marcantonio Speranza had been born.

They boarded the bus along with a number of their tour companions and bumped along the poorly maintained road for three hours. When they arrived hot and bedraggled, they looked around and didn't regret their decision. The picturesque fishing village, identical to all the others dotting the coast, looked like something from a movie set.

Peasants shuffled about stringing banners and lights along the main street, their feet scuffing up clouds of yellow dust that refused to settle. Some wore kerchiefs around their necks; others wore worn straw hats. Their shirts clung to bodies coated with sweat-soaked dust, but they didn't seem to mind. They had a purpose.

Three fishermen, their muscles bulging like weight lifters, measured and hammered with hands large and callused from hauling in fishing nets. They busily constructed the marquee to provide a bit of shade for the dignitaries who would help celebrate this day.

"Look at this," Gladys remarked with enthusiasm, "it's so quaint."

Emma was speechless. Her eyes soaked in the scene she might never see again. She took her digital camera out of her purse to capture the images. The women walked through the narrow warrens that led off the main thoroughfare. The stone houses cascaded down the hillside like a natural outcropping.

"Let's get out of this sun," Gladys said. "I'm wilting." She took a handkerchief out of her capacious purse and mopped her brow with no apparent effect.

They went into the church, the center of town life, that hugged the southern corner of the piazza, ancient and crumbling like everything else in the community. On this special day, flowers covered the altar, some already wilting in the heat. Emma and Gladys sat in the ancient church for a while until they felt rested, before going back out into the piazza, eager for a refreshing drink.

The other people on the tour began navigating to the small *trattorias* and *tavernas* lining the main street.

"One more picture," Emma said turning toward a group of small children following the tourists, their hands out in supplication.

The women walked into the nearest *taverna* and Gladys plopped herself into a chair, fanning her face with her hand. "Whew, it must be close to a hundred degrees out there."

Emma sat beside her and looked around, fascinated by the locals. One man in particular caught her attention. His face was a replica of a Roman coin: a hawkish nose, full lips, and an aristocratic bearing; he wore a perennial scowl. Emma was a natural linguist and had studied a number of languages, including Italian, so she was able to pick up bits of the conversation.

"Eh look," the man said to his companion, "all this fuss for the great Marcantonio Speranza." He spat the name in the sawdust on the floor then reached into the pocket of his fashionable slacks, took out a large red handkerchief and wiped his face. He laughed as he flexed his muscles, pulling against the sleeves of his expensive shirt, mimicking the men outside. His clothes were different from those of the peasants. His dress gave the appearance of someone important.

The women had ordered a pitcher of lemonade and gulped down the first glass.

"Umm," Gladys said. "This tastes so refreshing. She looked at her friend. "Why do you have that look of concentration on your face? Can you understand what they're saying?"

Emma held up her hand. "Shush," she whispered. She strained to hear bits of conversation from the nearby table. The two men spoke Italian, not dialect, so she could understand most of it.

"What can you do?" said the other man shrugging his shoulders. "He's a famous tenor for Christ's sake. He comes back to the town where he was born and the people feel honored." He sipped the colorless brandy in his glass, and sat back, apparently unimpressed by the flurry of activity outside.

"And besides, it's the feast of St. Guiliermo. He *is* our patron Saint. Even the town is named after him. They might as well celebrate both at once." He held his hands up as if that explained everything.

"Bah, St. Guiliermo forgot about this town a long

time ago. Nothing has changed in a hundred years. Do you see any tourists here, huh? Only those old ladies over there." He looked toward Emma and Gladys.

Emma frowned at the insinuation. After all she still considered sixty middle-aged. She strained to hear the rest of the conversation.

"There is nothing to see here except old people and old buildings," the man continued with scorn in his voice. "The young ones go to the big cities, Palermo, Roma, Milano." The taller man got up from his stool and paced, mumbling to himself.

"St. Guillierma may have forgotten," his companion said hurrying to the door, "but not these girls coming down the street. See there are young people here. Look at those beauties carrying all those flowers, *che belli figli.*" He ran his hand through his curly hair, waved, kissed his fingers and blew the kiss to the maidens headed for the church, their arms filled with flowers, their hips swaying provocatively.

He put one hand on his hip and, holding his other hand in the air, did a circular dance. The girls laughed and winked, then continued toward the church.

"You make a fool of yourself," the scowling man said.

"And *you* are too serious. Life is short, my friend. Like my ancestors, I live for today." He put his hand on his friend's shoulder.

The scowling man pushed the hand away, downed the *grappa* and watched the dust caress the ankles of the girls as they scurried about, chattering with excitement. "How many will still be virgins when Speranza leaves?" he asked.

"*Paisano,* let go of the past. You can't change it.

Speranza was born with everything, a handsome face, a divine voice, and the women love him. He's a world famous divo. Every opera house wants his name on their billboards.

"You and me? We just sing in the chorus. It's a living. We do okay. That's the way life goes, my friend. We have to accept it."

"Speranza can have anything he wants, and he takes it." The taller one stood still, shaking his head and balling his hands into fists. "Let's get out of this place." He stalked out, followed closely by his friend.

"What were they talking about that grabbed your attention?" Gladys asked.

"Sounds like they both sing in the opera chorus. One of them, the big one with the scowl, apparently hates Speranza. I wonder why. I have a feeling it's more than jealousy." Emma screwed up her face as she contemplated the situation.

"There you go with that 'sixth sense' of yours. Don't make a big deal out of it, Emma." Gladys frowned. "Oh look, there's a procession coming down the street. I think it's Speranza himself."

The women hurried outside and joined the crowds watching. The limousine crawled along, Marcantonio Speranza smiling and waving through an open window.

"No wonder women grovel at his feet," one woman said. "He sure is gorgeous."

But Emma wasn't watching Speranza. She squinted at the two men from the tavern. The scowling one looked at the great tenor. For a moment their eyes seemed to meet. Emma saw the scowling man's hand curl in some kind of sign. He smiled at the startled look on Speranza'a face. The tenor made the sign of the cross and drew back. The window slowly rose shut.

Emma felt a chill run up her spine as she watched the interchange between the two men. Something was very wrong here. She turned away, but the feeling lingered.

# Chapter 2

On her first night home Emma tossed and turned; disturbing dreams invaded her sleep. She sat up in bed, her heart pounding. What a strange dream. I dreamed I was in hell, again, and the scowling man from Sicily was there, too.

Emma's dreams were bizarre, to say the least. She, or someone else, always seemed to be on the brink of disaster just before waking. She opened the drawer of the bedside table and pulled out her journal. As was her habit, she jotted down the salient points of the dream, would look them up in her Dictionary of Dream Analysis. She had been doing it for years but never found anything of any significance. Someday she would throw the whole thing in the trash.

But through the years, her dreams always seemed to precede some disturbing event. She couldn't deny that fact. She remembered the look on the face of the man in Sicily as he communicated his hatred of Speranza. Did that presage trouble?

Since childhood Emma had experienced persistent premonitions, this 'second sight,' inherited from her grandma Lizzie. For Emma, it was a curse. Now at the beginning of her sixth decade of life, she was more than ready to set it aside. She had enough of premonitions and dreams.

"*Guardian Angel*," she said aloud, "*I want to resign. Give this gift to someone else. I've asked you that before, but you ignore me. I repeat, I resign.*"

Emma was a great believer in intervention from the spirit world. Too many things were unexplained, like the time she went downtown to look at Marshall Field's Christmas windows on an unusually cold December day. While walking from Union Station along Madison Street heading East, Emma stopped to look at a display of colorful boots in a shoe store window. As she pressed herself against the glass to get a better look at a buff-colored pair in the corner, she felt someone nudge her off to the side. At the same moment a huge slab of ice fell from the roof of the store, missing her by inches. When Emma looked around, she saw no one, no one of mortal substance that is.

Emma frowned as she adjusted the water in the shower, and tried to push these thoughts from her mind. She anticipated the pleasant afternoon she would spend with her daughter, Sylvia.

"Tell me all about the tour," Sylvia said, her eyes bright, her hands clasped together.

"It was fantastic: the picturesque look of Naples was just like a post card. Of course they took us only through the touristy section. I understand thieves and thugs abound in some areas. Pompei and Herculaneum were especially moving, all those plaster casts of people who suffocated from the ash of the volcano." She shivered. "They must have thought it was the end of the world."

"It *was* the end of their world, Mom," her daughter said. "Where else did you go?"

"We went to Palermo in Sicily and took a side trip to the small town where Marcantonio Speranza was born. It was quaint, but so hot." She fanned herself with her hand remembering the awful heat. She decided not to tell Sylvia about the incident with the chorus members. It was surely nothing, just her vivid imagination.

"Can't wait to see Speranza this season," Sylvia said. "It really is a feather in James's hat, getting the great man to appear at a small opera company like Midwest." She smiled, a look of pride on her face.

Emma broke off a piece of crusty French bread, dipped it in olive oil seasoned with rosemary and garlic and took a generous bite. After she swallowed it, she smiled at her daughter. "You and James are really happy. I can see it on your face."

"Oh yes, Mother, it's wonderful."

Emma studied her daughter's lovely face, so unlike her own which was birdlike with sharp features. Sylvia looked back at her mother with soft almond-shaped gray eyes trimmed with long lashes, the only feature she shared in common with Emma. "I see you're wearing a maternity top."

"Uh huh." Sylvia's face glowed. "Everything was getting so tight. And I really couldn't wait to wear this. It's like telling the world about the wonderful new life growing inside me."

Emma reached across the table and took Sylvia's hand. "I'm so happy for you and James." She swallowed the lump in her throat with a drink of water. For a moment she thought of her husband, Frank, and sighed. She had not adjusted well to widowhood. Then her thoughts turned back to her daughter.

"Now young lady, I know you have something to

tell me. I can see it in your eyes. Out with it."

Sylvia laughed. "I never could fool you. How would you like to be onstage at the opera?"

Emma blinked twice. "What are you talking about? You know I can't sing a note."

"Well," Sylvia continued after taking a sip of her strong espresso, "James said they're looking for more supernumeraries for the season. Thought you might be interested."

Emma's eyes grew wide; her eyebrows arched. "Me?"

"Yes, you. Why not?"

"On the stage of the opera house?"

"Mother, you won't be singing, you know; just standing around in a crowd pretending to be absorbed in conversation, or walking across the stage carrying something—that sort of thing."

Emma was speechless. She had dreamed of singing in the opera all her life. In reality she couldn't hold a single phrase on key. She had tried the church choir, but even she could hear the discordant notes. The choirmaster kindly suggested that her talents could be put to better use elsewhere. So she was relegated to the background, doing odd jobs, using her talent as a seamstress to repair ripped and torn robes, and making cookies for the bazaar.

Now she could actually be on the stage, in front of hundreds of people, dressed in elaborate costumes, an integral part of the production. She was so lucky to have a son-in-law connected with the opera company. "Tell him yes—yes! I'll do it."

"Good. It's too early to start interviewing, but, sometime in September, you'll get a call from the gal in charge of that department. I don't know her name, but James will give her your number."

"Maria, Maria," Emma called to her neighbor, as she gripped the wooden slats of the back fence. She bounced like an excited child, her hair peeking out from under a huge sun hat. She wore cotton white slacks and a long sleeved blue shirt buttoned high at the neck.

"What's the matter? Is the house on fire?" Maria Russo waddled down the stairs wearing an old-fashioned housedress, a patient grin on her face.

"I'm going to be in the opera! On the stage with all the great singers!" Emma clasped her hands to her flat chest melodramatically and closed her eyes. There was no doubt in her mind that she would be accepted. She had to be!

"You gonna sing?" Maria asked, a startled look on her face.

"No, of course not. I'll be an extra, a—a super-num-er-ary." She drew out the word slowly, emphasizing each syllable.

"A super what?"

"A supernumerary is someone who fills up the space on the stage. You know, crowds of people, soldiers marching, mothers with little children. They don't talk or sing; they're just—there."

"How did that happen?"

"Sylvia just told me that they need more extras for the season. They'll be calling me in September." She smiled, still unable to believe it. Would she be able to wait two more months?

"Hmm. You get paid for this?"

"Paid? I never thought of money. The honor of

being on stage with the great ones of music is enough for me."

"Eh?" Maria shrugged her shoulders.

Emma hadn't thought to ask about compensation. It seemed almost sacrilegious. "I don't think supers get paid, and I really don't care. Money doesn't enter the picture."

"And why you wearing that big hat?" Maria asked. "And you're all buttoned up."

"I don't want to get sunburned. You know how my face and arms freckle from the sun. That would never do onstage."

"Well, if you're gonna be in a whole opera, I better fatten you up. You're too skinny. Tonight I make spaghetti and meatballs. I bring you some."

Emma acted as if she hadn't heard a word. She swept off the hat, turned and walked back into the house, her head held high, her arms outstretched, wisps of hair standing out all over, the strains of an operatic overture ringing in her head.

# Chapter 3

Emma could think of nothing else but the coming opera season. She wondered how it would feel to be actually on the stage during a live production. Could she do it? Of course.

But the dreams kept interfering with her thoughts. They invaded her sleep nearly every night. If only I knew what they meant, she thought. She paced the floor, talked to her Guardian Angel, and tried to think of every conceivable reason for the nightmares, but no answer came. Nothing in her dream dictionary gave her a clue.

"Worthless thing," she muttered, casting it aside.

As if that wasn't enough on her mind, her children kept asking her how long she planned to stay alone in that old house. A recent call from her son, Stephen, had particularly annoyed her.

Emma had been on her own since her husband, Frank, died twelve years earlier. She was not ready to give up her independence, yet.

"Oh Frank, you always took care of things, always knew the right time to make changes. I wish you were here to advise me now." It was probably her subconscious mind, but Emma liked to think her husband was helping her from the other side.

"Why can't they leave me alone?" she mumbled.

"After all, folks are still young in their sixties these days. Just because the stairway gets steeper every year and the yard gets bigger and I tripped and fell down a few stairs doesn't mean I'm incapable of taking care of myself." She rubbed the ankle she had sprained. It still ached whenever the weather changed.

She still worked two days a week in a neighborhood bookstore. Yes, her life was busy and she felt fulfilled, didn't she? Now her role as a supernumerary would make it complete.

Emma reached for the phone and dialed a familiar number.

"Hi, Gladys."

"Emma, I was just thinking about you." Gladys' voice had a full robust quality that mirrored her body. "Have you recovered from the tour yet?"

"Just about. It seems so far away already, almost as if it happened to someone else."

"Yep, we get back to our mundane lives and put the exotic memories aside."

"Incidentally," Emma said with pride in her voice, "I'm going to be a supernumerary at the Midwest Opera for this upcoming season."

"Fantastic!" Gladys squealed. "I always wanted to do that, but I'm much too fat. You'll be great, as long as they can find a costume small enough to fit you."

Her hearty laugh brightened Emma's mood. "You're better for me than a therapist, always have been."

"I'll send you a bill. By the way, have you given anymore thought to Cornell's suggestion?"

Gladys' husband, Cornell Foster, was a successful businessman, co-owner of a small publishing company specializing in textbooks and how-to manuals.

Emma knew that sooner or later she would have to give him a definite answer. "Gladys, I may know a lot about opera, but I know nothing about writing. I couldn't possibly write an entire book!" She groaned.

"Nonsense," Gladys said. "All kinds of people write books and I've read plenty of them that should never have gotten past the junior editor. Here's Cornell now, talk to him."

Emma's head began to ache. She didn't need this added burden.

"Hi Emma, I hear my wife is badgering you again," he said in his soothing voice.

"Cornell, I don't know the first thing about writing. I wouldn't know where to start. I'd botch the whole thing." She squeezed the phone so hard her fingers lost all feeling.

"Just listen to me a minute. I've been toying with the idea of adding a new line for quite a while. Opera is really becoming popular with the younger set. I see more and more young people at the Met. I would like to put out a kind of manual, *Opera for Beginners,* something basic. My partner likes the idea, too."

"But why me?" Emma asked.

"Because you can tell it in everyday language that people can understand. I've heard you describe a particular performance, and when you finished I felt as though I had been there.

"I did talk to one of our writers, but what he came up with was much more complex than I had in mind. He wasn't interested in simplifying the material."

Emma let out the breath she had been holding. "Give me some time to think about it."

"That's all I'm asking. Don't take it too seriously. Here's Gladys. She's pulling the phone out of my hand."

"Did my loving husband put your mind at ease? You know, now that you're going onstage, you'll have first hand knowledge of how things really work. By the way, how are you doing with that new computer the kids gave you?"

"We don't talk about that," Emma said reaching for the bottle of aspirin. "You made your point. Now let me sleep on it. I'll talk to you later."

Sleep on it indeed. She frowned as she put down the phone and downed three aspirin tablets with a glass of water. If she wasn't dreaming about danger, she was being chased by a gigantic book, the blank pages opening and closing like jaws. And the computer, humph, she was still in kindergarten with that.

Her family and friends all seemed to be conspiring against her, trying to bring her up to date: a cordless phone that she was always losing, an intricate DVD player that she didn't know how to work, and now the computer.

She shook her head and sighed. I'll give it some serious thought. Even five-year-olds use computers these days. Why not me?

# Chapter 4
# Naples, Italy

Bruno Gentile and Gerard Torana sat in a small *tratoria* on a main street in Naples. The humidity in the air clung to their bodies leaving dark wet stains under their arms and down their backs. Gerard slammed his hand down on the table.

"Why didn't you sign the contract with the Naples Opera Company? Why?"

Bruno looked out at the people ambling by, tourists holding maps, groups of men arguing, their hands waving, women dragging crying children. A dog sniffed around, and lifted his leg against the building. Bruno grimaced and turned toward his companion. "Because I don't want to be stuck in this stinking place for the whole season."

Gerard blew out his breath in a loud snort and shook his head. "Then where will you sing? How will you pay the bills, eh? You want to be a fisherman like your father?"

Bruno shook his head and frowned. "Never! First I go to Venice, on a little business. After that I go to audition in Milano for three performances. They asked for me, said they need a good bass." He puffed out his chest. "And then, maybe—America. They always need singers for the chorus. We talked about going to America, remember? Singing in the big cities: New York, Chicago, San Francisco. Good opera companies. Come with me. We're a good team you and me."

Gerard thought for a few minutes. He frowned and looked at his friend, suspicion in his eyes. "What business have you got in Venice? They're not auditioning at La Fenice. What are you going to do there?"

Bruno held up his hand. "*Pacienza,* I have to do a favor for a friend. This is not your business. Meet me in Milano next week. They're auditioning Thursday and Friday. If we don't get hired, we can always come back to Naples. *D'accordo?*"

"And what about Francesca?" Gerard asked pursing his lips.

"Bah! I told her to find another lover," Bruno scoffed.

"My friend," Gerard said trying to placate him. "She's a good woman. She'll make a fine wife, give you strong sons. Besides, you promised."

Bruno exploded. "I did *not* promise anything! She expected me to marry her. I *never* asked her." He felt those words justified leaving the girl who had been faithful to him since childhood. He shook his head, threw some coins on the table and stormed out of the *tratoria.*

The sun beat down on Bruno's head as he walked rapidly away from his friend. He needed to think, to plan. He found a cool niche beside a fountain and sat down reaching his hand in the water and splashing it over his face.

Ah Francesca, what would he say to her? He felt a

pang of guilt as he thought about her. As children they had run down to the sea, where they waded in the warm shallows and searched for shells and tiny sea creatures. Many evenings they waited for the fishing boats to come in, dreaming of the future. Both their fathers had just managed to eke out a meager living in this harsh life.

Francesca was a lusty girl, her body a little too fleshy, but soft and yielding. Even as children she let Bruno touch her in private places. It had excited them both. It seemed only natural when they grew older to go farther . . . stolen afternoons in a protective copse of trees . . . moans of pleasure.

Bruno was always careful to wear protection. He knew that his future lay far from this poor village. The last thing he wanted was to be forced into a marriage that would tie him here.

No, Francesca did not belong in Bruno's picture of his new life. He had tried to tell her gradually, so as not to hurt her, but the girl was a stubborn Sicilian and would not listen. Besides, her family expected them to marry. What was he to do about her? How should he tell her?

## Venice, Italy

Bruno felt uncomfortable in the common clothes he had bought from a fisherman. He was used to dressing as a singer, always in fashion, but it was necessary here. Where he was going, he could not call attention to himself wearing fine clothes. He chose to remain an anonymous face in the crowd.

He boarded a boat on Venice's Grand Canal destined for Murano, one of the many islands dotting the lagoon. Since the thirteenth century Murano had been the center of glass production in Italy. The formulas and techniques for making this fine glass were jealously guarded secrets.

Bruno was not interested in the quaint canals and bridges of the island, or in the Venetian-Byzantine basilica. He headed directly to the furnaces and walked into a well-known glass blower's shop. When he opened the door, his eyes widened as he drew in a breath. It was like entering hell. He could see into the back through an open doorway. Heat radiated from the furnaces like a volcano ready to erupt.

Everything was still done according to tradition. Time stopped in the shops of Murano, the same instruments and the same techniques used for the past thousand years. Bruno was not interested in the exquisite goblets and vases still made in the old ways by the *Garzoni*, lackeys, and *Serventi,* trainees, turning white hot glass balls on long poles, expertly rolling, shaping, twisting.

"May I help you, Signore?" a pretty salesgirl asked. He saw by her look at his unkempt appearance that she knew he was not here to buy goblets and figurines.

"I want to see Donato."

"Is he expecting you?"

He smiled, but only with his lips, his eyes narrow and penetrating. He pressed a handful of Euros into her sweaty palm. "Donato. Now!"

The girl disappeared through a side door. Bruno tapped his foot and glanced at a painting on the wall of Saint Anthony Abate, patron saint of glass blowers. He shook his head and snickered, "Superstition."

A few moments later a small nervous man inched

his way through the door. Sweat poured from his bald head onto his dirty collar. He squinted through bleary deep-set eyes.

"What you want?" he asked straightening his bent back and looking suspiciously at the man.

Bruno took a folded piece of paper from his pocket and laid it on the counter. The little man stared at it, looked up at the bearer, and shook his head.

"No, not here. These are not made for hundreds of years. They are illegal. You must know that."

Bruno stood his ground. "How much?"

"I can't do it. I don't have the formula," the man stammered.

"Who does?" Bruno demanded. His eyes narrowed to slits as he took out a wad of Euros and began piling bills on the counter. The little man licked his lips and stared with greedy eyes. He grabbed the money and shoved it in his pocket, leaned forward and whispered.

"Go through the north alley. At the end there's a small furnace where I hear an old man makes special orders. Tell him I sent you."

"*Grazie.*" Bruno turned and left the shop.

He walked briskly to the north alley ignoring the weeds growing along the sides of wretched hovels. A starving dog dug through piles of rotting, stinking, garbage. He saw an old crone look out of a crumbling doorway, stare at him, then pull away, making the sign of the cross.

At the end of the alley, almost hidden by debris, stood an obscure shop with a small furnace in back. All was still. No fire issued from its dark maw. Bruno hesitated for a moment before he walked through the half open door.

"*Buon giorno,*" he called. No response. He walked to the back of the shop and called louder.

A wizened old man crept forward. He was dirty and smelled of sweat, his hands scarred from years of working at the furnace. He rubbed his eyes and frowned, apparently resenting this intrusion into his afternoon siesta. "What? Who are you?"

Bruno held up the paper. The old man squinted, took a pair of cloudy glasses from his pocket, wiped them with a dirty handkerchief, and perched them on his nose. He frowned as he carefully examined the paper, then looked up at his visitor. "Who sent you?"

"Donato."

"Huh, Donato. Why do you want this, Signore? Nobody wants these, too dangerous."

"That is not your business. Can you make it? How much?"

"I can make it. I can't guarantee it will be like the ones from the fourteenth century, but it will do what you want." He hesitated for only a moment. "One thousand Euros."

Bruno's eyes widened. "*Pazzesco,* crazy man. Too much. Five hundred."

The old man shook his head and frowned. "If the *polizia* catch me making this, I could go to jail. I have to pay them to look the other way. Seven hundred."

Bruno reached into his pocket. "Six hundred fifty." He counted out three hundred of the colorful new bills. "This now, and the rest when it is finished."

The old man thought for a moment, nodded and took the money. "Come back in two weeks."

# Chapter 5
# Brookfield

Summer came to an abrupt end with a cold spell in late September. Emma looked out her kitchen window at the drooping tomato plants, the wilted basil, the frost bitten squash vines. She spent the entire afternoon putting her yard to rest. Then she went to the local garden center and bought a large plant of yellow mums to herald the coming fall.

It was too early for the supers to be interviewed, but Emma received a packet of information from Cecily Cunningham, the super captain. As she filled out the required demographic information, she hesitated at the space for her birth date. I can trim off a few years, can't I? Who would be the wiser.

She looked at her reflection in the mirror, just a few wrinkles, no sagging jowls, a sprinkling of gray in her hair. Must do something about that.

Emma made herself three years younger and placed a postage stamp on the envelope with great care. She wanted Cecily Cunningham to see how precise she was. She walked to the corner and slid the envelope in the mailbox with a sigh of satisfaction. Her name was now duly inscribed on the list of folks willing and eager to stand around a stage for hours pretending to be involved in the plot of an opera. Their costumes might not fit properly; their scalps might itch under the ponderous wigs; and, undoubtedly, their feet would hurt from standing in one position for too long. But all Emma could think about were the music, the famous singers, the fabulous stage, the props, the footlights and hundreds of people watching her. The fact that she might be in a corner, unnoticed by anyone never entered her mind. She would be part of the drama and glory of the opera, and that was all that mattered.

The next morning Emma sat at her kitchen table pouring two-percent milk on her cereal of ancient grains with exotic names; spelt, millet, kamut, and quinoa. The morning rays of the sun streamed through the prism sitting on the east window fracturing the light into its soft spectral colors, which danced off the creamy walls, the appliances, and fell in splotches on the white tile floor.

Emma squinted through her thick glasses at the daily newspaper spread across the table. She hadn't yet put in her hard contact lenses. Emma refused to consider one of the new techniques for correcting severe myopia. The thought of someone manipulating her eyes in any way, shape, or form was a daunting prospect.

An article on the second page of the paper caught her attention.

*Last night, in the opera house in Milan, Italy, a heavy backdrop hanging in the fly space of the stage, came loose from its moorings and fell, narrowly missing the famous tenor, Mar-*

*cantonio Speranza. A stagehand was seriously injured when he pushed the tenor aside. Police are investigating, but, at this time, they have found no evidence of foul play. A faulty mounting device was to blame.*

"Oh, what a terrible accident. I hope the stagehand wasn't hurt too badly. What a brave man, to risk his life for Speranza. Could it have been deliberate? Who could possibly want to hurt such a famous man?" Then she remembered the incident in San Giullermo. How many men might hate the great singer? And why? Jealousy perhaps?

"I read about it too, Gladys," Emma said, holding the phone against her shoulder as she stirred the Bolognese sauce Maria had given her.

"I don't believe it was an accident," Gladys said.

"But that's what the newspaper said. Why would anyone want to harm someone with such a great talent?" Emma asked.

"Jealousy, or maybe an enraged husband. You know all the gossip that surrounds the rich and famous."

"I find it hard to believe. How could anyone do such a thing. Oh my, the pasta water is boiling over. I'll have to go now. Talk to you soon, Gladys. Bye."

Emma was eager to hang up before Gladys could ask her about the computer. Stephen had given her a lesson, but she didn't feel anywhere near proficient.

As she poured the linguine into the colander, her thoughts returned to Speranza and the backdrop. No, it couldn't be deliberate, just an accident, like the paper reported.

But something kept nagging at Emma.

The following day Emma walked into the study, a glass of wine in hand. She sat at the computer, looked at it for a moment, then turned it on. She opened a blank page and typed in *Opera for Beginners*. Hesitantly, she began to put down a few thoughts.

*Opera, as an art form, has been around for centuries, ever since man first composed some form of music and combined it with sounds and actions.*

She looked at the words, rather pleased with herself. Now, what would beginners want to know about opera? I should probably list the various kinds of opera, she thought. Let's see: grand opera, *opera seria, opera buffa, bel canto, verismo* … . She stopped — *verismo* — true to life. A number of operas were based on actual events. She remembered the article in the newspaper. Could Speranza be involved in something as melodramatic as an opera plot? Maybe someone wanted to harm him out of jealousy, revenge, family honor? She shook her head. I'm letting my imagination get the better of me. Stick to the facts, Emma Winberry, and mind your own business.

She turned her attention back to the computer, put in a few more sentences. Emma smiled, feeling self-assured. I can do this, she thought, certainly I can. I'll buy a book on writing techniques, there must be one of those for dummies. She promised herself to check on it the next day when she went to work. With a nod of satisfaction, she turned off the computer and walked out of the room.

# Chapter 6
# Milan, Italy

"That was some performance last night, no?" Gerard asked Bruno, a proud grin on his face.

"Yes. We sang well." He leaned back in the chair and looked at the walls of the restaurant filled with pictures of the famous singers who had dined there over the years. Some went back to the beginning of the twentieth century. He visualized his own image there, someday, among the great ones.

"We always sing well," Gerard said. "But I wonder what happened in the third act. That backdrop that fell could have killed Speranza." He picked up the bottle of burgundy-colored red wine and refilled both glasses.

"Too bad the stagehand was hurt, but the newspaper said he will recover," Bruno said, a hint of relief in his voice. "That sanctimonious bastard, Speranza. When we were singing, he looked right through us as if we weren't there." He downed the wine in one swallow, a small rivulet making its way down his chin, like blood.

Bruno remembered the day he and Gerard last sang with Speranza. They were members of the chorus in *Rigoletto*. When the great tenor, singing the role of the playboy Duke of Mantua, sang "*La Donna e*

*Mobile"*, Bruno could hardly contain himself. Speranza was not playing a role, he was portraying himself.

Gerard frowned. "We got pretty good pay for those three performances, don't you think?" he asked trying to steer the conversation away from the famous tenor.

"It was good," Bruno agreed, "but my mother is complaining again. Says she's sick and needs money for doctors and medicine."

"Don't you believe her?"

Bruno shook his head. "No! She's strong as an ox. I've seen her lift fifty pound bags of flour like they weighed nothing." He rubbed his hand over his eyes and sighed deeply. "She wants the money for Angelo."

"How do you know that?"

"I know, that's all. She'll never tell me. She knows how I feel about him." He shook his head and uttered an obscenity. All he wanted was to forget, but they were his family and he had to provide. Why had he been given this burden? Because it was his duty, always duty.

"Are you sending her the money?" Gerard asked refilling the glasses.

"Of course. Do you think I can call my mother a liar?"

"Eh, no, you can't. Soon we leave for America," Gerard said, taking a generous swallow. "That was a good idea you had. I always wanted to go to the United States, but my English is not so good."

"We get by. Lucky we got hired by both Lyric and Midwest in Chicago. We're making a name, eh?" Bruno playfully punched his friend's muscular shoulder.

Singers were usually hired far in advance, but some last minute cancellations had given them the opportunity to sing in Chicago, both in the chorus and in bit parts. The Naples and Milan Opera Companies had given them enthusiastic recommendations.

"In the spring we sing again with Speranza," Bruno said. "I look forward to that, especially *Un Ballo en Maschera.* Maybe Renato will really kill him in the last act." He threw his head back and laughed, but the sound was hollow.

## A Village in Sicily

*"Figghiu miu,* what do you mean you're going to America?" The elderly woman was dressed in mourning black, looked at her son through narrowed eyes, lined with years of hard living.

"Eh, Mama, I am going to sing in Chicago, a great city. You wouldn't want me to miss the chance to be someone important, would you?" He took her hand and patted it gently.

"No, I want you to sing. You have a great voice just like your father. He was a good singer, too."

*"Si,* only he never had the training, was only a poor fisherman."

She looked down at her knobby hands and shook her head. "But who will take care of us?" she whispered, clutching Bruno's hand.

"I'll send money, Mama. Don't worry, I'll always send the money."

The woman brightened and nodded. She reached up and tightened the bun in her white hair. "*Si, figghiu miu,* you are a good son. You always send money. How much?"

Her rheumy eyes looked at him with a cunning he knew so well. He sighed. It was always the same. "Enough, Mama. I will send enough."

"Enough for Angelo?" she persisted, a hard edge to her voice. This time she mentioned the boy's name.

He gritted his teeth and spat out the words. "For Angelo, too."

"And what about Francesca?" the old woman persisted.

"Eh, there is no place in my life now for a woman, Mama. I must think of my career." Bruno felt a pang of guilt. He knew this was a meager excuse.

His mother took his hand in hers and looked into his eyes. "She loves you."

"I know," Bruno said turning away. "But I cannot, not now."

"You will have to tell her. It is the honorable thing to do," she said, her eyes filling with tears.

Bruno nodded. He had wanted to avoid the encounter, but his mother was right. "I go now."

Bruno walked very slowly to the local bakery where Francesca worked. As the oldest of six daughters, her family depended on the added income from her job. Her father had hinted to Bruno many times that he would be happy to have him as a son-in-law. He had no sons of his own, and with six girls, he had stopped trying. Bruno knew that her mama needed Francesca at home. The woman was overworked, as were all these poverty stricken people.

Poor Francesca, short and plump, with her low forehead and round face, her hooked nose and too large sensuous mouth. But he grew excited at the thought of her. She was a lusty girl, and together, they had learned and refined the art of lovemaking. He would miss her.

She looked up from behind the counter as he entered the shop. "Bruno, you're back!" She ran out and threw her arms around him. "I missed you, *mi amore.*"

"Francesca, we have to talk," he said, disentangling himself from her arms. "When can you leave?"

She looked at the clock. "I can go now. Anna, I go now, okay?" she called to her co-worker.

*"Si, si*, go with your sweetheart." The motherly woman walked out from the back, a knowing smile on her face.

Francesca smiled back as she hooked her arm in Bruno's and gave him a playful peck on the cheek.

"We walk," he said.

"How was the opera in Milan?" she asked.

"Good, good." He told her all about the performances, relieved to be on neutral ground.

They walked down to the shore and looked out over the calm sea. The fishing boats were just coming in. Bruno heard the men calling to one another, some singing, others laughing. They must have had a good catch today.

He remembered his own father singing these songs. Until the day his boat didn't return. It was the fate of so many fishermen. He forced his thought back to the present and the task ahead of him.

The shore birds flew around squawking and swooping down to the sand anticipating their share of the catch. Bruno breathed in the familiar smells of salt air and fish. He would miss his community, but not the poverty and lack that went with it.

The water was just beginning to reflect the color of the clouds, pink and lavender tinged, heralding the approaching sunset. It was a peaceful sight.

"Let's sit here," he said motioning to a large rock.

"Remember when we used to come here as children?" Francesca asked. "Our Guardian Angels hid their heads under their wings when we touched each other." She smiled and blushed.

"Eh, we lived in a make believe world then. Things change." There was no easy way to do this. He turned to her. "I'm going away—to America."

Her eyes opened wide. She recoiled as if he had slapped her. "For how long?" she whispered.

"I don't know. I have a chance to become an important singer in America, to make a fine career." He looked out over the sea.

"What about us?"

"There's no place for you in America, not now. Francesca," he said turning to her. "Find another lover, somebody like your father. Get married and stay near your family. They need you." He knew it sounded cruel, but there was no other way to say it. Besides, what he planned might be dangerous. He had no right to involve anyone else.

"No!" She jumped up and glared at him. "You said someday we would get married. You promised!"

He winced at her words. Such a promise was sacred in this part of the world. "I'm thinking of what's best for you."

"No, no!" She shook her head vigorously. "You're thinking only of yourself. I mean nothing to you. I was just someone to play with. You never intended to marry me. Go to America. And I hope the airplane falls from the sky into the sea!" She ran away, sobbing and wailing.

Bruno felt a deep sense of shame. She didn't deserve such treatment. But he couldn't tell her what he had in mind, what he must do. He had another obligation, another promise to keep. Maybe he would come back for her.

No, it was better this way.

# Chapter 7

In early October Emma received a call for the general audition at the opera house. She took a number of deep breaths, clutching the arms of her chair. An audition! It sounded so theatrical. Sylvia had told her, but it hadn't registered until now. What will they expect me to do? Probably just walk across the stage, maybe a curtsy or a bow, certainly nothing of any importance.

After a few more deep breaths, Emma frowned, remembering a play in high school where she portrayed a slave girl. All she had to do was swing her hips as she seductively made her way across the stage carrying a water jug on her shoulder. Emma was so nervous she dropped the jug midway on her journey. It shattered into jagged pieces; water seeped across the stage. She was teased for the rest of her senior year. She had vowed that would never happen again.

"Sylvia, I have to go for an audition. Do you know what that's all about?" Emma clutched the phone, her knuckles turning white.

"I told you about it. I don't think you have to worry, Mother. They just want to make sure you can walk a straight line and follow directions. You can do that."

"Certainly," Emma said. At that moment she was so nervous, she wasn't sure about anything, felt as though she just might walk off the stage into the orchestra pit.

"They put marks on the floor," Sylvia continued. "All you have to do is remember your mark. You'll be fine."

"Hmm," Emma said as she hung up the phone. "I think I can do that." She screwed up her face and shook her head. "All I have to do is remember my mark!"

Two days before the audition, Emma searched her wardrobe looking for just the right outfit to wear. She grabbed one item after another tossing them to the side: a frilly white blouse, a dull beige-colored dress, a green plaid jacket.

"Why did I ever buy that? I remember. It was on sale. Serves me right, green was never my color. Have to buy some new patterns and make myself an updated wardrobe." She looked at the old Singer sewing machine in the corner, unused for too long. She was a fine seamstress in her youth, made all her own clothes because her petite figure was so hard to fit. But after Frank died, she lost interest in her appearance.

She looked in the mirror. "I look downright dowdy." She shook her head. "Well, no more of that. If I'm going to hob-knob with opera singers, I'll have to update my appearance."

Emma shook her head as she scrutinized her figure in the full-length mirror. There were no soft curves, no rounded hips and thighs, just a straight line. She never had anything even remotely resembling cleavage. When she was a self-conscious teenager her mother had called her budding breasts "dingle berries." But the buds never blossomed. They had remained small nubs protruding from her chest. Only when she breast-fed her babies did they enlarge enough to require the support of a brassiere.

She remembered her husband looking at her admiringly. "Maybe they'll stay like this."

"I don't think so, Frank. All my friends said they flattened out after they stopped nursing."

"Well, you can keep lactating, like the cows do," he had said jokingly. "It doesn't matter to me, my dear. You know I've never been a breast man. I love you just as you are."

Emma didn't see any humor in the matter. When she did finish nursing the babies, her breasts returned to their former state of insignificance.

She frowned, then made a monumental decision, one she had contemplated for a long time. She ran a brush through her unruly hair, picked up her purse, slipped into her long trench coat, plopped a hat on her head, walked out the door, and into the garage.

She climbed into her ancient Cadillac that had been sitting for too many years. The thing was a monster and drank gas like a camel filling up at an oasis. That was the name her son had given it years ago, the old Camel. Her children begged her to get rid of it, but Emma wasn't ready.

She backed out of the garage, looked around cautiously, and headed for a nearby shopping mall. Traffic was light, but Emma was always nervous behind the wheel. After three blocks she noticed a police car following her, its red light flashing. Oh Lord, I don't think I was speeding.

She pulled over to the curb, rolled down her window, and smiled at Officer O'Grady as he came up to her.

"Good morning, Mrs. Winberry," he said doffing his cap.

"Good morning, officer. What can I do for you?" Emma asked, an innocent expression on her face.

"How fast were you driving?" he asked trying to look stern.

"Was I speeding? I always try to stay well within the speed limit."

"More like well *below* the limit," the officer said. "I clocked you at fifteen miles an hour. I think we've been through this before. It's just as dangerous to drive too slow as too fast."

"Oh dear," Emma sighed. "I did it again. I will try to do better, I promise." She turned her huge gray eyes to him with such a look of innocence that he covered his mouth to hide the grin.

"You did promise the Captain that you would ride your three wheel bike, didn't you?"

"I do," Emma said emphatically. "When I go to the grocery store and ride around the neighborhood. But now I'm on my way to the mall. There are a few items that I absolutely *must* purchase." She placed great emphasis on the must.

"All right," Officer O'Grady said, "but keep your speed to at least twenty miles an hour. Can you do that?"

"Certainly." Emma nodded, pulled away from the curb, and gunned the engine. In her rearview mirror she saw the officer grimace and shake his head as she took off with a bounce, and slowly resumed her crawl down the street.

Emma walked through the crowded mall looking for just the right store. It was a school holiday and teenagers sauntered along flirting with one another. One clothing store followed another, the mannequins dressed in tight fitting jeans and skimpy tops. Why do young women think it fashionable to show a navel? Now they even put rings in them. What can they possibly be thinking?

She spotted a new store advertising the latest CDs and DVDs. On a whim, she walked in. There was a small classical section, the rest of the racks touted country western, jazz, rock, all the things young people were interested in.

She walked up to the desk and looked at the girl with spiked hair and a dagger-like piece of hardware sticking through her eyebrow. Emma winced. "Do you have the latest CD of *A Masked Ball* with Marcantonio Speranza in the title role?"

The girl looked at Emma as if she were speaking in tongues.

"It's an opera."

"Oh, just a sec." She disappeared to the back of the store and soon an older man came forward. He must be the manager, Emma thought.

She repeated her request as the man punched the information into the computer. I must learn to do that, Emma thought. It looks so easy.

"We don't have it in stock, but I can order it for you."

"Please do." Emma gave him her credit card. "And can it be sent to my home?"

"Certainly." He wrote down her address and gave her a receipt.

As Emma walked out of the store, she gritted her teeth and looked around. On her left she spotted Fredrick's of Hollywood. She averted her eyes from the blazing red teddys and lace garter belts hiding little of the plastic mannequins. Two boys pointed at them and laughed. Emma blushed as she overheard their remarks.

She hurried along spotting Victoria's Secret. The lingerie in the window was a little more tasteful. She would probably find what she wanted in there. After all, she reasoned, if Victoria had a secret, so could Emma Winberry.

"Frank, I know you wouldn't approve of what I am about to do, but, sorry, I'm tired of the way I look," she muttered as she walked into the store.

"May I help you, Ma'am?" a shapely young clerk asked.

"I need a bra," Emma said softly.

"What size?"

Emma hesitated, and felt her face flush as she whispered, "One that makes me look a little — bigger."

"Oh, a padded bra." The clerk led her to a rack with a sign that touted the 'Miracle Bra.' "This is our most popular seller." She took one down and showed Emma the generous padding in the cup. "This will make you look much larger, I guarantee it."

"I'll take one," Emma said feeling that everyone in the store was staring at her. "I'm not sure about the size."

The clerk led her into a fitting room and measured her chest. She took a bra off the rack in the section marked small. "This should fit. Do you want to try it on?"

"No, no. I'll take the black one."

"Is there anything else I can get for you?"

"Maybe there is." Emma got close enough to whisper in the girl's ear.

"Sorry, we don't carry those. Try Fredrick's of Hollywood."

Emma nodded, paid for her purchase, and hurried out of the store. She walked back and forth, hesitant to go into that place. The teen-aged boys were gone and no one else was peering in the window. This entire business was so embarrassing. Finally she pursed her lips, clenched her fists, and walked through the door. Fortunately there were no other customers at the time.

"May I help you?" asked another curvaceous clerk.

"I need, umm, I need something to enhance my figure."

"What part of your figure, Ma'am?"

"My backside," Emma whispered.

"Sure. We have the invisible 'Fanny Panty.' Here, let me show you."

She led Emma to a rack at the rear of the store where panties in various colors hung on individual hangers. "See, there are two pockets in the back holding removable pads. They do wonders to enhance the curves. We even have this one with pockets on the sides, as well."

Emma looked around, to make sure no one had entered the store. She felt her face flush again. "I'll take the first one," she said without making eye contact.

"Did you want a black one?" the clerk asked.

"They come in small, medium and large. I think a small should fit you."

"Fine." Emma paid for the panty and asked the clerk to put it in the Victoria's Secret bag. Then she hurried out the door.

The mall was more crowded now, filling up with mother towing small children. Head down, Emma made her way to the parking garage. She felt as if everyone knew what was in her parcel. She was perspiring by the time she reached her car. The speedometer registered two miles over the speed limit all the way home.

# Chapter 8

Nate Sandler stood looking out the window of his condominium on Lake Shore Drive. From the east he had an unobstructed view of Lake Michigan. He enjoyed sitting on the balcony in summer watching the sailboats and excursion vessels. Stormy nights excited him: dark clouds rolling in, the wind bending trees, waves crashing against the shore. On clear nights he watched the heavens, identifying all the constellations he could recognize.

To the south lay Navy Pier with the fifteen-story Ferris wheel continuously moving. He was just able to make out the visitors and tourists scurrying along the pier, running in and out of theaters and eateries like ants busy in the hive.

On the Fourth of July and other momentous occasions, Nate had a front row seat for the fireworks displays. He had paid dearly for this view and never regretted it. He loved the city with its excitement, the opera houses, the many theaters and museums, the fabulous restaurants, the ethnic milieu. He vowed to stay here, always.

In his huge walk-in closet, Nate closely examined his tie rack trying to decide which of the thirty-plus ties to choose. He grabbed one festooned with musical notes, frowned, and decided it was too gauche. He picked up another splashed with impressionistic colors and shook his head. What made him buy *that one*? After a minute of indecision, he chose a navy blue with tiny red dots, put it around his thick neck, and deftly tied a Windsor knot. It added just enough color to light blue shirt, the navy slacks and his favorite sport coat, a dark blue silk with a muted red thread running through it.

Nate chose his clothes with care, liked expensive things, the way they felt, and the way they looked. He was not a handsome man, a little thick around the waist, his hair thinning at an alarming rate. He knew he needed all the help he could get.

He was on his way to the audition for supernumeraries for the Midwest Opera Company housed in the Lakeshore Center for the Performing Arts. It was an old theater building built at the turn of the twentieth century along Chicago's picturesque North Shore of Lake Michigan. In the 1960s a philanthropist purchased the building and completely refurbished it, naming it for the local theater groups, choral, and symphony fledglings that took advantage of its wonderful acoustics. With the resurgence of interest in classical ballet, a new resident company staged three first rate productions a year. Nate never missed a performance.

He was delighted when, ten years earlier, a wealthy financier provided the backing for the Midwest Opera Company. Nate had been a supernumerary ever since. He knew the audition was just a formality, but he enjoyed watching the new folks, their nervousness, their awkwardness, their sense of awe at the prospect of being part of an opera performance.

He wondered if that sensuous red head would be

there again this year. She had flirted, let him know she was interested, but she was a little too buxom for his taste and much too forward. Perhaps she had slimmed down since last year.

Nate liked women, enjoyed their company, liked the feel of soft skin under his hands, the sound of their laughter. But he tired quickly of most of the women he met. A few dates, perhaps a night or two in bed, but no intellectual conversation, no real communication, soul to soul. The ones he had dated who were intellectually stimulating were not sexy enough for him. He never had found all he wanted in one woman, but, ever the optimist, he kept looking.

# Chapter 9

Emma arrived at the opera house a half-hour early. She hesitated for a moment before going in, as if she were waiting for permission. A woman at the entrance nodded to her; a man smiled. Were they staring at her newly acquired figure? She did like what she saw in the mirror. For a change, her breasts poked out the front of her rust-colored wool sweater with more than an apology, and her tweed skirt hung seductively over her enhanced backside.

A gust of wind off the lake pushed her through the door. Emma tried to smooth her hair, but unruly strands stuck out behind her ears. I should have worn a hat, she chided herself. But few women wore hats these days. She would stand out from the others, and she certainly didn't want that. She smoothed it back once more and looked at the letter in her hand — Room 110.

A few people had arrived ahead of Emma, two women and three men. Most were dressed conservatively. She was glad she had chosen the skirt and sweater. Emma nodded, took off her coat, and sat down.

"Has anyone ever done this before?" a heavy-set woman asked. She sat forward in her chair, hands clasped tightly on her knees.

Emma shook her head, as did the other woman and two of the men.

"I have," said the third man. He was sitting back, one knee crossed over the other, his foot keeping time to a beat only he could hear. He exuded an air of nonchalance.

Emma looked at his round head, balding, except for a fringe of white hair around the base. Rather large ears protruded from each side. He had eyes like an owl and a slightly hooked nose. A friendly sensual mouth and a deeply cleft chin balanced the more severe features. All in all she thought it a notable face.

"Nate Sandler," he said, nodding. "I've been a super ever since Midwest started."

"Why do we have to audition?" the heavy-set woman asked, obviously uncomfortable in the straight-backed chair.

Nate laughed. "They just want to make sure you don't trip over your own feet. The stage manager and the super captain will both be here today. They'll have us walk and stand and follow simple directions. Nothing to it." He clasped both hands over his knee, a smug expression on his face, obviously enjoying his superior position.

Emma fidgeted, wondering if she was cut out for this role. She felt uncomfortable. The man with the owl eyes kept looking at her, but she tried not to make eye contact with him. More people wandered in and sat down, waiting for direction.

A few moments later a tall slender woman with short red hair curling around her freckled face waltzed into the room. She wore a muted green suit with a purple scarf around her long neck. Behind her walked a gray-haired man wearing horn-rimmed glasses. He could have been thirty or forty-five. A suit designed for someone taller and thinner exaggerated his stocky build.

The woman smiled as the men rose from their seats. She nodded to Nate Sandler. "Thank you all for coming. I'm Cecily Cunningham, the super captain, and this is George Ross, the stage manager. You'll meet Carl Wilcox, the stage director, later. He's the one in charge of the production. He'll tell you all where to stand and what to do."

Emma smoothed her errant locks as she nodded and murmured, "Hello."

"Please sit back and relax," Cecily Cunningham said sliding into one of the straight-backed chairs. "We'll give you a run down on what we expect of you. Then we'll take you out onto the stage so you can get a feel for things. First I had better check my list and see if everyone is here."

She picked up a clipboard that was lying on the desk and quickly scanned the names. The door opened and a man and woman stood for a moment unsure of what to do. "Sorry," the man said. "It looks like we're late."

"Not at all," Cecily Cunningham said. "We were just getting started. Please, sit down and make yourselves comfortable." She read off the names and those present responded with a "here" or a "yes" or simply raised a hand.

"It looks like we have two missing, but they may show up in a bit." She looked at the nervous group and smiled.

"Relax everyone, this is an informal gathering. We, here at Midwest, are very proud of our opera company. In just ten short years a number of wealthy patrons have donated a great deal of money and we're attracting some major stars. I'm sure you have heard that Marcantonio Speranza has agreed to perform his signature role in Verdi's *A Masked Ball.* And, we just learned that the famous soprano, Rosa Finelli, will be singing opposite him."

Emma raised her eyebrows. She knew Finelli was scheduled to sing at the Lyric, but the Midwest, too? How did they ever manage that? She would ask James.

Everyone nodded. Murmuring from the group.

The super captain cleared her throat, and continued. "Our first production, *Die Fledermaus,* will be presented in January, the third Wednesday and Friday evenings with a Saturday matinee. We need supers for the second act." She stopped to make a note on the page. "The second opera, in March, is *The Pearl Fishers* by Bizet. No supers for that one; members of the chorus assume all the roles. Then, for *A Masked Ball* in May, we'll need supers for the ball scene in the third act.

"Now I think I've said enough. George, will give you a general introduction to your duties."

George Ross stood up and clasped his hands behind his back. The gesture pulled his suit jacket across his protruding belly, but he didn't seem to notice.

"As most of you know, supernumeraries are a necessary part of any opera production. They are the folks who fill up the stage with crowds, soldiers, peasants, and all that. You will be required to be at rehearsals and all the productions. It can get tiresome waiting around for your part, which may not come until the last act. But we will provide a comfortable room where supers and other cast members can relax.

"You will have to fit into stock costumes, wear wigs and sometimes heavy makeup."

Emma squirmed at the thought of so much fussing, but she relaxed as she visualized herself changing from a lowly caterpillar into a magnificent butterfly. She envisioned herself as tall and regal wearing a fancy ball gown with layers of petticoats underneath; on her head a white wig with large curls hanging down the back, perhaps an elaborate fan giving her the look of a coquette.

The vision melted away as George Ross continued. "This is a general meeting to get you acquainted with the functions of the supernumerary. Auditions for each opera will be announced shortly before the scheduled rehearsals. The staging rehearsals are held after seven in the evening on weekdays and any time on weekends. These are for the purpose of learning when and where you are to be on the stage. Carl Wilcox and I will be there to guide you." He stopped for a minute, poured a glass of water from a pitcher on a side table and took a generous swallow.

"There are piano run-through rehearsals with full scenery, lights, and costumes. These are mandatory." He looked around at the group to make his point clear. "Then there is the dress rehearsal which is exactly like a performance. Needless to say, you must attend.

"We know this is a tremendous commitment of your time, so decide now if you really want to do this. Any questions so far?"

A few people squirmed in their seats. Nate Sandler looked around at the group mentally calculating which ones would follow through and which would drop out. His eyes rested on Emma. He wasn't sure about her, but something intrigued him. She was not attractive, but he liked her figure. It was a little sparse, but she had nice breasts and a nice ass. She definitely drew his attention. Perhaps it was the faces she made. She kept biting her lower lip and grimacing. He found her humorous. She'll stay, and, maybe I'll get to know her. Just then she looked at him with luminous gray eyes rimmed with long lashes and he decided that he would definitely get to know her.

Emma raised her hand hesitantly. "I have a question."

"Yes?"

"What if the costumes don't fit us?"

"Good question," Cecily Cunningham said smiling. "I don't think you need to worry. If they're a little too loose, we either pin them or take them in with large stitches that are easily removed. Most of our problems with fitting are with folks a little too large."

A few titters around the room. Emma blushed, took a deep breath and couldn't help looking at Nate Sandler who was nodding and smiling at her.

"I have a question," one of the men said. "Do we get paid?"

A few eyebrows raised. Emma thought the question in poor taste.

"That's a good point," the super captain said. "Yes, you get $100 for each opera you participate in. I know it isn't much, but it's all we can afford at the present."

"Any more questions?" she asked. "No? All right. Please come with George and me." The group followed them through winding corridors, past dressing rooms, and onto the stage.

"The stage directions are given from the performers' point of view. Keep that in mind when you are told to enter and exit either stage left or stage right," George Ross said.

"It is my responsibility, as stage manager, to call all the cues. I call the singers, actors, and supers, to the stage as well as calling the lighting and engineering cues. I'll be around throughout the entire performance." He made eye contact with each of the hopeful supers.

Emma felt disoriented. She looked out over the vast array of seats doing her best to visualize them full of bodies. How would she feel? Could she actually walk out there with all those people watching her?

George Ross walked to the back of the auditorium and flipped on the stage lights.

"This is what you will see when the performance is in progress," Cecily Cunningham said. "The audience becomes a blur behind the glow of the lights."

"After a while you forget they're there," Nate Sandler whispered to Emma. "Don't be scared. There's nothing to it."

She nodded trying to seem matter of fact, but she gripped her stomach to stop the butterflies.

"Now we would like each of you to walk across the stage and perform a small task," The super captain said. "Everyone stand over here in the wings." She led the nervous group off to the side. "George, will you go ahead?"

"One at a time I want each of you to pick up that pitcher over there, walk across the stage, and put it on the table at the rear. Then go and stand on one of those Xs marked with tape. Mr. Sandler, since you've done this before, why don't you begin."

Nate nodded and proceeded to carry out the instructions. One by one the novices imitated him.

When it came to Emma's turn, she hesitated for a moment, then practically ran across the stage and knocked over the pitcher as she put it on the table. Remembering the disaster in high school, she stood still staring at the floor, her face burning.

"Oh dear," she said.

"Don't be nervous," George Ross said. "It happens to all of us the first time."

Emma walked slowly over to the others and stood on a piece of tape.

Nate whispered to her, "I tripped the first time and fell flat on my face."

She dared not answer for fear she would burst into tears. She bit down on her lip and stared at the floor.

"Good job, everyone. Are there any questions?" Cecily Cunningham asked.

"What are all the huge hanging things up there?" a woman asked pointing upwards.

"That area is called the fly space. Those are scenery backdrops. They can be lowered and raised as needed. That way, as one act ends, the backdrop is pulled up and another lowered in a matter of minutes. The ones up there now are for the ballet."

Emma remembered the newspaper article of Marcantonio Speranza almost being crushed by one in Milan. She shook her head as she stared at the extremely large backdrop hanging right over their heads. There was no way that could happen by accident. Someone was trying to kill the famous tenor, but who and why? Emma felt a chill as she looked again up into the fly space. She shivered before turning back to the group.

Next on the agenda was a backstage tour. The

wardrobe room was crammed with stock costumes owned by the company, racks of shoes tucked in each corner. They came in all shapes and sizes.

"We're fortunate to own quite a number of costumes. The rest we rent from a local agency. Some prima donnas though, like their own special ones," George Ross said. "Many of the stars wear their own shoes and I can't say I blame them. Sore feet could make anyone miss a note."

The heavyset woman giggled as she glanced down at her orthopedic oxfords.

"This room is also shared with the theater and ballet companies, so they keep things here, too. All the wigs are rented," Cecily Cunningham continued.

The next room looked like a beauty parlor. "This is the makeup room. For some operas you may apply your own makeup. For others, it will be done for you. The principal singers are all professionally handled."

They walked into another room where Emma cringed at the sight of swords and sabers, axes and spears hanging on the walls.

"Again we are fortunate to have a good collection of weapons. The theater group uses these, too. They look surprisingly authentic," George Ross said. "Even though they are fake, they *can* inflict damage to human flesh.

"The stars are given lessons to make the fighting look real without hurting each other. Still, some of them get carried away." George Ross smiled at the group. "Some of you men may be asked to carry a weapon, but nothing more."

Emma recalled something she had read, didn't remember where, about some kind of dagger made of glass and the glass objects that kept invading her dreams. That certainly didn't seem very serviceable. She shook her head and looked at the variety of weapons. Nothing came close.

"I think that's enough for today," Cecily Cunningham said. "We don't want to overload you. Thanks for coming in. You'll be notified when the auditions are scheduled for each individual opera. The first, as I said, is *Die Fledermaus* in January. We will need supers for the second act at Prince Orlofsky's ball. If some of you can waltz, it will be helpful."

Nate Sandler looked at Emma and winked. "Do you waltz?" he asked as they filed out of the room and down the stairs.

"I used to. My husband and I danced a lot when we were young."

"And you don't dance anymore?" he persisted.

"No, I've been a widow for a long time. Haven't danced in years." She sighed.

"Well, maybe you'll permit me to rectify that," he said assuming a gallant pose. "We compliment each other in height. Maybe we can do the same on the dance floor. Why don't we discuss it over a cup of coffee?"

Emma hesitated for just a moment. *He's rather forward,* she thought but why not. She nodded. "All right."

Noticing some of the other supers heading for a coffee shop on the corner, Emma and Nate followed. They ordered *cappuccinos* and *biscotti.*

"And," she said, "your last name is? My memory fails me a little too often these days."

"Nathaniel Sandler. It's part Jewish, plus a sprinkling of this and a little of that."

Emma raised her eyebrows and nodded.

He laughed. "If anyone asks what my ethnic background is, I answer either Heinz fifty-seven or thirty-one flavors, depending on how much of a smart ass I want to be."

Emma smiled. He certainly was amusing.

"And what about you, Emma?"

"Winberry," she answered.

"That's a melodious name," he said. "Win-ber-ry. I can visualize you in an English garden carrying one of those baskets on your arm, collecting exotic flowers."

Emma laughed. "You do have an imagination. I have a small garden in my backyard, but nothing exotic: roses, zinnias and a few snapdragons."

They talked about their families and their lifestyles. Nate told her he was divorced, had two grown children living out of state, and that he lived in a condo on North Lakeshore Drive.

She told him of her house in Brookfield and her children. Neither mentioned age, but she presumed by their conversation, that they were in the same age bracket.

When Emma checked her watch, she was surprised at the time. "There's a Metra train in a half hour. I had better get to the station."

He frowned. "I can drive you home. I live just four blocks from here. We can get my car in a few minutes."

Emma thanked him but decided it would not be appropriate, but he insisted on waiting at the bus stop with her until a bus came headed for the station. When he said goodbye, she turned for just a moment and thought he might have blown her a kiss.

She smiled. Strange man. Kind of forward, but nice, and he made me laugh. It had been many years since a man had paid attention to her. A warm feeling settled over her as she sat back and waved goodbye.

Nate watched the bus recede into the distance. What an interesting woman, not pretty, definitely too skinny, and a little klutzy, but a great conversationalist. And those eyes . . . They radiated a deep intelligence and, perhaps, something more? Yes, she was definitely a woman he wanted to get to know better.

# Chapter 10

As excited as Emma was at the prospect of being a supernumerary, she couldn't get the thought of danger out of her mind. What is it that's bothering me so?

She punched down the bread dough with renewed vigor. Someone has a vendetta against that tenor, I feel it. But who? And why? And what can I do about it? With a sigh she put the dough in a bowl, covered it with a dishtowel and set it on the counter to rise.

At breakfast that morning, while reading the newspaper, she saw an article about another near miss in Naples. During a performance of *Rigoletto*, Speranza had tripped on a loose step and sprained his ankle. Only the intervention of another singer had prevented a more serious accident. How can these both be coincidences? Some folks are accident prone, but I have a feeling something is seriously wrong.

*Guardian Angel, what can I do about it?*

*Wait and see,* the inner voice said.

Emma sat in her favorite chair, screwed up her face and thought. Maybe it's another singer. What if I can find out who was in the cast of those two operas, in Milan and Naples, where the so-called accidents happened? But how can I do that?

If I ask Sylvia to present my dilemma to James,

they'll both think I'm loony. Hmm . . . If I remember correctly some of the members of the Lyric Opera Chapter went on an opera tour recently. It was shortly after Gladys and I returned from Italy. Maybe they went to those two performances. No harm in asking. And what about those two men in Sicily? One of them certainly hated the famous tenor.

Emma searched the small address book issued by the chapter. There were a number of these chapters in the Chicago and suburban area. Their main purpose was fundraising for the Lyric, Chicago's premier opera company. Emma enjoyed the regular meetings, the speakers so knowledgeable about various singers and legendary performances. One of the members was a well-known authority. Maybe he could help her. But what was his name?

Emma decided to call the president of the chapter and ask her if anyone had the playbills from the operas on the tour. That way, she reasoned, she could compare the casts and see how many singers appeared in both performances.

*Singers frequently perform together*, her inner voice said. *That will prove nothing.*

"It might give me a clue," she said aloud. "These dreams mean something and I intend to find out what that something is."

After she put two loaves of bread in the oven to bake, Emma punched in the phone number of Joy Devon, the chapter president.

"Hello, this is Joy," a melodious voice answered.

"This is Emma Winberry. I'm a member of the chapter."

"Of course. How are you, Emma?"

"Fine thanks. I have an unusual request to make."

She hesitated for a moment.

"Yes?"

"I'm looking for the playbills from the opera tour."

"May I ask why?"

"Well, I'm doing a little research to see how often some of the famous singers perform together. You see, I'm trying to put together an outline for a book I've been asked to write." Is she buying this? Emma wondered. It sounded a little far-fetched.

"That's impressive. Let me see who went on that tour. I'll have to get back to you."

"Thanks very much." Emma gave her phone number and a cheery goodbye. At least it's a start, she thought.

She took out a pad of paper and wrote a heading.

**Investigation**

1. Find out who's consistently in the cast with Speranza.
2. Find a link between them.

Emma had no idea how she was going to accomplish this task. It was a challenge. She felt like a sleuth, one of the ordinary women she read about solving mysteries, sometimes accidentally. It gave her a tinge of excitement. She put the pad in her top desk drawer and went to check on the bread.

# Chapter 11

"Emma," Maria called out the back door waving to her friend.

"*Ciao,*" Emma answered.

"How is the opera star?"

Emma had put all thoughts of dangerous portents out of her mind as she waited for a call from Joy Devon. "It's so exciting," she said waltzing to the fence. "I went to an audition and I'm probably going to be in *Die Fledermaus* in the middle of January."

"What kind of opera is that?" Maria asked as Emma did a graceful turn around the fence post.

"It's light and funny with beautiful music and lots of waltzes. I'll be in the second act at a fancy ball at the home of a prince. In fact, I may do a little dancing, myself." Emma looked pleased at the thought.

"Who you gonna dance with?"

"One of the other supers, a man named Nate Sandler. We've been practicing," she said feigning an air of nonchalance.

"Uh huh." Maria raised her eyebrows. "Is he nice?"

Emma shrugged concentrating on Maria's question. "Nice enough. He took me out to dinner and then to a club. A band played some of the old time songs that Frank and I used to dance to. It felt so good." Emma clasped her hands and looked off into the distance. For a moment she relived the big band sounds of Glenn Miller and Artie Shaw in the quiet ambience of the old fashioned dance hall. They had waltzed, done the fox trot, some jive, and even a Polish hop. Emma felt young again. She followed Nate as if they had danced together for years. When the band played Stardust, he held her close and hummed in her ear. The scent of his after-shave was subtly masculine, and Emma had found herself taking a deep breath. She felt stirrings deep inside that she hadn't felt in years.

"Do I see stars in your eyes, neighbor?"

Emma shook her head. "No, we're just friends."

"Sure, with friends you don't get that look."

"What look?"

"You know what I'm saying." Maria studied her friend critically. "Can I get a ticket?"

"But I thought you didn't like opera."

"If you're in it, I want to go, even if I don't understand what they're saying."

"Now they have supertitles," Emma said.

"What's that?" Maria looked puzzled.

"There's a screen above the stage and they project the words on it."

"In English?"

"Of course in English." Sometimes Maria was impossible.

"Eh," Maria said shrugging her shoulders. "I try."

Emma smiled visualizing her friend sitting through a three-hour performance. "I'll see that Sylvia gets you a good seat. Now I have to go shopping for a new dress. Nate is taking me to the Lyric Saturday night." She gave Maria a sheepish look.

"Oh, it's Nate, and a date. What you gonna see?"

Emma studied her fingernails making a mental note to get a manicure while she was downtown. "It's an opera by Handel. There's a new counter-tenor performing and he's supposed to be great."

"What's this counter-tenor? I never heard of that." Maria looked puzzled.

"It's a male singer who is able to bring his voice up into a high register so that he sounds like a woman. You know, years ago, when this opera was written, women weren't allowed to perform on the stage, so the men sang the women's roles."

*"Madonna mia."* Maria clasped her hands around her drooping jowls. "I thought they didn't do that no more!"

"Do what? Why are you getting so upset?"

"You know," she answered, embarrassed.

"No, I don't know." Emma was becoming annoyed; the woman could be exasperating.

Maria whispered, "Cut off the balls of little boys so they sing soprano."

"Oh God!" Emma burst into peals of laughter. "Maria, they don't castrate boys anymore. They did that centuries ago. Today families don't sell their boys to become sopranos."

"Are you sure?" Maria asked.

"Yes, I'm sure."

*"Grazie,"* she said, heaving a sigh of relief.

"The counter-tenors sing in a falsetto voice. I've heard them in recordings, but never in a live performance. It should be interesting."

Maria shrugged her shoulders and shook her head. "I don't understand. Go buy your dress and have a good time."

Emma dialed a familiar number waiting impatiently for an answer.

"Gladys? I auditioned for *Die Fleidermaus*. This is like a dream come true." Emma still couldn't believe it.

"Terrific," Gladys answered. "What are they going to do about the costumes?"

"Well, I bought some new lingerie, you know those with—figure enhancers?"

Gladys laughed with a loud guffaw. "Remember when I had my breast reduction? I offered you some tissue, but you refused."

"Silly, you know that's not how it's done."

"You know my youngest daughter is built just like me. She keeps telling me she's going to have her boobs bobbed one of these days." More laughter.

"There's something else I have to tell you. I met a man, a fellow super. He's nice, witty, and a great dancer."

"That's wonderful, but why do you sound hesitant?"

"I'm feeling a little guilty, like I'm being unfaithful to Frank." Emma grimaced and bit her lip.

"Listen, my friend, there's nothing better than a warm loving relationship. It's time to move forward. Frank has been gone a long time. He would want you to be happy, so go for it!"

Emma bit her lip again, this time so hard that she tasted blood. "He calls me his little Sparrow, like Edith Piaf, that French singer during World War II."

"That's so romantic!"

"Right now I have to be careful and try not to read anything but friendship into this relationship, at least, not yet."

"There's something else, isn't there?" Gladys asked. "I can hear it in your voice."

Emma groaned and let out a deep sigh. "Lately I'm afraid to go to bed at night because of terrifying dreams."

"You're still having them?"

"Yes, and they're getting more specific. In my dream, Marcantonio Speranza is in danger, but if I tell that to anyone but you, they'll think I'm crazy."

"Well, you have to admit, you are a little out of the ordinary."

"See, even you, my dearest friend, thinks so," Emma said, hurt by Gladys' words.

"What can you do about it?"

"I don't know, but I'll think of something."

"Okay, keep me posted. I'm starting to worry about you."

When Emma took in the mail a few days later, she noticed a catalogue from Triton College. She usually threw them away without a cursory glance. After all, she was not going to college at her age. She had a degree in Liberal Arts. "Useless thing," she muttered. It hadn't prepared her for anything specific. "It will broaden you," her mother had said. "Make you well rounded."

"Nothing ever made me well rounded," Emma said, glancing at her reflection in the mirror.

She sat down in her favorite chair and sorted the mail, most of it advertising, offers for credit cards with fabulous perks: air miles, free gasoline, cash back. Emma shook her head and deposited those in the recycle pile. The few bills she placed on the end table. And there was the catalogue. It was not the regular one of all the credit courses, but a short four-page flyer of evening, weekend, and non-credit classes. "It won't hurt to take a look."

She scanned the listings and shook her head at all the computer classes, then ran her finger down the alphabet. There it was, staring at her, almost daring her to read the course description.

Computer Basics: Four Weeks, Wednesdays, 7-9PM. November 1-22. $100.00

That's it! I'll take a course, learn to use the damn thing, surf the net, as they call it, and, perhaps, learn more about Speranza.

The four weeks passed quickly. As it turned out she didn't have to tell anyone about it. She knew her children would tease her, but, on the other hand, they might be proud.

She didn't feel exactly competent, but she had lost her fear of the blank page and actually put down a skeletal outline of the proposed book. The book she had bought, *An Introduction to Creative_Writing,* was very helpful, had given her confidence.

Perhaps I'll discuss this project with Nate after the holidays. He did tell me he writes for an investment magazine. He might be interested in getting involved.

*Is this a way to intensify the relationship?* the inner voice asked. She wondered.

The following day a call from Joy Devon brought the Speranza dilemma back in full force.

"Sorry it took me so long to get back to you, but I had difficulty contacting Alonzo Duncan. He was out of town, but he went on the opera tour and saves every playbill from every performance. He has stacks of them."

"Stacks?" Emma envisioned playbills piled to the ceiling.

Joy laughed, a tinkling sound. "He's a bit eccentric. He said he'd be willing to lend you some, and he stressed the word lend, as long as he gets them back without any damage."

"Of course," Emma assured her.

"Which ones are you interested in?"

"Perhaps I should start with the ones from the tour and those covering the previous six months. That way I can check the casts and maybe come up with some general statements." The woman is going to think I'm really balmy, Emma thought, but it's worth a try.

"All right. I'll ask him to bring them to the chapter meeting. Let's see, that's next week. Will that be soon enough?"

"Just fine," Emma said. "I'll see you then."

After Emma placed the phone back on the charger, she fixed herself a cup of tea and sat in her favorite chair. "*All right, Guardian Angel, I guess that was a reminder that I can't abandon my quest. I wish I had never heard of Marcantonio Speranza. I wish I didn't have this . . . gift. Oh well, that old song about wishing will make it so was certainly a fallacy.*"

*Don't be such a skeptic,* the inner voice said. *Didn't you always wish to be on the opera stage? Now that dream is coming true with a mystery to solve as an added bonus.*

Emma sighed. "You win. I accept the challenge."

# Chapter 12

The chapter meeting took place two weeks before Thanksgiving. Alonzo Duncan seemed reluctant to hand over his 'treasure' to Emma, but she gave him her most gracious smile and did a little eye batting. She assured him she would return them right after the holidays. He frowned as he handed them to her wrapped in heavy brown paper.

Thanksgiving came and went. With shopping, Christmas cards, and baking, Emma put all thoughts of writing aside. She had just finished the class. Promised herself to continue the investigation after the holidays.

She hung wreaths of holly and pinecones around every window and doorframe. Evergreen sprays lying on the window seats filled each room with the scent of balsam. She stuck cloves into oranges and tangerines and tucked them near the radiators adding the tang of citrus to the air.

The sounds of Christmas Carols filled the living room and echoed from speakers in the kitchen. Emma rolled out piecrust to the strains of "O Little Town of Bethlehem." Cans of pumpkin and mincemeat lined the countertop waiting for their turn to become part of the feast. Kitchen towels with Santa Clauses and Christmas Trees hung over the rod near the sink. A bar of soap with green and red faux fruit sat in the dish. No one would use it, of course, and Emma would carefully wrap it in foil, put it in a cupboard and display it again next year.

A real tree stood majestically in the living room, the angel on the top branch sat an inch away from the ceiling. Her son, Martin, and his girlfriend, helped her pick it out.

"Mom, this one's too tall," Martin had said. "It'll hit the ceiling."

"No, it won't," Emma answered. "It's the same size I buy every year." She noticed the girlfriend studying her fingernails and twisting her body from side to side itching to get away. Emma frowned. "I want this one."

"Okay." Martin shrugged. "But I still say it's too tall."

After he put the tree into the stand, he smiled sheepishly at his mother. "You were right. It's perfect."

"I'm usually right," Emma said, looking at the girlfriend, who was inching toward the door. If only she could tell him what a mistake this girl was, but, hopefully, he would find that out for himself.

She sent them on their way and proceeded with the trimming. Some of the ornaments were as old as Emma herself. She handled each with tender loving care, never let anyone else touch them. She loved all the tasks associated with Christmas and performed the ritual every year.

When she placed the last pie in the oven, Emma was tempted to read over the playbills. They lay on her desk and seemed to call to her every time she passed the study.

But she had promised to take some cookies next door to Maria. Better do it now. Five tins sat stacked in a corner on the kitchen counter top. Emma grabbed the top one, slipped on a jacket, and closed the door behind her. She didn't hear the phone as she walked carefully down the steps, grasping the railing. A thin sheet of ice had taken residence over night. The sun, beginning to warm the air, would soon turn it to slush.

"Ah, Emma, *buon giorno.* You're out early," Maria said ushering her into the warm hallway.

"I brought you some cookies to take to your daughter's for Christmas Eve dinner tonight." Emma always suppressed a smile as she looked at Maria's living room. "Are you ever going to take those plastic covers off the furniture?" she asked, knowing the answer.

"Eh, when I have company they sit on the couch and get it dirty. This way, it looks just like when I bought it." Maria nodded in satisfaction.

Emma smiled at the wallpaper mural of Roman ruins behind the flowered sofa and the traditional Italian lamp sitting on an ornate table in front of the picture window, a half-dressed nymph holding up the fringed shade.

"Come in the kitchen," Maria said. "Have coffee."

"Just for a minute. I have pies in the oven."

The two women chatted about family, gifts, and Christmas dinner.

"What about your boyfriend?" Maria asked.

"My boyfriend?"

"That Nate somebody from the opera. Don't pretend you don't know who I mean."

Emma dunked a *biscotti* into her coffee and took a

bite. "First of all, we're just friends, and second, he's gone to Florida to spend the holiday with his son's family. Why do you ask?"

"Umm. I was just wondering, that's all. Do your kids know about him?" Maria raised her eyebrows.

"There's nothing for my family to know. He's a fellow super and when the opera season is over, I'll never see him again. End of story. Now, I have to check my pies. Thanks for the coffee, Maria, and *Buon Natale.*"

Emma's eye caught the blinking light on the answering machine. "Nobody calls all day, and the minute I walk out of the house . . . ," she mumbled depressing the play button.

"Emma," Nate's voice called. "Sorry I missed you. I'm leaving for the airport in a few minutes and wanted to say Merry Christmas. I plan to be back before the New Year and, if you have no other plans, maybe we can spend it together. Give it some thought. Good-bye."

Emma felt a tug at her heart. She wished she had been able to talk to him. The oven timer and the doorbell rang at the same time. She switched off the oven and hurried to the door.

"Emma Winberry?" a delivery man asked. "Sign here."

Emma signed and took the huge Poinsettia plant from a neighborhood florist. She ripped off the Christmas paper to reveal magnificent white leaves with pink radiating down the center. She blushed as she read the card, and tucked it away in a drawer.

The holiday came and went in a blur of activity. The

house filled with the smell of turkey and sage . . . a champagne cork popped . . . gifts exchanged . . . too much food . . . talk of the coming baby. Stephen and Pat's little girl, Susan, toddled around pulling at the ornaments on the tree and tripping over the boxes. Finally her mother handed her a bottle of milk and the child snuggled amid the colorful Christmas wrappings and fell asleep.

"Mother," Sylvia asked, "whatever happened to the electric train Dad used to snake around the Christmas tree?"

"It's packed up in the attic. If you want it, help yourself. That is, if the others have no objection." Emma looked at Stephen and her youngest son, Martin, who was clutching his girlfriend a little too close.

They shook their heads.

"We don't have room for it," Stephen said. "And we have a girl. You know that your baby is a boy." He smiled at his sister.

"We'll take it next year," James said. "The baby will be old enough to be inquisitive about it then." He looked at his wife who was sitting on the edge of a chair, her belly stretching the fabric of her dress.

"How much longer?" Stephen's wife, Pat, asked.

"Six more weeks," Sylvia answered, the words coming out in a long sigh. "I don't think I can stretch anymore." She groaned. The women empathized with her.

"You'll forget all about the discomfort as soon as you hold that little one in your arms," Emma said remembering the joy of her own babies.

"Mother," Stephen said, "you still haven't told us who sent that gorgeous Poinsettia."

Emma pretended she hadn't heard as she set out a

plate of cookies decorated with colorful sprinkles.

"Mother?"

By now the others were looking curiously at Emma.

"Just a friend," she said, "a fellow supernumerary."

"My friends don't send me plants like that," Martin's girlfriend said in a piping nasal tone.

Emma winced. There was nothing she found endearing about this girl, particularly her voice.

"We're only friends," Emma said trying to sound matter of fact.

"I remember a couple of years ago," James said, "one of the operas sparked a romance between two of the supers. I think it was *La Boheme.*" He looked at Emma waiting for a response.

"James, nothing like that is going on between me and Mr. Sandler. We're going to dance together in *Fleidermaus,* so, naturally, we have to practice. That's all there is to it."

"You didn't tell me you were going to dance," Sylvia said. "I think that's great."

"Don't get excited. The professional dancers and the chorus will be in front. Nate and I will stay in the back."

James winked at Sylvia, at the familiarity Emma insinuated. Sylvia smiled back at him.

"Emma wrinkled her brow. "I heard that Rosa Finelli is going to sing with Speranza at Midwest. How did you manage that?" She looked at James, the question in her eyes.

"That was a real stroke of luck. The soprano we had scheduled had to cancel because of personal reasons. They never tell you just what those reasons are." He raised his eyes and shrugged. "We contacted Finelli's agent and he convinced her that, as long as she was already in Chicago, she might as well add a few more performances. She agreed, which really surprised me. But, as I understand, she's been canceling too many engagements lately. Her agent pretty much laid down the law. Either she appears in public or her career is over." He took a swallow of cold coffee and shook his head. "That's the real reason she agreed to sing at Midwest. There's no love lost between her and Speranza. There was gossip at one time that the two of them had an affair. It ended rather suddenly. It'll be interesting to see how they interact."

"Hmm," Emma said wondering just how much Finelli hated the famous tenor.

"Besides all that, they play one-upmanship. For instance, they both want to stand on the same spot onstage. It's supposed to bring good luck or some kind of superstition. Their voices really compliment each other but all the time they're staring daggers with their eyes." He sat back and laughed.

The word dagger, sent chills up Emma's spine. Just because they dislike each other was no reason to suspect the soprano, or was it more than that? Could she be responsible for the 'so called' accidents?

*Not Finelli,* her inner voice said.

"And," James continued, "she's got hang ups and superstitions galore. Has to set up an altar in a corner of her dressing room and I hear she burns some weird smelling candles shortly before a performance."

"That should be interesting," Emma said.

*It will be more than interesting*, the inner voice said.

Emma frowned and tried to dismiss the thought.

"Ma," Martin said, changing the subject, "how are you doing with the computer?"

The others turned to Emma.

"Very well, thank you. I'll tell you now that I took a course at Triton Junior College and feel quite comfortable with the beast."

"I'm impressed," Martin said.

"Mother, you didn't tell me," Sylvia said, a hurt tone in her voice.

"Do I have to tell you everything? After all, I am a healthy independent adult and still able to care for myself and make my own decisions." She raised her chin and gave them a look that said end of discussion. "Right now I don't want to think about anything but the baby and my role as supernumerary."

Soon they all left and Emma was alone with her thoughts. She was weary, but satisfied to have her family around her. She sat in her favorite chair, the arms a little frayed, a colorful old afghan across her knees, sipping a night-cap of warm milk.

"Oh Frank, it's times like this that I miss you most. You always loved the holidays. I'm trying to keep up the tradition the way you always did. But you won't be here to see our daughter's first child." She wiped away a stray tear. "Oh why did you have to leave me so soon?" Another tear slid down her cheek as she pondered the years gone by, so many happy holidays, so many precious memories.

And what about Nate? Was he just a friend? He indicated he wanted to be more. And what did she feel for him? Why not give it a chance to grow. She would wait and see what the New Year would bring.

And what about her suspicions of danger? Emma felt the nagging fear return as she thought about the coming opera season.

# Chapter 13

Every time the phone rang Emma jumped. The following day was New Year's Eve and Nate hadn't called. Maybe he wasn't back yet. Maybe he had changed his mind. Maybe something had happened to him. She had called his number frequently, but always hung up before the answering machine responded. Initiating the call seemed too forward.

Emma went through her closet a half dozen times examining one outfit after another. If he did call, she wanted to have something special to wear. She settled on a long black skirt with a sequined sweater. It was dressy but not ostentatious. With her 'enhanced figure,' it would look nice. She had bought two new fashionable dress patterns and yards of the latest fabrics, but hadn't gotten around to cutting and sewing yet.

When the phone finally did ring that evening, she had just about given up on him, had decided to begin studying the playbills.

"Emma, it's Nate. Please forgive me for not calling sooner. I didn't have your number with me and I just got back a few minutes ago." He took a deep breath.

"Did you have a nice time?" she asked, trying to sound nonchalant.

"Hectic. My grandson fell off his new bicycle and

broke his arm. That's why the delay. It wasn't a serious break, but he wanted his grandpa with him at the hospital."

Emma smiled as she pictured Nate holding the little boy as the doctor put the cast on. "How old is he?"

"Eight, and full of hell. I'm getting too old for this." He laughed and took another deep breath. "Did you make any plans for tomorrow night?"

"No, I have no plans."

"I just talked to a friend of mine. He can get two tickets for *Shadow's End* at the Schubert."

"On New Year's Eve? What kind of friends do you have?" Emma was amazed. She heard that play had sold out weeks ago.

"You might say, influential ones." He laughed. "We can have dinner first," he continued. "I'll get reservations at Rivers on Wacker Drive, then we'll go to the play. If you wish, we could welcome in the New Year at the Pump Room."

Emma couldn't believe her ears. He had just quoted an evening costing hundreds of dollars.

"Are we on?" Nate asked.

"We're on."

The dinner at Rivers was elegant, breast of pheasant on a bed of wild rice, asparagus spears covered with a heavenly sauce, a salad with spiky looking greens that titillated the taste buds followed by crème brule for dessert. Nate chose a dry white wine Emma had never heard of. It was divine.

The play was all the reviewers had claimed and more, the story a modern version of *Camille*. The heroine was dying of AIDS instead of tuberculosis. Emma cried at the poignant ending as Nate held her hand.

Afterwards they walked into the Ambassador East Hotel and into the famous Pump Room modeled after the one in Bath, England. The Wall of Fame touted photos of celebrities who had dined there through the last six decades.

The small dance floor was reminiscent of the Hollywood supper clubs of the 1930s and 40s. A net stretched across the room fastened to the oak pillars on each side. At the stroke of midnight the Master of Ceremonies cut the rope as balloons and confetti tumbled onto the patrons below.

"Happy New Year, Emma," Nate whispered in her ear. He brushed his lips along the lobe, down her cheek, and found her mouth. The kiss was much more than friendly. She surprised herself by her response. Chills, tingling, goose bumps up her arms.

"I'm growing very fond of you," he said. "I'm feeling things I thought I buried long ago."

Emma didn't answer. She was afraid to betray her own emotions. She just clutched him as they danced cheek to cheek to the strains of "Auld Lang Syne."

A few days later Emma took all the decorations down and stored them for next year. The dreams were back, almost every night. She went into the study and stared at the packet of playbills. She had promised to return them after the holidays. Get to it, she told herself.

Carefully she unwrapped the parcel and laid the playbills on the kitchen table. She searched for the dates of the tour that took place in Milan and Naples and found three different operas for each city.

"Okay. I must go about this systematically." She took her pad and pencil and compared the casts. Marcantonio Speranza sang the lead in four of them, but the other principal singers were different. Only one woman's name appeared twice, in Milan and Naples.

"It can't be a woman," she said aloud. "How could she maneuver that huge backdrop without help?" Nevertheless, she wrote the name down. "Now what?"

*Check the chorus*, the inner voice said.

"Of course, the chorus."

The members of the Milan opera chorus were the same in all productions, as were those in Naples. But when she compared the chorus names of the two companies, she found that two male singers appeared in both cities.

Goose flesh broke out on her arms as she wrote down the names and dates, Gerard Torano and Bruno Gentile.

"Now I'm getting somewhere, but where? And what am I going to do with this information?"

She checked the other playbills for the past six months and the same two names surfaced in Palermo, Sicily, where Speranza, again, sang the lead. The image from San Guiliermo surfaced. Could those two be the same ones she had seen in Sicily? She added that date to her list.

"Now, I must find out if those two are scheduled to sing in Chicago. I'll ask James to get me the names of the cast, including the chorus. What reason shall I give him? I can't say that I have a premonition, that these two men send a chill up my spine. I'll tell him the same thing I told Joy Devon, but he may not be so easily convinced. I'll just have to cross that bridge when I come to it."

Emma took a few notes to add to the outline of the book she was attempting to write. They might be useful. She repackaged the playbills and, with a note of thanks, walked to the post office and sent them back to their owner.

She called James the following day, but he was out of the office. Emma left a message to call her, but nothing urgent. When he called back a few days later, Emma repeated her request, citing the book as the reason.

"I'm tied up right now, Emma, but give me your e-mail address and I'll have my secretary send you the lists."

He didn't sound surprised, and Emma sighed in relief. She knew her family and friends had learned to expect the unexpected from her.

She waited eagerly for the information, but nothing came. Dare I call again? Yes. This time she talked with the secretary.

"I'm so sorry, Mrs. Winberry. I got busy and forgot about it. I'll get you the information as soon as I can."

Now all Emma had to do was wait.

# Chapter 14
# A Village in Sicily

"I did my duty, spent Christmas with the family. Now I want to get the hell out of this stinking place." Bruno frowned. His hands clutched the glass of wine on the table of the neighborhood *taverna.* He went back to his hometown only out of a sense of duty, but he felt trapped there. All he saw around him was poverty and inertia.

"Did you see Francesca?" Gerard asked.

*"Sì."*

"Eh, what happened?"

"Nothing."

Bruno grimaced as he remembered the painful encounter with her.

Without telling Bruno, his mother had invited the girl to go to midnight mass with them on Christmas Eve. When Francesca knocked on the door, he opened it, surprised and uncomfortable. She wore a simple black dress with trim lines, an old fashioned broach at her throat, and a flower perched provocatively behind her ear.

*"Buon Natale,* Bruno," she said, her face like that of

a dying heroine in an opera.

"Why are you here?" he asked rudely.

"Your mother invited me. Aren't you glad to see me?"

"Sure, sure. Come in. We go to mass."

"I go with you," she replied.

Bruno ignored the glare his mother gave him.

"Where is Angelo?" Francesca asked searching the tiny rooms.

"He is already at the church," Giovanna Gentile answered. "He sings in the Christmas choir tonight, like an angel." Her eyes shone with pride.

Bruno said nothing. The women threw black lace shawls over their heads and accompanied him to the festively decorated church. Where had all the flowers come from? No matter how poor these peasants were, they would spend their last coins decorating the church for the greater honor and glory of a God who had forsaken them long ago. Superstitious fools!

But as the priest intoned the time-honored phrases, something touched Bruno's heart. The voices in the choir, slightly off key, lent a raw simplicity to the setting. For a moment he was transported back to his own childhood and the security he had felt in youth.

Francesca touched his hand and slipped a small package into his coat pocket. He felt a stab of pain. He had nothing for her, hadn't given it a thought. He promised himself to send her something nice from America.

"Eh Bruno, what are you thinking about? Are you already in America?" Gerard asked.

Bruno shook his head to erase the painful memory of his leaving. Francesca had clung to him weeping, begging him to return to her. He had merely walked away.

"Did you hear from your cousin?" he asked.

"I got a letter yesterday. We can stay with his family in Chicago, but we have to share a bedroom," Gerard answered.

"Fine. I don't want to stay with strangers and it will be cheaper than staying in a hotel. We have to be there for rehearsal next month." Bruno felt a great relief. Everything was falling into place. He felt as if an unseen hand directed him.

He frowned as a thought crossed his mind. Sometimes at customs they did a thorough search of some of the baggage. They would take it away from him! No, he had better be safe.

"Gerard, I want to send a box to your cousin to keep for me. Give me the address."

"What do you have to send? Can't you pack everything in the suitcases? What's going on? First you go to Venice and don't tell me why, and now you send a box. What are you up to?" He gave Bruno a glowering look.

"That's my business. Just give me the address." He poured more wine as he ogled a dark eyed *Putana* sitting at the next table. He would have her tonight.

Bruno carefully wrapped his prize in layers of newspaper. He wadded up more paper and stuck it in the box cushioning the object. When he was satisfied, he sealed it and addressed it to himself in care of Gerard's cousin to an address on Taylor Street in

Chicago. He went to the post office, paid the fee.

# Chapter 15

"A winter storm is predicted for the Chicago area. The snow will begin this evening around rush hour and may accumulate to eight inches by morning."

Emma turned off the television and paced. She dialed the super hotline and listened again to the recorded message.

"The final piano rehearsal of *Die Fleidermaus* is scheduled for two P.M. All performers and supers are required to attend."

It was almost noon on this early January morning, and the sky was clear, the sun shining. She shrugged and decided the meteorologists were probably wrong. Emma always gave them a fifty percent margin of error. She put on fur lined boots, bundled up in a down coat, and pulled a woolen hat over her head and ears, tucking in the stubborn strands of hair that kept sneaking out. With a pair of fleece mittens and a scarf, she was ready to face the winds of downtown Chicago and anything else Mother Nature had in store.

Emma trudged the three blocks to the Metra station, the wind snaking under her coat, chilling her legs. She pulled her scarf tighter around her nose and mouth and hunkered down. The train took her to Union Station in the downtown area. From there she boarded a bus which stopped a block from the Performing Arts Center. Fortunately the trains and buses were on schedule and she got there in plenty of time. The sun still shone, but the lake winds blew harder.

Other supers and cast members got there about the same time as Emma, shivering and eager to get into the building. The singers also wore heavy scarves wound around their throats, noses and mouths, protecting their valuable instruments.

The stars went straight to their dressing rooms. The chorus, dancers, and supers congregated in a lounge lined with sofas and comfortable chairs. Coffee, tea, and hot cider sat on a table in the corner, enticing the chilled performers.

Emma nodded to a fellow super and helped herself to a cup of herbal tea as Nate came up beside her, his nose and cheeks apple red.

"That's a biting wind out there," he said. "How are you?"

"I'm fine, but you had better have a hot drink. You look nearly frozen. Tea or coffee?"

"I'll have coffee, thanks, black with three spoons of sugar." He smiled. "I need the energy. I decided to walk because, if the weather prediction is correct, the roads will be bad." He took the cup between his hands and let the steam warm his face as he inhaled the invigorating aroma.

"They predicted it won't start snowing until tonight," Emma said, a worried look on her face. "We should be finished rehearsing well before then."

"I never completely trust the weathermen," Nate said. "It was starting to cloud up when I came in."

Emma felt uneasy. She certainly didn't want to be caught up in a snowstorm; anything could happen!

The rehearsal lasted longer than originally scheduled.

"No! No!" Carl Wilcox the stage director shouted. "Not like that." He ran his hand through his hair and took a deep breath, pacing across the stage.

"Please, let's try it again. Mr. Gorsky, stand over here and look at the audience," he said to the flustered baritone. They repeated the passage over and over until, at last, he was satisfied.

"I'm sorry I've kept you so long," Wilcox said. "But it's essential we get this right. As you all know, there are no more rehearsals until the dress rehearsal."

A stagehand came up to him and whispered something in his ear. "I've just been told it's snowing pretty hard, so you all better get on home." He took the weary baritone aside and the two talked in hushed tones.

When Emma and Nate walked out the door they found themselves in a white world of whirling snow. Like a surreal painting, cars crawled like sugar-coated insects. A few pedestrians struggled against the driving snow.

"I had better call a cab to take me to the train," Emma said shaking her head.

"You'll never get a taxi tonight," Nate said. "Come on, the best thing to do is walk the four blocks to my place and wait it out there."

A limo pulled up to the curb plowing its nose into a snow bank. The stars piled in, destined for their hotels. Other members of the cast made their way to the coffee shop on the corner. One chorus member had the foresight to bring a four-wheel drive all weather terrain vehicle. He piled in as many of his fellow singers as possible. The rest went back into the theater to wait out the storm.

Nate took Emma's hand and they trudged, heads

down, into the bitter north wind. The four blocks seemed more like four miles. Huge wet snowflakes made their way down inside their collars; toes and fingers lost feeling after a short time; the skin of their faces felt tight and the hair in their noses froze. Nate tried to keep his arm around Emma to hold their bodies as close as possible, but the wind kept clawing at them, as if it were a living thing.

When Nate finally put the key in the lock and opened the door, they almost fell into the warm hallway. Emma's teeth chattered; her whole body shook.

"Come on." Nate took her hand and led her to the elevator. He punched five and put his arm around her, holding her as close as their heavy clothing would allow.

Once inside the apartment, Emma stood near the heat vent. She thought she would never stop shaking. Nate put the teakettle on the stove and turned up the thermostat.

After a bowl of soup and two cups of hot tea, Emma finally began to thaw. She walked to the window and looked out on an alien world. She could hardly see the street. Swirls of huge snowflakes danced crazily before plunging to the ground.

"Oh my God! Look at the snow."

"You're not leaving here tonight," Nate said, an authoritative tone to his voice. "I won't let you." He smiled as she visibly relaxed. "This sofa pulls out into a comfortable bed. I'll sleep here and you can have the bedroom." He held up his hand. "I promise to be a perfect gentleman."

Emma took a deep breath and smiled. "I guess I really have no choice. There's no way I can get home tonight, but I'd better call Sylvia. She knew about the rehearsal and will be worried sick."

Nate nodded and handed her the phone. Her daughter answered on the first ring. "Sylvia, I just want you to know that I'm all right. Yes, I knew you would be worried. I'm going to stay with one of the supers who lives near the theater. No, there's nothing for you to do. I'll go home tomorrow when this mess clears up. Don't worry, I'm in good hands." I certainly hope so, she thought glancing at Nate.

"Do you mind if I make another call?"

"Of course not. Make as many calls as you like." Nate busied himself pulling out the sofa bed and bringing sheets from the bathroom.

"Maria, this is Emma. Yes, I'm downtown. Won't be able to get home tonight. I didn't want you to worry. I'm staying with one of the supers. Never mind who. I'll talk to you when I get home tomorrow. Do me a favor, please, and call the boy across the street to shovel my snow in the morning. Thanks."

Nate smiled. "They're very protective of you, aren't they?"

"Yes, they are, but my neighbor is so nosey. She wants all the details. Who? What? When?" Emma smiled. She could imagine what Maria was thinking now.

"It's good to have people care about you," Nate said giving her a look she couldn't quite understand.

Later Emma snuggled under a down comforter in the middle of the king sized sleigh bed, lost in a pair of Nate's pajamas. She wondered where some of the other cast members were spending the night, but within a few minutes she fell asleep, lulled by the sound of the howling wind, feeling protected and cared for.

In her dreams she sat on a huge snowflake, swirling round and round until it landed on a mound of soft snow. Instead of lying on top, she began to sink farther and farther down until she was surrounded by a warm, soft, world of white.

"Are you up?" Nate asked after gently knocking on the door.

Emma looked around, confused and disoriented by the unfamiliar surroundings. Then she remembered the storm and the dream.

"I'm up," she called. "Be dressed in a minute."

"No rush. If you want to shower, there are clean towels in the bathroom. I'll start breakfast."

She walked into the large bathroom and looked appreciatively at the expensive ceramic tile in a muted beige color covering the walls and floor. She turned on the tap, stepped into the deep tub, noticing the jets on the sides, and stood under the hot water luxuriating in its warmth. When she got out, she wrapped herself in the soft absorbent towel. Nate certainly didn't skimp on luxury.

She dressed and tamed her hair as much as possible, made the bed and walked into the kitchen. The aroma of strong coffee made her eyes widen.

"Help yourself," Nate called from the living room. "Then come look out this window."

Cup in hand, Emma stood next to him staring at the tableau on the street below. A plow crawled down the center piling snow on the cars parked along the curb.

"I feel sorry for those fellows," Nate said. "It'll take them hours to dig out. Glad my car is in the garage."

Emma shivered. A few people trudged along the sidewalk, but they didn't get far. Drifts of snow blocked the intersections and whole portions of the walk. Most gave up and returned the way they had come.

Nate switched on the television, tuned into the news. "Over a foot of snow fell on Chicago and many of the northern and western suburbs. The CTA hopes to have buses running by late morning. Metra trains will resume their schedules later today. Residents are asked to remain in their homes and give the cleanup crews time to clear the streets. Salt trucks and snowplows have been out all night. Only emergency vehicles are running at the present time."

"It looks like you're stuck with me," Nate said, smiling.

A knock at the door interrupted what might have been an uncomfortable moment. "Nate, are you there?" a shrill voice called.

He cringed as he cracked open the door. "I'm here, Sadie."

"Thank God. I was worried about you with all this weather. How about you come to my place for some breakfast? I got fresh bagels and lox."

"Thank you, but I have company. Some other time." He closed the door as she stretched her neck trying to see around him.

He turned to Emma and shook his head. "I'm sorry if that sounded rude, but that woman is impossible." He threw up his hands. "Never lets me alone."

"She must be after you," Emma said smiling.

"She's after every unattached male in the building. None of us is safe. On top of that, she's six axe handles wide and has a mustache."

The previous night Emma had been too cold and tired to look at anything except warm blankets. Now she gazed around the room noticing the décor. The floor was a light-colored planking, the center covered by a two tone green area rug. Its color complemented the muted green and blue stripes of the sofa and armchair. Neither drapes nor blinds obstructed the large windows, just a sheer soft green swag across the top, draped unevenly along the sides. A walnut Yamaha upright piano stood along one wall, sheet music strewn across the top. A number of original watercolor landscapes gave the room a homey look.

"This is a lovely room," Emma said. "It doesn't look like a bachelor's pad."

"No," Nate said, laughing. "Shortly after I bought this place, my brother and sister-in-law came to visit. She took one look and said, 'Yuck! Let me fix this room up for you.' She's an interior decorator."

Emma nodded and smiled.

"My brother said, 'whatever you do, don't give her your credit card.' I followed his advice, but I went shopping with her and got caught up in the excitement. She didn't have to ask me to give her the card, I gladly handed it over myself. When the statement came in the following month, I almost fainted."

Emma walked over to the piano and caressed the keys with her fingers. "This is a wonderful piano."

"Do you play?" Nate asked sitting down on the bench and thumbing through the music.

"No," Emma said with a sigh. "I'm sorry to say, I

never learned. My children all took lessons. When we bought the house there was an old relic in the living room, you know, one of those old uprights that weighs a ton."

Nate nodded.

"My older children kept up their skills. They each have pianos in their homes. The youngest one hasn't decided what he really wants to do when he grows up, if he ever does."

Nate laughed as he ran through a few scales, and played one of the oldies. "I learned about ten years ago," he said. "I play just enough to amuse myself. When I throw a party, I entertain my guests, but only after they've had a few drinks. Shall we have breakfast?"

After they stuffed themselves with eggs and toast and fruit, they watched a video of *A Masked Ball.* Nate pointed out the scenes where supers were needed.

After switching off the video, he sat opposite Emma. "Now, I want to know more about you, Emma Winberry. You've told me that you're a widow with three children and you've lived in Brookfield for ages. But who are *you*?"

"Who am I? You want my life history?"

"An abbreviated version, please. You see, I haven't met a really interesting woman in a long time."

Emma settled back in her chair and sighed. "Well, I was born into a middle class family, the first of two girls. I was skinny and plain with straight mousy brown hair and my sister, Clara, was chubby with blond wavy hair and green eyes." She smiled remembering those years. "I asked my mother if I had been adopted since I didn't look like anyone else. She told me I looked like myself, and that was good enough. It was what I amounted to that mattered."

Nate nodded. "Sounds like a wise woman."

"Yes," Emma said, "but she was always praising Clara, the way she played the piano, sang in the choir, her acting in the school plays."

"Did she have any real talent?"

Emma shrugged. "She did join the Community Theater when she was older. She got so involved in every part she played that she actually lived the role."

"Well," Nate said, "there's nothing wrong with that. Most good actors do that to some degree."

"Yes, but I thought it was going too far when we all had to address her as the Duchess of York or Madame Bovary." Emma shook her head. "She was impossible to live with."

Nate leaned back in his chair and laughed.

Emma considered asking Nate about his early life, but the portents of danger haunted her. She said, "I have a favor to ask. I'm not too proficient with the computer, yet. Can you pull up some information on Marcantonio Speranza for me?" She didn't want to say anything more just yet.

"Certainly. A high profile entertainer like him, there will be lots of sites. Let's fire up the machine."

Emma followed him into the study and watched every move he made, making a mental note to remember them.

"We'll start by typing his name, up here where it says search, see?"

"But don't you need all that http/www?" Emma asked.

"Only when you have a specific address. We're only looking for information. There. See? Lots of sites about Speranza: videos, DVDs, CDs. Here's a biography."

"Yes," Emma said, her voice shrill with excitement. "Pull up that one."

"Just click on it and there you have it, a picture of the great man himself."

"Amazing." Emma was still in awe of all the marvelous fetes technology could accomplish.

"Do you want me to print this?"

"Yes, please."

Within a few seconds Emma held three pages in her hand. She folded them and put them in her purse.

"Anything else you desire, dear lady?"

"Not at the moment." She felt a little uncomfortable with that question.

"Give me your e-mail address," Nate said. "And I'll give you mine. It's simply another way to communicate."

"Yes, Stephen did set me up with one." They exchanged e-mail addresses, then Emma got up and walked to the window. It was such a beautiful view. She was sorry to see that traffic was almost back to what passed for normal in a bustling city.

"I guess it's time for me to go," she said, looking at him with regret. "That's the first installment of my history. More next time, and you can give me yours." She laughed as their eyes met wondering how many next times there would be.

Nate drove her to Union Station. As she was about to get out of the car, he said, "Emma, wait." He reached over and pulled her to him, and held her for a long time. He tilted up her face, kissing her tenderly with just a hint of passion and a promise of things to come.

She felt goose bumps and a deep stirring inside. Where would this lead?

When Emma got home, she was relieved that her driveway and walk were shoveled. She would give the boy across the street a generous fee. Now she could hardly wait to look up the two names that plagued her, Gerard Torano and Bruno Gentile. She turned on her computer and did exactly as Nate had done, but could find no information about either man. I guess they're not important enough, she thought.

How about Rosa Finelli? Rumors abounded about the legendary soprano. Emma typed in her name. Her picture flashed across the screen. As with Speranza, there were lists of recent performances, but Emma could not find a bio. She frowned then stretched, feeling a tightness across her shoulders. That's enough for now. It must be somewhere else. I'll ask Nate. She suddenly realized how much she was relying on him already.

She turned off the computer and brewed a cup of tea, took the pages about Speranza out of her purse and began to read. After scanning the list of operas in which he had performed, she read his personal information: born in a small town in Sicily, San Guiliermo, voice training in Palermo, first performance in Palermo Opera in . . . .

It went on to say he owned a villa in Tuscany where his wife and three children lived. Emma highlighted the personal information then put the pages in the folder she had marked **Investigation.** She sat back and waited for enlightenment. Something was going to happen, her senses told her. But what? Perhaps I can intervene, she reasoned.

*And how do you plan to do that?* The inner voice asked.

*I have no idea, but I expect some help from you, Angel. After all, you seem to be directing this show.*

# Chapter 16

The transcontinental flight that had originated in Palermo made a two-hour scheduled stopover in Rome. Bruno stretched his stiff legs as he and Gerard deplaned.

"Now we have to stay in this stinking airport for what? Two hours?" he complained.

"What can you do?" his friend said. "Let's go get a beer."

They pushed themselves through the crowds to the counter selling beer and soft drinks. After downing two bottles each, and an extra half-hour delay, they finally reboarded and headed for Chicago. The men dozed fitfully until they heard the pilot's voice.

"We are making our final approach to Chicago's O'Hare International Airport. Flight crew, prepare for landing. The temperature in Chicago is ten degrees above zero with a wind chill of ten below. Welcome to the Windy City."

"What did he say? How am I supposed to sing if my lungs are frozen?" Bruno growled, as he tightened his seat belt.

"Just take that scarf that your mother made you for Christmas and wrap it around your throat, your nose, and your head. It's about six feet long," Gerard said smiling. "My cousin will be at the airport to meet us. We won't be outside long."

They had been in busy airports before, but neither of them was prepared for the bustling crowds, the long lines at customs, the delays, the babble of so many different languages. It was disorienting. Bruno wondered if he had made a terrible mistake. Maybe they should turn around and go back home, but he had come this far. He had to complete his mission.

It seemed like hours before they passed through customs and picked up their baggage, so many people, so many questions. They were crabby, tired and hungry. Gerard looked around, then smiled, as he called to a drab figure flanked by two young children, waiting outside the gate.

"Antonio." He hurried to his smiling cousin. The two men embraced pounding each other on the back. "So long since I see you. This is my friend, Bruno," he said grabbing the other man's arm.

"Welcome," Antonio said shaking the man's hand. Bruno nodded as the children hid behind their father. "Come, come, Tony, Sammy," he said, pushing them forward. "Here is our cousin from Sicily and his friend, famous opera singers."

Gerard shrugged at the word famous, but smiled as he shook the hands of the children. Bruno simply grunted.

The men loaded the luggage into the trunk of a battered Chevy that had long ago turned over one hundred thousand miles. The trip to Taylor Street took almost two hours in the rush hour traffic on this dark, freezing January evening. Cars honked, pedestrians hurried along the sidewalks, everyone eager to get home. The restless boys bounced and argued with each other, settling down temporarily after a reprimand from their father, but before long, they were making noise again.

When they finally reached their destination, they trudged up three flights to Antonio's flat, where the mouth-watering smells of tomato sauce, basil and oregano greeted them. The two men were relieved to unload their burdens into the spare room in the back.

"Antonio," Bruno said. "Did a package come for me?"

"Yes, yes. I put it away so nothing would happen to it." He went to the closet and reached up into a corner. "Here, Bruno, safe and sound."

"*Grazie*." Bruno put it in his suitcase with no explanation, and tucked the case in a corner of the closet.

"When you are ready, come into the kitchen and we'll have some supper. My wife, Amalia, is anxious to meet you."

"I'll come with you, Antonio," Gerard said. When they had walked down the hall, he whispered to his cousin, "That box of Bruno's, did you see anything on the customs notice?"

"I couldn't help but look. The value was $500 dollars. He must have a girlfriend in America."

"He doesn't know anybody in America. I wonder what's in that box," Gerard frowned, afraid his friend was up to no good.

"Eh, it's none of my business. I'm just glad to have you two here, for company and for the extra money. Josie, my youngest, is sick, bad lungs. She needs medicines and treatments. Costs so much. You know how it is. I can't afford it on a butcher's salary."

"I'll help you with the little one," Gerard said, grabbing his cousin's arm. "Don't worry."

"*Grazie*. Ah, here comes Bruno. Now come into the kitchen and meet my wife."

"Amalia, here is our cousin, Gerard and his friend Bruno." Antonio put his arm around the buxom woman, dressed in an old housedress, cotton stockings sagging at the knees, her puffy feet encased in old worn slippers. Strands of hair escaped the bun on top of her head, and hung around her cheeks.

She smiled from a face worn with care and work. She smelled of garlic, basil, and exhaustion. "Welcome to our home. It is an honor to have famous opera singers here," Amalia said wiping her hands on an apron tied around her generous waistline; her sagging breasts hung well below.

Bruno looked at the woman, the meager surroundings, the ragged children, not with compassion, but with disdain. Old lumpy furniture lined badly stained walls, in need of repair and paint. The flat shouted out neglect, overcrowding, and something else that Bruno knew little of and didn't recognize—love.

Josie, the youngest peeked out from behind her mother, her face thin and ashen in color. Her breath came in shallow rapid gasps, all that her failing lungs could provide. An angelic smile spread across her face as she stared at Bruno. He frowned in return, but something in that smile tugged at his heart.

"Children," their mother said, "go into the parlor and finish your homework. We are going to sit here and visit. No noise."

Obediently the three boys and two girls filed out of the room.

Amalia quickly set the table and poured wine for the men. She put out a plate of tomatoes and fresh mozzarella cheese, sprigs of basil nestled between the slices. She poured thick green olive oil over the top. Then she cut crusty country bread in thick chunks. Another plate held provolone, mortadella, and salami, with green and black dried olives scattered between.

"Eat," Antonio said. "You must be starving."

The men shared the simple meal and drank the wine. Gerard and his cousin talked in the familiar way of caring family members. Bruno said little. Amalia stood near the sink and observed.

Later in the bedroom, Gerard threw himself on one of the twin beds. "I'm tired. All I want now is sleep." The two men settled in and turned out the lights, but the sound of bedsprings squeaking disturbed their attempts at sleep.

"That cousin of mine, he's a lusty guy, eh?" Gerard said, a laugh in his voice.

"He's a fool," Bruno responded. "He's got five kids that he can't afford, one of them sick, and he's in there making another. Bah . . ."

Bruno lay on the lumpy mattress for a long time, staring at the cracked ceiling and thinking. He glanced at the dresser where he had placed the picture of Francesca that she had slipped in his pocket on Christmas Eve. He thought of her soft responsive body, her sensuous mouth and was aroused by the memory. Why am I here in this freezing country? I should have stayed in Italy where I belong, gone back to Naples where it's warm. But I might not get another chance. *Promesso.* He must fulfill his promise.

# Chapter 17

Emma eagerly checked her e-mail twice a day. When the message from James's secretary finally arrived, she was so excited, she almost deleted it. She caught herself just in time and printed out the pages. She sat at the desk and, with trembling hands, scanned the names on the lists.

The Lyric Opera performances of *The Elixir of Love* showed no members of the cast who performed in the operas in either Naples or Milan. But when she looked at the chorus, there they were—Gerard Torano and Bruno Gentile. Goose bumps crept up her arms when she scanned the cast for *A Masked Ball.* They appeared again. This time they were to sing, not in the chorus, but in subordinate roles.

"That's it!" she cried aloud. "It has to be one of them. Wait until I tell Nate." But how could she prove anything? If she told anyone about her suspicions, they surely wouldn't believe her. She gave a deep sigh and sat back. She would have to wait for the answers to come.

The night of the first performance of *Die Fleidermaus* finally arrived. The dressing room filled with the excited bantering and chatter of the performers. The sounds grew louder in Emma's head making her hands tremble as she tried to fasten her costume. Can I really do this without something terrible happening?

"Guardian Angel," she whispered, "help me, please . . . ," She fiddled with her dress, adjusting the ruffled bodice over and over. The three-layered skirt sagged around her body. No matter how many tucks the wardrobe mistress had taken, it was still too large. She tugged at her wig a dozen times, and touched up her make-up until she was tempted to take it all off and start over again.

When she heard the stage manager call for the chorus and supers to come to the holding room, her heart began to pound so loud she was sure everyone could hear it. Her breath came in short gasps. She became lightheaded, was certain she would faint. Then she felt a firm hand grasp hers and turned to see Nate smiling at her.

"Don't be nervous," he said. "We've practiced this a dozen times."

"I know," she said, "but this is the real thing. My mouth is so dry, I can't swallow."

"Bite your tongue," he said.

She looked at him quizzically, and bit down. "Ouch."

"I don't mean you should draw blood, silly. Just bite down gently a number of times. It stimulates the flow of saliva. The singers do it all the time."

She followed his instructions, then nodded. "It does work."

He gave her a smug look, slipped one arm around her waist and said in a commanding voice, "Now, take a deep breath and let it out slowly. Now, another."

She did as she was told and felt calmer as she chewed on her tongue and let Nate lead her to the wings at the stage manager's instructions. She tried to remember where her mark was on the floor, but couldn't. Oh God, I'll just let Nate take over. He'll know what to do.

"Everyone on stage," George Ross called out.

Emma took another deep breath and followed Nate. She gasped as she was transported to another world. The stage looked like a palace ballroom, with back lighting reflecting off of ornate chandeliers. Red velvet drapery fell in soft folds around tall French doors. Marble-like columns lined the walls. The dazzling colors of the costumes ranged from rich ivories to bright peaches and blues. It was really a fairy-tale world, more so than the dress rehearsal. Emma found herself held firmly in Nate's arms, just the way they had practiced.

"Lights, curtain," the stage manager called. The lights went on, the curtain went up and the audience applauded the colorful tableau.

When the music started, Emma began to relax as she followed Nate's lead, waltzing around the stage. She felt like she was actually part of the story. She was no longer Emma Winberry of Brookfield, Illinois, but an important guest at the home of Prince Orlofsky. She lifted her head, smiled, and lost herself in the music.

Everything went smoothly until the tenor came onstage and began a duet with the soprano. The prompter whispered, "Your fly is open." The embarrassed singer clutched the soprano to him and clumsily zipped his pants, hoping the audience hadn't noticed. When they finished the duet and attempted to pull apart, something held them together. The soprano frowned as she tugged hard. A loud ripping sound . . .

At that moment the tenor began singing a reprieve. As he faced the audience holding out his arms, a tail of white lace hung from his zipper, brilliant against his black tuxedo. The audience went wild with laughter as they applauded with shouts of "Bravo." The tenor was at first unaware of his faux pas. When he looked down at the lace, he turned crimson. The soprano swore under her breath. The chorus and supers snickered. The orchestra continued playing and everyone resumed the waltz as the curtain descended to riotous applause.

In the wings Emma and Nate laughed as they listened to the stage manager and the tenor. "It's a good thing this is a light opera," George Ross said. "What if that happened in *Il Travatore* or *Aida.*"

The tenor huffed. "There is no lace in *Aida*," he said and stalked off to his dressing room.

Later Nate and Emma sat in the coffee shop on the corner reliving the evening. Emma was still lost in the magic of the music, the costumes, the sets. She didn't think she would ever come down to earth.

"Is it always like this?" She asked.

"Like what?" Nate looked at her, a quizzical expression on his face.

"Magic. I felt like I was somewhere else, in a real palace." She clasped her hands and stared off into space.

"Well, sometimes it's like that but other times it's downright boring, standing around at the back of the stage; seems like hours when it really isn't."

"To me it will always be magic," Emma said lifting her cup to her lips.

"That business with the zipper and the lace was pretty funny," Nate said chuckling.

"Yes," Emma said. "I guess lots of things can go wrong during a performance. I remember once, during *Rigoletto,* when the Duke was romancing Gilda, he grabbed the doorknob to go into her bedroom for a romantic tryst, and the entire door pulled away in his hand." Emma laughed at the picture in her mind of the robust tenor holding a door in the middle of an emotional love scene.

"What happened then?" Nate asked.

"He just laughed and put the door back, then went on with the aria."

For a moment Emma remembered the newspaper article about Speranza's mishap in the same opera. She wanted to say something to Nate, but it didn't seem to be the right time.

Nate smiled. "There's a delightful little book about operatic disasters. I'll have to get you a copy. *Tosca* is the opera that seems to have the most mishaps. At one opera house, a very difficult soprano was singing the title role. When she jumped off the parapet after her lover is shot at the end, instead of a mattress on the floor, the stagehands had put a trampoline in its place. She bounced up and down two or three times." He threw his head back and guffawed. "I would love to have been there. Another time the stagehands didn't get the mattress in place on time, and the soprano ended up with a broken pelvis."

"I'll bet the lawyers grabbed a hold of that one," Emma said, sipping her hot chocolate.

"Whenever animals are part of the act, accidents are bound to happen. Can you imagine the triumphal scene in *Aida* with all those horses and, in Verona, sometimes elephants going across the stage?" Nate smiled visualizing animals obeying a call of nature while walking across the stage to Verdi's powerful music.

"Once in a performance of *Andrea Chenier*, I was one of the soldiers waiting for my cue," he continued. "One of the new supers was so nervous, he kept pacing back and forth looking for the stage manager. I told him to relax, she would be there. He finally calmed down when she appeared. When the tenor had finished his aria, she signaled her approval by saying, "go man, go." The super thought it was his cue and ran onto the stage to find himself out there, alone, the audience staring at him expectantly. He hesitated, looked around, then shouted, 'Has anybody seen my horse?' and ran off."

Emma laughed, but her expression soon became serious. "Have there been any instances of one performer intentionally injuring another?"

"There are heated arguments from time to time, but I'm not aware of anything serious. Why do you ask?"

"I was thinking of the accidents, if you want to call them that, to Speranza in Naples and Milan."

"I'm sure they were just that, accidents."

She shrugged and smiled, "I'm just a silly woman who reads too many mystery novels."

# Chapter 18

Emma paced from one end of the house to the other. She stopped in front of a picture of herself with her late husband. It was the last one they had taken together.

"Oh Frank, I have to talk to you. I've met a man, a really nice man, and I like him a lot. In some ways he's like you, in others, not at all. Sometimes I feel as though I'm being unfaithful to you. I know it's foolish," she continued, as if he had answered her. "You've been gone for such a long time, eight years, long ones. I know I have the children, but sometimes I get lonesome — for — you know, a touch, loving words — a man." She whispered the last words as though someone might be listening, then blushed. She held the picture to her chest, kissed his image, opened a dresser drawer and tucked it away under rarely used items.

The previous night she had dreamed that she and Frank were shopping downtown. There were crowds of people pushing and pulling. She lost sight of him — called for him — then, when she did see him, he turned and smiled at her, waved, and slowly walked away. Emma felt it was a message.

"I just wanted to tell you that I invited him to dinner, and, well, if something happens, I won't try to stop it."

She felt relieved, as if she had done her duty to her late husband's memory. Maybe nothing will happen, she thought, but in her heart she was hoping it would. In the bedroom she laid out a pair of midnight blue silk pajamas. She had bought them at Victoria's Secret when she bought more padded bras and more panties from Fredrick's of Hollywood. The curves made her look and feel feminine, and she liked that.

Of course, if her relationship with Nate did get to the intimate stage, he would find out the truth, but she hoped he would understand. She would just have to deal with that when the time came.

As she rolled the silk between her thumb and forefingers, she remembered something. "I think they were the same color," she said aloud. "Now where did I put them?" For the next ten minutes Emma searched through drawers, shelves, and cupboards until she finally found what she was looking for in the bottom drawer of a little used chest.

She unzipped the plastic cover to reveal a set of satin bed sheets and pillowcases almost the identical color of her pajamas. They had been an anniversary gift, but Frank had died soon after and Emma had put them away unused.

Did she dare? Why not. If they didn't use them, she could store them away again, and if they did . . . She carefully made the bed, placing lavender sachets under the pillows. There was nothing more she could do here.

She walked into the kitchen and began peeling apples for a pie. The room soon filled with the succulent scents of baking apples and spices. When the pie was done, she put a chicken with sage dressing and two baking potatoes in the oven. With a tossed salad and some rolls, that should be enough. She put a bottle of *Pinot Grigio* in the refrigerator to chill.

Anxiously she looked at the clock, the hands pointing to five thirty. He would be here in an hour. She had better hurry. She laid out her clothes and was about to get into the shower when the phone rang.

"Hello. Oh, hi James. What's going on?"

"Sylvia's in labor," he said, his voice an octave higher than normal.

"Oh my, when did it start?"

"A couple of hours ago. We're at the hospital now. They're just admitting her."

"Do you want me to come?" she asked, not wanting to sound uncaring, but tonight of all nights. "I'm having company for dinner, but if you need me, I'll certainly be there."

"No need, Emma. There's nothing you can do. The doctor said everything is progressing normally and it will be hours."

"All right then, keep me informed. I'll be here. And, James, tell Sylvia I love you both." She heaved a sigh as she stepped into the steaming shower hoping to loosen her tense muscles. She felt guilt-ridden. Maybe I should be with my daughter, but first babies usually take a long time and the doctor did say everything was all right. She agonized for the next ten minutes until she looked at the clock again. It was too late now. Nate would be here any minute.

The doorbell rang at six thirty sharp. Emma smoothed back her hair, loaded with styling gel. For now, anyway, it stayed in place. She looked at herself in the full-length mirror, a black tunic length sweater fell softly over a rust colored mid-calf skirt. She had finished it just yesterday. A strand of pearls nestled provocatively between her enhanced breasts. She nodded with approval at her reflection. When the doorbell rang again, she jumped, her heart skipping a few beats.

Nate stood at the door, a bouquet of flowers in one hand, a bottle of champagne in the other, and a big grin on his face. "Hi," he said.

"Hi yourself." Emma accepted the flowers and closed the door behind him. "How lovely." She buried her nose in the spicy carnations, a bicolor pink with baby's breath and ferns artistically arranged around them.

"Take off your coat while I put these in water." She watched him from the kitchen as he hung his coat in the hall closet and wandered around the living room. Emma took her time arranging the flowers, her hands shaking, her heart beating wildly.

"Something smells good," Nate said walking into the room. "Is that pie homemade?"

"Nothing but," Emma said putting the cut glass vase holding the flowers on the dining room table.

"This is a comfortable house," he said approving of the long narrow windows with leaded glass inlays. "You can't buy those windows today."

"No, they're genuine antiques, but they do let in a lot of cold air. Every year I say I'm going to get new storm windows and every year I put it off. My children are encouraging me to sell the house; they say it's too much for me to keep up, but where would I go? I enjoy my garden and I do love this place. I'm certainly not ready to give up my independence." She shook her head as the phone rang.

"Hello, how are things going? She's dilated three

centimeters." Emma frowned as she listened to her son-in-law. "Okay, keep me posted." She turned to Nate. "My daughter is in labor, first baby. She dilated to three centimeters then stopped. They're going to let her sleep a while and see what happens." Emma shook her head.

"First babies take a long time," Nate said. "I sometimes wonder why women ever have a second one."

Emma raised her eyebrows. "We soon forget, that's why, and you boys have something to do with it, too."

Nate looked at her with a mischievous grin. "Aren't you glad we don't have to worry about that anymore?"

Emma certainly wasn't ready for this conversation, yet. "I think I had better check on dinner." She hurried into the kitchen, her chest heaving, her heart galloping.

Nate came after her carrying the champagne. "Shall we?"

Emma nodded, glad for the diversion. She reached into the cabinet and took down two flutes. After Nate popped the cork and poured the bubbly wine, he walked into the living room, glass in hand. Emma followed.

As they sipped the champagne she wondered when would be the right time to show Nate the 'evidence' she had collected. Probably after dinner. Just then the timer sounded and she hurried back into the kitchen.

Nate helped her carry the succulent food to the dining room. The chicken was tender and juicy, and the potatoes oozed with melted butter. Everything was perfect.

Over pie and coffee they talked about the coming opera season. Now's the time, Emma thought. I'll take him into the study and show him the folder.

But Nate had other ideas. He poured more champagne and toasted the opera, the new baby, and a lasting relationship.

Emma began feeling a little tipsy. I'll tell him later. She turned on the stereo to a program featuring light classics. They cleared the table together sipping the last of the wine, loaded the dishwasher, then it seemed only natural that she would be in his arms. The strains of the "Merry Widow Waltz" filled the living room. They dodged furniture and moved around as one until Emma's foot caught on the leg of the end table and she toppled against Nate. He fell backwards onto the sofa pulling her on top of him.

They laughed; their eyes met and exchanged a message that needed no words. They kissed slowly at first and then with passion. Nate's hands caressed her back and slid down her body. She froze when he grabbed her buttocks.

"Wait," she said sliding off the couch. "There's something I have to tell you."

"Not now," he whispered, his voice husky. "I want you, Emma—please."

Without another word she led him up the stairs.

# Chapter 19

Emma hesitated at the bedroom door. When she turned and saw the love and longing in Nate's eyes, she knew it would be all right, it had to be.

Nate began pulling her sweater up, but Emma stopped him.

"Wait," she said, "let me get ready." She hurried into the bathroom, stripped off all her padding, and put on her silk pajamas.

When she came out, Nate was sitting on the bed in his underwear. He was surprised to see her buttoned up to the neck, but decided it was old-fashioned modesty. He reached for her and held her close, his hands exploring her body under the silk. Her breasts pressing against his chest felt like two plums instead of the oranges they had appeared to be. He ran his hands down her buttocks and stopped.

"Emma, what happened to your ass?"

She pulled away and covered her face with her hands. "Oh Nate, that was what I was trying to tell you. It was all padding, the panties, the bra. I have no figure at all. I'm built like—like, Olive Oyl." She sat on the bed and cried in wrenching sobs.

Nate stood for a moment, then began to chuckle. He sat down next to her and put his arms around her. "Listen to me. When I first saw you, I thought you were cute; I liked your figure." Her body shook with more sobs. "No, no, stop that. Now that I've gotten to know you, it doesn't matter. When I looked into those bottomless gray eyes of yours, I knew you were someone special. I'm falling in love with *you,* Emma Winberry, my little Sparrow." He rocked her back and forth, humming and stroking until she was quiet. "Now, I'll just use the bathroom and be right back."

Emma felt a tremendous sense of relief. He knew and it didn't matter. If he had been turned off, then he wasn't the man she thought he was. It would have broken her heart. But he didn't mind. He loved her just as she was.

She smiled as she turned down the comforter exposing the shimmering satin sheets. She crawled between them feeling their smooth, slippery surface, anticipating the pleasure to come.

After a few minutes, she heard the knob on the bathroom door being twisted violently.

"Emma," Nate called. "I can't open this door."

Oh God, now what. She jumped out of bed, grabbed the knob from the outside and turned it, but nothing happened. She tried again and again, but the mechanism inside was jammed. She had been having trouble with that lock, but it was just another thing she had put off.

They continued twisting and turning from both sides for another ten minutes. She heard cursing and swearing.

"Maybe I should call the Fire Department."

"No! Get a piece of plastic, like a credit card. They're always opening doors like that in the movies."

Emma rummaged through her purse and found her credit card from a neighboring department store.

"Now what do I do with it?"

"I'm not sure. Try running it down the side of the door."

She stuck it in the crack between the door and the jam and began pulling it down. When she reached the lock it stopped and would go no further. "That doesn't work," she said pulling harder.

Nate blew out a long frustrated breath. "Try pushing it in straight and wiggling it from side to side."

Emma tried to inset the card alongside the locking mechanism but the fit was too tight. Finally she did manage to get it into the tiny space and pushed. With a snap the card broke in two. "No good," she said slumping to the floor. "It broke."

"Damn!" Nate said. "We'll have to take the door off. I need a hammer and a large screw driver so I can take the pins out of the hinges."

Emma still thought it would be easier to call the Fire Department, but then she envisioned the truck screeching down the street and all the neighbors coming out to see what was happening. The humiliation would be too much.

"I'll have to hand them to you through the window," Emma said.

"But we're on the second floor."

"I'll put up a ladder. It's not too high. I've done it lots of times to wash the windows." God, if somebody sees me at this time of night with a ladder at my window,_they're sure to call the police.

"What's this on the inside of the window, this plastic?" Nate asked, his voice rising in pitch.

"It's an inside storm window; the room was so drafty. I'm afraid you'll have to take it off before you can open the window. It's held in place by small screws."

"So where do I get a screw driver?"

"They're in the basement," Emma answered biting her lip.

"Great, that's just great." More muttering as she heard Nate opening drawers. "Is there anything in here I can use?"

Emma thought for a moment. "There's a fingernail file in the top drawer. That might work."

"I found it. Damn, I haven't got my glasses. I can't see these blasted things." More cursing and swearing.

By now Emma was totally devastated. All her beautiful plans were slowly sliding down the drain.

More muffled sounds and cursing. "I got it," Nate called. "I got this damned thing off. Now just get me the hammer and screw driver and we're in business." His voice sounded triumphant.

Emma took off her silk pajamas and slipped into a sweat suit. She put on her boots, a heavy jacket, and pulled a cap over her head, then went into the basement for the tools.

When she opened the back door, a blast of frigid air slapped her in the face. She trudged through two inches of frozen snow to the garage to retrieve the metal ladder.

Emma looked around as she struggled with the ladder, then, with some difficulty, stabilized it against the house. Everything was quiet. Carefully she climbed up, the tools protruding from her pocket.

Nate watched anxiously from the open window. As she handed him the tools and quickly climbed down, a light went on in Maria's kitchen. Emma saw her back door open and heard her neighbor's voice call out, "Emma, are you all right? What's wrong? Are you locked out?"

"Everything's fine, Maria. I'll talk to you tomorrow." She pulled the ladder through the snow and stowed it in the garage. She could see her neighbor watching her every move.

Back in the house Emma heard pounding from the second floor as she pulled off her boots, coat and hat leaving her hair sticking out in all directions. She ran up the stairs just as Nate took the pin out of the last hinge.

"I'm back, Nate."

"Okay," he said. "All clear. Just push the door along the hinge side and it should fall inward."

It took more than one push. The door had warped and fit too tightly. They pushed and shoved and pounded until it finally gave way. They looked at each other, Nate standing in his underwear, perspiration staining his underarms, Emma with her hair askew, and burst out laughing.

"You'll have to get this lock fixed," he said. "I'll take it out for now." It took a while for him to get out the old rusted screws. He rehung the door as Emma examined her ruined credit card. She would have to apply for a new one.

"I think it might be a good idea if I go home," Nate said.

Emma nodded. The spell was broken. She knew they couldn't recapture it now.

Nate looked at the bed as he dressed. "Put those fancy sheets away 'till next time." At the door he took her face in his hands and smoothed back her hair. He kissed her eye-lids, the tip of her nose, and her mouth. "Good night my little Sparrow. It's been a most interesting evening."

As Emma watched him drive away, she wondered if she would ever see him again. She hadn't told him about her suspicions, the danger to Speranza. She had flubbed the whole evening.

# Chapter 20

The following morning Nate sat at his kitchen table drinking a cup of strong black coffee. He stared out his window at the rows of vintage buildings on north Lakeshore Drive as he mentally reviewed the events of the previous night. Did he really want to be involved with this quirky woman? He started to chuckle as he recalled running his hands down her straight body. Olive Oyl indeed! His belly shook as he relived their attempt to open the bathroom door. By the time he had gone through the entire fiasco, he was groaning with laughter.

"Yes," he said aloud, between breaths. "Yes, I certainly do."

After a restless night punctuated by bizarre dreams, Emma sat at the kitchen table drinking endless cups of coffee. "What a catastrophe. He'll never call me again. He probably thinks I'm a crazy old fool!"

*Guardian Angel, why did you let this happen? Now I'll never be able to enlist his help in my search for the villains.* How melodramatic, she thought. Maybe I am going round the bend.

She jumped at the sound of the phone.

"Hello. Oh, hello James." She had waited for his

call most of the night, waking and dozing, until finally she slept a few hours.

"Emma, you have a grandson!"

"How wonderful," she whispered swallowing the lump in her throat.

"He weighs seven and a half pounds and is nineteen inches long, and has blond fuzz on his head, and, of course, he's beautiful." A deep sigh from the proud father.

"Certainly. How is Sylvia?" Emma asked, a note of anxiety in her voice.

"Tired, but fine."

"You sound pretty tired yourself."

"Yeah, having a baby is hard work," he said yawning. "Do you want to come to the hospital with me this afternoon?"

"Absolutely! What time?"

"I'll pick you up at two."

"I'll be ready. And what name did you finally decide on?"

"James, Jr. Okay, Grandma, I'll see you at two."

Emma heaved a sigh as she poured another cup of coffee. Maybe she could relax now. Not with all that caffeine in her bloodstream, besides, someone wouldn't let her. She was startled by the sound of the doorbell, wasn't going to answer it, but the caller was insistent. She dragged herself off the chair and walked slowly to the door.

Maria stood outside bundled against the February cold. "So, I came to talk," she said handing Emma a plate of *biscotti.*

"Come in, the coffee's hot." Emma shuffled into the kitchen.

"You look tired," Maria said taking a mug from

the shelf and pouring herself a cup of the steaming brew. "What happened that you're climbing up a ladder in the snow in the middle of the night?"

"It was a disaster." Emma covered her face with her hands. "He'll never want to see me again." Tears made their way down her cheeks.

"Now, now, tell me about it," Maria said, patting her hand. She sat back in her chair and cradled the cup in her hand.

Emma started from the beginning and told her friend the entire story, describing the dinner, the satin sheets, the body padding. When she got to the locked bathroom door, she started to laugh, then broke out in a loud guffaw. "I wanted to call the Fire Department."

Maria laughed with her. "*Mama mia,* can you imagine what would have happened? Old Mrs. Cooper with her wagging tongue. The whole neighborhood would know."

By the time she finished the story, Emma felt the relief of confession. Both women laughed as they nibbled on the *biscotti* and drank coffee.

"Maria, I have a grandson. James just called. He was born at six this morning."

"*Buona fortuna.* Such good news. And Sylvia? She's all right?"

"Fine."

At that moment the phone rang. The women looked at each other as Emma went into the living room to answer.

"Hello," a note of hesitation in her voice.

"Hello, little Sparrow," Nate's cheery voice asked. "And how are you this morning?"

"Oh Nate, I'm so sorry about last night."

"Don't apologize; it wasn't your fault. You have to admit, it was pretty funny."

"It was, wasn't it?" Emma breathed a sigh of relief. "I could hear you swearing behind that door because you didn't have your glasses." She began to titter again.

"And your neighbor saw you on the ladder, didn't she?"

"Yes, she's here now drinking coffee and hearing all about it."

"Well, I'm certainly glad you didn't call the Fire Department. It would probably be all over the front page of the neighborhood newspaper. Tell your neighbor I said hello and I'm looking forward to meeting her. How about dinner tomorrow night□ in a restaurant?"

"Wonderful, I'll look forward to it."

"I'll call you in the morning and, Emma, I wouldn't have missed last night for anything."

Emma's eyes were shining when she walked back into the kitchen.

"It was him, eh?" Maria asked.

"Yes, and everything is all right. We're going out to dinner tomorrow night. He said 'hello' to you."

"Good. I told you he would call. Now you better get some rest before you go see that baby."

Temporarily Emma put aside all thoughts of Speranza and the two suspects. She had a new grandson to welcome into the world.

Emma was dressed and ready when James pulled into the driveway. He still looked tired, but was beaming with pleasure.

"I feel different already, Emma," he confided as they drove to the hospital. "I've been so involved with the Midwest Opera these past years and now I'm suddenly responsible for a wife and a child, one so tiny and helpless. It's a little scary."

"It is at first, but you'll get used to it. You know, my husband said the same thing when Stephen was born." She sat back and remembered the look of wonder on Frank's face as he had looked down on their first born son. At times like this she missed him more than ever.

When they entered the hospital room, Sylvia was nursing the baby. She appeared tired, but happy and fulfilled.

Emma got to hold little James for a few minutes. As she gazed at the small creature in her arms, she realized how good life was. This is the way it's supposed to be, not worrying about tenors and vendettas.

She and Nate met the following evening at a new restaurant on Rush Street called the Opera Club. The walls displayed colorful posters of opera performances through the years. Muted background music, orchestral versions of various operas filled the air. A huge mural of the *Café Momus* from *La Boheme,* with the revelers in the background, covered an entire wall. The patrons sat at tables in front of the mural taking them back to nineteenth century Paris.

"You're glowing, my dear," Nate said.

"I saw my new grandson yesterday afternoon. He's so perfect. It's truly a miracle." Emma sighed with satisfaction as Nate adjusted her chair.

"Yes, it's a totally different experience being a

grandparent, satisfying and fun without the responsibility."

Nate picked up the menu fashioned like a libretto. "Now, what are you in the mood for?" he asked picking it up, raising his eyebrows, and grinning.

She ignored the innuendo and stared at the entrees. "I think I'll have the Pasta Primavera. It says here that it has three different kinds of mushrooms, capers, artichoke hearts, and chunks of eggplant."

"Good choice. I'll have the same."

When their dinner arrived, Emma took a deep breath inhaling the smells of garlic and Italian seasonings. She took a bite, closed her eyes, and groaned with pleasure.

Nate laughed. "A total sensual experience. That's one thing I like about you, Sparrow, you indulge yourself completely. We must come here often."

They relished their meal with a robust red wine to complement it, talked about opera, their favorite singers, and memorable productions.

Emma looked at Nate and squirmed in her chair. "Uh … There's something about me you ought to know."

"Oh? More than Fredrick's of Hollywood?" Nate asked raising his eyebrows and suppressing a grin.

She scratched her head, and tucked an errant strand of hair behind her ear. "I … have sort of a *sixth sense*."

"A *sixth sense*," he repeated. "And just what do you mean by that?"

"Well, sometimes I know things without anyone telling me, that is, no one on this plane of existence. You see, my Guardian Angel sometimes tells me things, not in actual words of course. I know how this sounds," she interrupted herself, watching his face for a reaction, "but ever since I was a child I could sense things before they happened. It was frightening. I seem to have inherited it from my grand mother. She told me it was a gift; I think it's a curse. The other kids thought I was a witch." Her eyes begged him to understand.

At that moment the waiter came by with the dessert menu. "Would you like any dessert?" Nate asked.

"I'll have some *tiramisu,*" she answered, a dejected tone in her voice. "You think I'm crazy, don't you?"

"No, I don't think that. You're just—different. That's part of your charm." He folded his hands under his chin and looked at her.

"Emma, you can believe anything that works for you. I may not agree with your philosophy, but I certainly won't try to dissuade you. I expect you to do the same, okay? Now that you got that off your chest, do you feel better?"

"Much better," she answered, taking a generous bite of the delectable dessert.

"I've done some research," she said suddenly. That went well, now it was time to tell him the rest of what she was feeling.

Nate's fork stopped halfway to his mouth. "What kind of research?"

"Hear me out before you look at me like that, Nate. Speranza is in real danger. Some one is out to harm him." She told him about her dreams, the playbills, the list of singers for the Lyric and Midwest performances and the two names that consistently appeared in all of them.

Nate finished his dessert without saying a word. He looked at her skeptically. It was a lot to take in for one dinner. "That's all coincidence, my dear. It's not unusual for singers to perform with a number of opera companies. Your research, as you call it, proves nothing."

She sighed and hung her head. "But I feel it. I know something is wrong."

He looked at her for a moment, his eyebrows knit together. "If you feel that strongly about it, who am I to disagree? What can I do to help?" He reached for her hand and gave it a squeeze.

"I don't know. Just think about it, please."

"I will."

"And, I tried to find some information on Rosa Finelli, but all I got were performance schedules. Could you try?" She gazed at him, widening her large gray eyes.

"You don't have to take on that helpless little girl look," he said sitting back and laughing. "La Finelli is a very private person. I know she lives somewhere near Rome, but that's about all. I'll do some digging. Okay?" He smiled as one conspirator to another.

Nate sat in his study, hunched over his desk, a glass of scotch in hand. He reread his article for an investment magazine one more time, made a few corrections, then gave a sigh of satisfaction, done, and well before the deadline.

He sipped the scotch, sat back and thought about Emma's premonitions. She seemed to really believe them. And she was worried, he could see that.

Who was he to doubt her ability? Did he believe in 'second sight' or a 'sixth sense'? Not really, but he remembered the old woman down the block who had cautioned his mother not to let Nate and his brother go to the movies one particular afternoon. The boys had been angry, had stomped around the house pleading, but to no avail. That afternoon the theater caught fire and five children suffered serious burns.

Nate frowned. Maybe Emma was right. Maybe I'll do some investigating myself, he thought, just to put her mind at ease.

# Chapter 21

In the flat on Taylor Street, Bruno sat at the kitchen table, brooding and fingering a letter. He read it for the third time. "Agh!"

"What's the matter?" Gerard asked, pouring a cup of coffee.

"A letter from my mother."

"When did your mother learn to write?"

"Fool, she didn't write it. The priest, Padre Martino, did."

"Eh," Gerard said sitting down and dipping a piece of stale bread into his coffee.

"With what we pay your cousin to stay here, he should give us more than stale bread for breakfast," Bruno complained, breaking off a piece.

"Little Josie is so sick," Gerard said. "Did you hear her coughing last night? Poor little thing. Amalia used all the old cures, mustard plasters on her chest, garlic rings around her neck, but nothing works. So they took her to the clinic. Antonio picked up the medicine from the pharmacy and it cost over a hundred dollars for just one bottle. *Que peccato,* how are they to live?" He shook his head and dipped more bread into the bitter coffee.

"So what does the priest say? Is everything all right at home?"

"Angelo is singing in the choir," Bruno said.

"The choir? He's just a little kid."

"The Padre says he's good, a voice from heaven he writes. He says there's a teacher in Palermo, three hours away by train. He wants to take the boy there for lessons." Bruno's voice filled with scorn.

"Maybe he *is* gifted," Gerard said. "After all, you're a singer, and your father was a singer, and Angelo's father . . ."

"Don't mention Angelo's father," Bruno snapped.

Gerard shrugged and poured another cup of coffee. "So, will you send the money?"

"*Si,* I'll send the money. *Io promesso* . . ." he whispered, shaking his head.

"*Zio* Bruno," a small voice piped. "Will you read me a story?" Little Josie walked unsteadily into the kitchen clutching *The Cat in the Hat* by Dr. Suess.

"I'm not your uncle," Bruno said frowning, but he felt a tightening in his chest as he looked at this thin bit of humanity tenaciously clinging to life. "Come on. I'll read to you."

He picked her up and felt the frail body shiver underneath the footed flannel pajamas. Her cold hands gripped the book and Bruno noticed the bluish tinge on the tips of her ears and nose. He felt the little heart pounding beneath her ribs. Holy medals and scapulars hung around her thin neck. Bruno felt afraid as he held the child close. She had wormed her way into his heart, no matter how hard he tried to prevent it. Her tender smile, the huge brown eyes, the dimple that appeared just above her chin, seemed to bore into his very soul.

He took the book, worn and stained by all the sticky hands that had turned the pages. The centerfold had come loose from the binding. Bruno tucked it back in carefully and began to read.

# Chapter 22

March came in with below zero temperatures and a virulent flu epidemic. Emma had cold symptoms for about five days: a stuffy nose, sore throat and mild cough. But she recovered quickly. She attributed her strong immune system to a healthy diet and the many vitamin/mineral supplements she swallowed every morning.

Nate, without all this protection, coasted through. He walked along the lakeshore every day, ate whatever he pleased, and rarely succumbed to viruses or bacteria. He attributed his good health to his stubborn nature.

One frigid morning Emma received an urgent call from Cecily Cunningham, the super captain from the Midwest Opera. She said she couldn't even pull herself out of bed: high fever, sore throat, and aching muscles.

"I have a request to make." She hesitated, coughing and hacking. "A touring opera company is appearing at McCormick Place. They're putting on *Aida*." More coughing and sneezing.

"What can I do?" Emma asked.

"They need supers for the triumphal scene. So many people are sick. They're calling both Lyric and Midwest for help." At that point her voice gave out.

Emma heard her sip something, then clear her throat.

"But there aren't any women in that march; aren't they all soldiers?" Emma asked.

"Not to worry. They'll dress you like a young man."

"All right," Emma said with some misgivings.

"Thanks, Emma. Call this number and talk to Jack." She gave her the number and hung up with a groan.

Poor thing, she sounds miserable. Emma decided to call Nate. He had received a similar call and had already talked to Jack Martin from the touring company. They were to be at McCormick Place the next day at four in the afternoon to prepare for *Aida,* Verdi's masterpiece set in ancient Egypt. Emma pictured the opulent sets, the exotic costumes, heard the powerful music playing in her head.

"Emma," Nate said, "Since there are two performances scheduled, we'll be busy downtown most of the week. It would be silly for you to go back and forth. Why not plan to stay here, with me?" There was a hint of mischief in his voice.

That certainly sounded like a practical idea. Perhaps a romantic one, too. "All right," she answered. "I'll pack a suitcase." She thought for a moment then decided to take the blue silk pajamas, just in case.

I'd better call the kids, she thought. They'll worry if I don't answer the phone. She gave them Nate's number, should anyone need to contact her.

"Oh God, if I don't let Maria know, she'll undoubtedly think the worst," Emma said aloud picking up the phone again.

"Hallo."

"Maria, it's Emma. Are you well with all this flu going around?"

"Eh, I got garlic around my neck. So far, no flu."

Emma chuckled. "I just wanted to tell you that I'll be staying with Nate all week. We have to help out with the opera."

A long drawn out "Ohhh" from the other end. "You be good now. Remember what your mother taught you."

"I don't know what you think I'm going to do, Maria, but I can assure you I won't do anything unacceptable. Here's the number in case you have to get in touch with me."

After Emma hung up she smiled. Garlic indeed. Old fashioned superstitious Maria. *Well Guardian Angel, I'm relying on you to tell me what's acceptable in today's relationships.*

"My, this parking lot is immense," Emma said as Nate pulled as close to the entrance as possible.

"You can say that again. When they have conventions here plus the auto show, and the RV show, they need every bit of this space."

They made their way inside and into the lobby of the Aire Crown Theater. Emma was amazed at the lovely modern décor. Midwest could use a little sprucing up, she thought.

As Emma and Nate walked backstage they heard the buzz of excitement. Emma clung to Nate's hand. The size of the place made her uncomfortable. The large community room was filled with people. Jack Martin, the stage manager, called them to attention.

"I want to thank you supers from the Midwest and

Lyric Opera companies for helping us out. If we didn't have enough folks, we would have to cancel the performances, or whittle down the triumphal scene."

The supers laughed. They knew that would be a disappointment. It was one of the most dramatic spectacles in all of grand opera.

"We've already replaced one of the stars with his understudy. Now, those of you who are our regulars, please help the new folks. Most of you will wear tunics. The men who have no chest hair, or who have shaved their chests, will be bare from the waist up. All you have to do is march across the stage. One of the regulars will partner up with each of the new people. Just watch your partner and keep in step. Thanks again." His beeper went off and he hurried from the room.

"Come on," A masculine looking woman said to Emma. "I've been in this scene for years."

Emma obediently followed her into a dressing room crowded with female members of the chorus and dancers.

She searched the clothes rack. "There's not much to you, is there. Here's a tunic that should fit. Go through these sandals 'till you find your size."

Emma rummaged through the box of sandals but saw no sizes marked. She held them up and found two that looked about right. Their long laces wound around the calf. She went into a fitting room and took off her clothes. The tunic fit like a tent. She slipped out of her shoes and socks and shoved her feet into the sandals. She wasn't sure which was right and which was left, but it didn't seem to matter. She locked her clothes in a locker and pinned the key inside the tunic.

"Oh boy, you are tiny," said one of the seamstresses. "Come over here." She began pinning the back and left side of the garment. "You'll be entering from stage left so your right side will be toward the audience. This won't show." She finished, looked Emma over, and nodded her approval. "Now go over there for a wig and makeup."

Emma followed another woman into the makeup room. "We need some body paint here," yelled the designer looking over Emma's white skin.

A young girl ran over with a bucket and a sponge. She told Emma to take off her tunic and sandals. She sponged Emma's face, arms, and legs with a thick dark pasty liquid.

"It'll dry in a few minutes," the girl said, running off to find her next super.

Emma stood holding her arms away from her body, clad only in a shift and panties.

"Okay, you're dry," the makeup artist said touching Emma's arm. "Get dressed and let me finish the job."

Emma felt as if she were having an out of body experience as she sat before a mirror and watched the woman work her magic. She put dark eyeliner under both eyelids, curving it to the sides reaching almost to the hairline. Then she applied heavy purple eye shadow.

With a black curly close-cropped wig adjusted to her head, Emma didn't recognize herself.

"Let me see," the dresser said. "Great. You pass for an Egyptian boy. Next."

Emma went into the community room and sat in a corner, waiting. She studied a playbill scanning the cast members' names. Goosebumps formed along her arms when two names jumped out at her: Gerard Torano and Bruno Gentile. At that moment a man walked in wearing a priest's robe. He was scowling and muttering under his breath. He took a letter from under his tunic, read it, shook his head, balled it up and threw it in the wastebasket. When he looked up, his eyes met Emma's. With a scowl, he grabbed a bottle of water and stomped out of the room.

I wonder if he's one of them? He did look vaguely familiar even under all that makeup. Emma looked around to be sure no one was watching her as she sidled up to the wastebasket. She picked up a napkin and dropped it into the basket. With trembling fingers, she reached down to retrieve it, wrapping it around the letter.

"Has your research led you to picking up wastepaper?" a man said coming up to her. He, too, wore a tunic and sandals and a wig similar to hers.

"Nate?"

"You look just like a boy," he said.

Emma wasn't sure if she should take that as a compliment, but decided it was a tribute to the artistry of makeup.

"And what was that you took out of the basket?" he asked.

"I dropped something, that's all." She held the crumpled letter behind her back trying to decide what to do with it. There wasn't time to go back to her locker. On the pretext of adjusting her wig, she shoved the letter under the netting, and pulled the wig securely in place.

"Bruno Gentile," the stage manager called.

"Here," Bruno answered. He and Gerard, with other members of the chorus, stood elegantly dressed in white priests' robes.

"You're Alan Benson's understudy, aren't you?"

"*Si,* the part of Ramfis, the high priest."

"As you know, Mr. Benson is not well. He thought he could perform, but he's running a high fever and is unable to get out of bed. You'll have to sing in his place."

"Bruno," Gerard said. "What a break. That's a big part." He slapped his friend on the back. "What do they say here in America? Break a leg?"

Bruno grunted and followed the stage manager to the star's dressing room. The manager had called him that afternoon and told him he might have to sing the part, but Bruno hadn't told Gerard.

"You're sure you know all the cues?" the man asked.

"Of course. I know everything." What's the matter with these Americans? How can I be the understudy and not know the cues? He relished the part of the cruel high priest who condemns Rhadames, the traitor, to death.

As the curtain went up on scene two of the second act, the audience was transported to the temple of the god, Ammon; two massive statues flanked a dais holding two ornate thrones.

Emma heard the applause of approval. The orchestra began the moving music as the Pharaoh and his daughter, Amneris, entered. They marched slowly across the stage, and took their places on the thrones. The priests led by Ramfis followed them. Emma's eyes widened as she recognized him, the man with the letter.

She trembled in anticipation, taking one deep breath after another and biting her tongue. She stood next to her partner, each of them carrying sheaves of grain. The dried wheat tickled her nose and for one terrifying moment she thought she might sneeze. The sensation passed as she heard the beginning of the Triumphal March. The stage manager said "go."

Suddenly Emma was no longer a woman living in the twenty-first century in a suburb of Chicago. She was transported back in time, to the land of the Pharaohs, a young Egyptian warrior returning victorious, carrying the spoils of war. She marched proudly across the stage keeping perfect time. She could almost feel the hot Egyptian sun beating down on her, almost feel the sand under her feet. It was so real. All around her, other supers carried banners, sacred vessels, and statues of the gods.

When she and her partner exited the stage, she shook her head for a moment reorienting herself. They were quickly given shields and helmets and instructed to go around the back and march again across the stage. The music soared; Emma again felt the centuries melt away.

This time they followed a horse loaded with objects of plunder. Emma could smell the earthy odor of the beast, could hear it snorting. Halfway across the stage the horse began raising its tail and expelling gas.

"Don't even think it, horse," Emma's partner muttered. But the horse followed nature's call and just as he reached the exit, dumped a pile of manure on the stage. The barnyard odor hit Emma as she tried not to breathe. Her partner muttered a few expletives. At that moment Emma's helmet began slipping to the side. She raised her left hand to steady it and stepped directly into the manure. "Ugh," she said as someone pulled her into the wings.

Two stagehands quickly cleaned up the mess and wiped the bottom of Emma's sandals. She grimaced as she felt the warm sticky manure squishing between her toes like mud on a rainy day.

"Hurry, take this spear," someone said.

"But I have horse manure in my sandals," Emma moaned.

"Keep going," the voice said. "No one will know."

Emma's partner grabbed her and propelled her around again and onstage. This time she was marching with the group of soldiers escorting the horse drawn golden chariot carrying Rhadames, the victorious leader. The animal kept snorting and breathing down Emma's back. It didn't want to be there and was making its discomfort known to all those around. Emma felt warm drops of saliva drip down the back of her tunic. She had visions of being trampled. Horses never liked me. *Guardian Angel, protect me from this vicious beast.*

When the chariot stopped in front of Pharaoh, the soldiers, including Emma, marched off stage.

"That's it," the stage manager said. "You're done. And thank you so much."

With a sigh of relief, Emma followed her partner back to the women's dressing room. She took the crumpled letter out from under the netting and tucked it into her purse, then went to a shower stall, stripped off her costume, wig and sandals and stood under the hot water. She held up her feet, one at a time and grimaced as she worked the manure from between her toes. After ten minutes of scrubbing she felt fairly clean, but the makeup stubbornly clung to the creases in her skin. She washed the sandals as best she could and was exhausted by the time she dressed, stored her costume where she was instructed, and went out to find Nate.

"Are you all right?" he asked when he found her in the community room sipping a cup of tea. "I saw what happened."

Emma giggled. "I'm okay now, but I really freaked out when that horse lifted his tail."

"The trainers are supposed to see to it that accidents don't happen, but—you've got makeup on your neck," he said, massaging her shoulders.

"I'll take another shower when we get to your place," Emma said.

Nate winked at her. "I have a better idea. Come on, let's go home."

When they reached Nate's condo, Emma saw his neighbor's door open a few inches, then immediately close.

"Your girlfriend is looking for you," she said, raising her eyebrows.

Nate closed the door firmly. "I've been rude to that woman more than once. I wish she would just leave me alone. Come on, forget about Sadie. Let's open a bottle of wine."

Emma took off her coat and hat, plopped into a chair and yawned. She hadn't realized how tired she was.

Nate walked into the living room and handed her a

glass of chilled *Pinot Grigio.*

"Mmmm," Emma murmured. "This is just what I need."

He raised his eyebrows. "Are you sure that's *all* you need? I'm running the water in the tub with a special herbal mixture guaranteed to promote complete relaxation or your money back."

A few minutes later, Emma smiled as she walked into the bathroom. The tub was half filled with water; a fragrance she couldn't quite identify filled the room.

"Get in when you're ready; I'll turn on the Jacuzzi," he said.

Emma took off her clothes and settled back in the warm water bubbling around her. She closed her eyes and felt the tension slowly ebbing from her body. In a few minutes she heard the door open. She looked up to see Nate enter the room carrying two more glasses of wine. Her eyes opened wide. He was naked.

"You didn't think I was going to let you luxuriate in here alone, did you?" He put the glasses on the floor next to the tub, got in, and settled behind her pulling her body between his legs and up against his chest. "There, isn't this nice?"

"Oh yes, very nice."

After a few more minutes and a few more sips of wine, Nate took a wash cloth and a bar of soap and began scrubbing the rest of the makeup off Emma's arms and neck. Soon his hands began to roam.

"Wait a minute," she said. "There's no makeup there."

"There better not be."

"Now, you'd better let me wash your neck," Emma said snatching the cloth out of his hand. She got on her knees between his legs and before long the wash cloth settled at the bottom of the tub as their hands explored each others' bodies.

"Come on," Nate said, pulling her up. "Let's get in bed."

They finished the wine. Between kisses, they dried each other with thick towels. Coyly Emma walked to the king sized bed holding the towel around her.

Nate pulled it away and lifted her chin with his hand. "Now little Sparrow, I'm going to show you just how much I love you."

Emma was transported again to another world, but this time it was real.

Later, as they lay in a state of complete relaxation, Emma stared wide-eyed at the ceiling. "Nate," she said.

"Huh?"

"The bass who sang Ramfis was Bruno Gentile. I heard the announcement."

"So what?" he groaned turning on his back.

"There was something evil about him. I could feel it," she said.

"Just your imagination. He was the stand in. Nice voice. He's supposed to be evil; really threw himself into the part."

"No, it was more than that. He's one of the two men."

"Go to sleep, Emma." The words slurred as he dozed.

Emma lay there for a long time thinking about the bass. Was he the one trying to harm Speranza? Perhaps the letter would give her a clue.

# Chapter 23

The following morning Emma could wait no longer. When Nate went out to the neighborhood deli for fresh bagels and lox, she took the letter and envelope from her purse and smoothed them out on the kitchen table.

First she examined the envelope. It was addressed to Bruno Gentile in care of Patano to an address on Taylor Street, a well-known Italian neighborhood. Her heart skipped a beat when she looked at the return address□ San Guillermo, Sicily, the same town Speranza came from, the same town where she had seen the two chorus members. Yes, she was getting somewhere, she was sure of it.

Eagerly she looked at the letter, the cramped handwriting difficult to read. She could only make out a few words since it was written in dialect. She screwed up her face. This is going to take some time, she thought. When she heard Nate's key in the lock, she quickly shoved the papers back into her purse.

The next performance of *Aida* went well with no mishaps from the horse. When it was over, Emma breathed a sigh of relief. That night she, again, stayed with Nate and enjoyed his ardent love making.

The next morning, as usual, he went to the neighborhood deli for fresh bagels and lox. When he returned they went into the kitchen, sat down at the table and he gently kissed her neck. It seemed so right, to be here, like this, with him. Nate toasted the bagels and slathered his with cream cheese.

"What were you like as a little boy?" Emma asked.

He took a bite and chewed, then thought for a moment. "I grew up on the West Side of Chicago. It was a rough neighborhood and my brother and I soon learned to defend ourselves against the bigger, tougher boys. We had no choice; it was a matter of survival.

"My father owned a shoe repair shop. In those days people weren't so quick to throw away their footwear. There was no money to buy new ones. On Saturdays my brother, Sal, and I helped out, polishing shoes and cutting leather. I hated every minute of it. That was not what I wanted to do with my life." Nate stopped for a moment, took a generous bite of bagel and washed it down with coffee. Emma sat quietly, sipping her coffee and listening.

"Pa wanted us to take over the business. He said it was an honest living and would put bread on the table, but I wanted more on my table than bread.

"Sal and I looked at each other and shook our heads. The smell of leather and glue was not for us. We ended up selling real estate. It was the right time. The economy was stabilizing and people were making money. I was a born salesman and did quite well."

Emma tried to suppress a smile at those words. How well she knew. She bit her lip and kept looking at her untouched bagel.

"Pretty soon Sal and I started buying run down

stores, fixing them up and renting them out. Money rolled in. Pa sold the shoe repair business and we set him and Ma up in a little house in Florida. Eventually Sal settled there, too, married a nice Jewish girl and did well in real estate." He looked at her, but she still averted her eyes.

"Mine was a different story. I loved Chicago, the excitement of the city, the nightlife; something was always going on. One night, just for a lark, I went to the opera with some friends. I couldn't believe what I was hearing, music I didn't know existed. I went back again and again; I was hooked." He stopped and spread cream cheese on another bagel, then added a generous helping of lox.

"Oh I made my share of mistakes when I was young, everyone does. And I paid for them, dearly." He looked away, a pained expression on his face.

Emma didn't ask more. She knew that some things were better left unsaid. There were things in her life that she wouldn't share with anyone either.

Nate continued. "Through the years I invested my money wisely, married, had two sons, divorced, and now am comfortably retired. Does that satisfy your curiosity?" He hooked his finger under her chin and gently raised her head to look into her luminous eyes.

Emma took a deep breath and bit into her bagel. "What was your wife like?"

"Hmmm—Estelle. What can I say? She was beautiful and sexy. I was young and hungry. We clicked in bed, but that was the only place." He looked out the window and hesitated a moment.

"The first few years were okay. The boys were born two years apart. Then she decided that children were ruining her figure. There would be no more, even though I had always wanted a daughter." He shrugged. "I went along, but nothing I did satisfied her. She wanted a bigger house, I bought her a bigger house. She wanted domestic help, I hired a maid. She wanted to join the Country Club, so we did. Then she decided I was too crude and should polish my social skills.

"Enough already," he said bitterly. "By then the boys were in high school and we were in separate bedrooms. When she said she wanted a divorce, I was relieved. My lawyer saw to it that my rights were protected. I signed the papers without a word of regret." He closed his eyes and traveled back over the years, a sad but determined expression on his face.

"Did she remarry?" Emma asked.

"Oh yes, someone with position and lots of money. But the last I heard, she was tired of him, too. I feel sorry for the guy."

"What about your relationship with the boys?" Emma asked.

"They always respected me; knew what a greedy woman their mother was. We've stayed close through the years. The older one, Alex, lives in Oregon, got involved in the lumber business. He married, but soon divorced. The younger one, Nate, Jr., lives in Florida near my brother. He has two sons. There, now you know all about me, and my family." He gave her a wicked smile.

All you want me to know, she thought. "I'm new at this," she confessed. "You see, this is the first relationship I've had since Frank died. I feel so — vulnerable."

"I can understand that. And, as far as women are concerned, I'm still a virile man, as you well know."

He smiled at her blush. “I like women, their softness, their coy little ploys. I like to be seen with them, find them entertaining. But, there has to be more to a relationship, my dear. When the sex is over, I want to be able to have an intelligent discussion with the lady. I don’t want to ask a question and have her answer, ‘Huh?’”

He hesitated a moment, as if trying to find the right words. “When I met you, I felt something deep, something lasting. It’s hard for me to explain. You make me laugh, Emma, make me feel fulfilled. I want to be with you, always. Do you understand that?”

She nodded, unable to say anything. Her heart began to pound. Could this really be happening?

He took her hand and pressed it to his lips and she didn’t want him to stop.

After Emma left, Nate’s phone rang. He really didn’t feel like talking to anyone just now, but he decided to answer it. He froze at the whiny sound of the voice on the other end.

“Hi, lover boy, did you miss me?”

“Marsha, what a surprise.” He was about to say an unpleasant one, but decided to hear her out.

“Do you miss me?” she asked, again.

“No, actually, I don’t.”

“That’s not very complimentary.”

“Listen, you’re the one who suddenly decided to run off to California. You’re the one who ended the relationship. What do you want now?” He gripped the phone and paced back and forth.

“Don’t be mad at me. I miss you. Maybe I’ll come back to Chicago. Would you like that?”

"You can go anywhere you like, but don't expect me to be waiting for you."

"Well, you sound serious."

"I am. Now I have an appointment, so, if you have nothing else to say, good bye." He hung up the phone, clutched his fists and gritted his teeth. He willed his body not to react to the memory of Marsha's soft curves, her sensuous mouth, her erotic lovemaking.

"No. No! I'm through with women like her," he shouted trying to convince himself. "I love Emma, yes, I do. And I won't let Marsha or anyone else spoil it."

# Chapter 24

Emma sat at her kitchen table with a cup of tea, the folder with all the information she had gathered, her English-Italian dictionary, and the letter smoothed out in front of her.

She began translating as best she could. Her knowledge of Italian was good, but the letter seemed to be written in the Sicilian dialect. It referred to someone named Angelo singing somewhere, she couldn't quite make out the words. Something about lessons in Palermo. A request for money. It was signed by a Padre Martino. She began to extrapolate from all the information she had so far.

On a blank page she wrote:

1. Gentile and Speranza born in the same Sicil ian town.
2. A child named Angelo has talent.
3. Priest requesting lessons in Palermo.
4. Who is Angelo? Bruno's brother? His son? Some other relative?
5. How is Speranza connected to Bruno and Angelo?

*Guardian Angel, I think I'm getting somewhere. I know*

*the answer will come. Guide me, please.* She felt satisfied, as if she knew her celestial guardian would intervene.

Just as she put the folder away, the phone rang.

"Hello."

"Hi Emma," Gladys' voice boomed. "How did your stint as a super for the visiting opera company turn out?"

"Oh my, let me sit down and I'll tell you all about it."

For the next twenty minutes Emma recounted the episode with the horse manure.

Gladys roared. "I can always count on you for a good story. So—you stayed with Nate?"

"Yes, it would have been foolish to go back and forth."

"And?"

"And what?"

"Did you *do* it?"

"Do what?"

"Don't play coy with me, Emma Winberry. You know what I mean."

"Oh, that. As a matter of fact we did."

"Was it good?"

"More than good. It was great. I never imagined I could be so responsive at my age." Emma blushed at the memory of their lovemaking.

"Nonsense, age has nothing to do with it. If you're both in reasonably good health and the attraction is mutual, I say, go for it." Gladys let out a low earthy laugh. "Why when Cornell and I get going . . ."

"That's enough, Gladys. No details please." Emma felt this conversation had gone far enough.

"Okay my conservative friend, but I am delighted to hear that the relationship is progressing nicely. Before you hang up, has there been any progress with the manuscript?"

Emma grimaced. "I did write a couple of pages," she lied, "but got caught up with this supernumerary role. After the opera season is over, I'll get back to it, I promise. And, I told Nate about it. He thought it was a great idea and wants to get involved." Emma felt more comfortable talking about the project now.

"Fantastic!" Gladys gushed. "I'll tell Cornell."

"Okay, but tell him not to expect instant results. This is going to take me a while. Now I must get to more mundane tasks. The laundry awaits. Talk to you soon. Bye."

"Nate, my grandson is going to be baptized on March 23, that's a week from Sunday. Would you be interested in coming? My family wants to meet you," Emma said, a note of anxiety in her voice.

"Let me check my calendar. Hang on a minute."

Emma paced, clutching the phone and wondering how he felt about meeting her children.

"That day is clear. I'd love to come. I think it's time your kids found out what kind of man has been making love to their mother." He laughed, a lascivious tone in his voice.

"Nate, what a thing to say."

"Well, it's true. They're adults. You bring out the earthy side of my nature, my sexy little Sparrow."

"You shouldn't be saying such things over the phone." Emma fidgeted, feeling embarrassed.

"Why? Is your line tapped? Maybe the CIA is listening? Oh my dear, you are naïve. Perhaps that's why I'm so fond of you. Now, what time and where for this solemn religious observance?"

"The service is at the Church of the Trinity in the western suburbs at two in the afternoon. I'm not sure of the address, but I'll let you know. Will you be comfortable in a Catholic Church?"

"Dear Lady," he said, "I feel comfortable in any church, and I have visited most denominations. I will be at the baptism and behave in a most dignified manner."

She heard the mirth in his voice, took a deep breath and let it out slowly. "Afterwards, there will be a catered supper at James and Sylvia's place just a short distance away."

"Count me in. Now, where shall we go for dinner tomorrow night?"

When Emma stepped on the scale the following morning, she noted a weight gain of two pounds. Love agrees with me, she thought. She realized that her relationship with Nate filled a vacancy she had ignored for too long. Her family noticed the change in her, approved, and were eager to meet this dynamic man.

Was this really love she felt? She looked forward to their time together with such anticipation her heartbeat doubled. Not only was he an ardent lover, he was well read, considerate, generous, had a great sense of humor, and she knew he was financially comfortable. What more could she ask for?

That night Emma dreamed about another disturbing image.

*Emma is at the baptism, but the church is a very old church like the ones in European towns. The choir begins to sing. A boy's voice rises above the others in clear lucid tones.*

*Suddenly Bruno Gentile walks into the church. He stares at Emma.*

*"Don't interfere," he warns.*

Emma woke in a cold sweat, her heart pounding. "I'll never rest until I resolve this mystery," she said getting out of bed and pacing the floor.

*Oh Guardian Angel, please give me some guidance.*

The day of the baptism dawned sunny and unseasonably warm for the middle of March. Emma wore a new dress of soft light blue wool that she had worked on all week. An orange print scarf, a gold bracelet and matching earrings set off the outfit to perfection.

Maria came lumbering up the front stairs holding onto the railing. "Ah, my knees are going bad," she said, as Emma led her into the living room.

"Sit down. What did the doctor say at your appointment yesterday?"

"He said I have to lose twenty pound before he can give me new knees. Oh *Mama mia*." She shook her head and rubbed her painful joints.

"So?" Emma asked. "Are you going to take his advice?"

"Eh, I try. No more baking. I eat *verdure e fagioli*, greens and beans, and a little pasta, that's all. He says I should exercise in a swimming pool. Can you see me in a bathing suit?" The woman patted her abdomen, today restrained by a tight corset. She shook her head and moaned.

Emma commiserated with her friend, but had never faced a weight problem in her life. She thought of Gladys and her life long battle with the scale, until she had finally said, "To hell with it!"

Stephen picked up Emma and Maria at half past one. They arrived at the church a few minutes before two. Emma looked at the modern façade, only a stained glass window of colored designs, no spires, no bell tower reaching toward heaven. Inside was one huge room with benches in a semicircle. A Spartan altar sat in the center. There were no side altars to Mary and Joseph as there had been in the churches when Emma was a girl. The stations-of-the-cross were of such modern designs, she had to look carefully to determine what they were. She frowned, not to her liking at all.

She thought of her dream, almost expected to see Bruno Gentile glaring at her from somewhere inside the church. She shook her head free of the image, and hurried over to the proud parents standing near the baptismal font. She took baby James in her arms, looking down at him in awe, her first grandson, so innocent, so perfect. She caressed the velvet soft cheek with her finger, smoothed the down-like blond hair. Was Frank watching? Yes, he had to be. She could feel his love surrounding them. "This is our daughter's child," she whispered as if he were right behind her.

"Oh Mom," Sylvia said. "Your gentleman friend is here. He seems very nice."

Emma looked at Nate standing off to the side. He smiled as he came toward her and slipped his arm around her waist.

"You've already met James and Sylvia," Emma said. "This is my neighbor, Maria Russo. My son Stephen, and his wife Pat, and their daughter Susan."

The little girl wore a ruffled pink dress with a matching bow in her hair. Pat held her hand tightly but she kept pulling away, eager to explore.

Nate shook hands, welcomed by everyone.

"Where's your brother?" Emma asked.

"Not here yet, and he's the godfather," James said tapping his foot and looking at his watch.

"Typical," Emma muttered.

"By the way," Stephen said, "I hear that Martin has a new girlfriend."

I hope she's better than the last one, Emma thought.

Martin and his latest girlfriend, Bertie, came rushing in as the priest was making his way to the baptismal font.

Emma looked with approval at the petite girl, her dark hair in a pixie cut, her smile exuding friendliness.

"Sorry," Martin whispered, taking his place next to his sister.

The ceremony lasted an hour, three babies receiving the sacrament. Baby James slept through the whole proceeding. As the priest poured the holy water over his head and uttered the time-honored phrases, Emma wondered what life had in store for this little one. Frank, please watch over him, she prayed, and little Susan, too.

Later they all gathered at the proud parents' house. The catered meal was delicious, various hors d'oeuvres, sliced ham and cold beef, crunchy rolls, salads, and a beautifully decorated whipped cream cake.

After most of the guests had left and the baby was sleeping peacefully, Emma, her children, Nate and Maria sipped coffee and chatted. Her family had all accepted him without question.

"How are you doing with the computer, Ma?" Martin asked.

Emma, a smug expression on her face, answered confidently. "I'm happy to tell you all that I'm doing very well." She looked at Nate and smiled. "Nate is going to help me with the manuscript, just as soon as we have time."

He nodded. "It's a challenge, and there's nothing I like more."

"How are preparations going at the Lyric for the opening of *The Elixir of Love?"* Emma asked James.

"Speranza came in a few days ago to begin rehearsals and so did Finelli. Boy, she's something else. I was talking to the stage manager at the Lyric the other day and he said she complained about everything. She said the stage was too small, it was too cold, the piano was out of tune. She told the director she might never come back to Chicago."

"I'll bet he was glad to hear that," Nate said laughing.

"He was, and so were the other members of the cast. She refuses to stay in a hotel, shuns all reporters and has a deathly fear of the paparazzi."

"Where does she stay, if not in a hotel?" Emma asked.

James shrugged. "With some family members on the north side. She keeps it a guarded secret. Comes and goes in a limo, a real weird one."

"But aren't most of them like that?" Pat asked.

"Not really," James continued. "That temperamental diva bit is really a myth. Most of them are very nice."

"And what's Speranza like?" Emma asked.

"A great guy! Of course he has all the women eating out of his hand. He's handsome, suave and debonair. A little too cocky, but that's to be expected with a voice like his."

"Wasn't there an accident at one of the rehearsals?" Nate asked. "I heard something on the radio."

"My sources tell me that a balcony he was leaning against gave way and one of the other singers grabbed him. It was a near miss. The man seems to be accident prone."

Emma frowned and shook her head. She wanted to tell them all she had learned, but, she hesitated; at this point it was all conjecture. There was no proof, but she was compelled to say something. "I have a feeling it wasn't an accident, like that backdrop in Milan and that incident in Naples. I believe the man may be in danger."

"There goes Mom with her prophecies," Sylvia said rolling her eyes.

"Yeah, we heard plenty of those when we were growing up," Martin agreed.

Emma frowned. "Never mind, all of you. Wasn't I right most of the time? Remember when you lost your gold ring, Sylvia? I told you just where to find it, in your locker at school. And your watch, Martin?"

"I have to admit," Sylvia said, "I did think you might be a witch."

"This opera singer," Maria said, "maybe somebody put the *malocchio* on him, you know, the evil eye. I saw that happen when I was a girl in Italy. Somebody needs to take it off!" She nodded and folded her hands in her lap.

"How would you do that?" Martin's new girlfriend, Bertie, asked. She was a quiet girl who thought before she spoke. Emma approved of his choice. This might be the one to make a man out of him.

"Eh," Maria said. "He should go see a *strega!"* She nodded vigorously.

"I don't think people advertise as witches in this country, Maria," Emma said.

"When I say *strega,* I mean a good witch. Somebody born on Christmas Eve with the power to remove the curse, a *Jettatore."* She whispered the last phrase and made the sign of the cross.

Nate stared at the ceiling suppressing a smile.

"In my town," Maria continued, "there was a *strega* with a mark on her face, like somebody spilled *vino roso* down the side. People went to see her for headaches and all kinds of bad luck caused by the *malocchio.* She helped them every time." Maria clasped her hands and nodded her head forcefully as if to add credence to her words.

"And how did she do that?" Martin asked. He was sitting on the edge of his chair, drawn into Maria's story.

"Eh," she said raising her hands, "with oil and water!" She looked around to make sure she had everyone's attention. She leaned forward and took a saucer from the table. "She took a bowl, filled it with water and put a few drops of olive oil in the water to make the sign of the cross." She crossed her hand slowly over the saucer. "Then she held the bowl over the head of the sick person and moved it around, very slow." Maria raised the saucer and rotated it counterclockwise.

"If the oil spread out across the water, it was the sign of the *malocchio:* jealousy or bad luck. She would say special prayers, then throw the water out the window." Maria took a deep breath, put down the saucer, and sat back, a self-assured expression on her face.

"Hmm," Emma said, "anything is possible."

She didn't want to embarrass her friend, besides, if she could talk to her Guardian Angel, wasn't the *malocchio* possible? Maybe it was the man from Sicily, or possibly Finelli. Could the two be working together? Emma remembered the stage bills. The soprano had appeared in the Naples production but not in Milan. She dismissed the thought and reconsidered.

Nate shrugged. "And who is going to suggest this — exorcism to Signor Speranza?" he asked winking at Emma.

Since he was involved with the Midwest, all eyes turned to James. He squirmed in his chair and cleared his throat. "Well, that's a little unusual, but let me think about it."

# Chapter 25

Bruno and Gerard sat in Antonio's kitchen drinking wine and studying the musical score to *A Masked Ball.* The family was in the living room talking in hushed tones so as not to disturb the singers.

"What happened at the rehearsal of *Elixir of Love* when Speranza almost fell off that balcony?" Gerard asked, giving Bruno a suspicious look.

"Why are you asking me? Is it my fault the man is a clumsy oaf?"

"He could have broken something. It's a good thing Mario caught him."

Before Bruno could respond, they heard raised voices from the living room.

"Why can't we go, Poppa?" Sammy asked, his voice rising. "My teacher says it's a big, big dinosaur, and his name is Sue."

"Sh," his father warned, "not so loud. You mustn't disturb my cousin and Bruno. You know why you can't go. The museum costs too much money. I have to spend the extra on medicine for Josie." His voice softened.

"Josie, always Josie," the boy wailed. "What about the rest of us?"

A resounding slap followed by more crying.

"No more," Amalia said.

Bruno put the score down and frowned as Josie inched her way into the kitchen, huge tears sliding down her cheeks, her breath coming in gulping sobs. She went to Bruno and buried her face in his lap. The child reeked of camphor and garlic.

He looked at Gerard's pained face. "Come on, little one, don't cry," he said patting her head and lifting her onto his lap.

"Bruno," Gerard said, "we take them to the museum, huh? We pay."

*"Sì,"* Bruno agreed.

The two men walked into the living room, Bruno carrying Josie on his shoulder.

"Eh," Gerard said, "Sunday we *all* go to the museum, to see this big bag of bones, this Sue. What you say?"

"But Gerard . . . ," Antonio began.

Gerard lifted his hand. "No. We pay. Everybody goes. Okay?"

The children began jumping up and down. Josie smiled as Bruno wiped her face. Amalia turned around and dried her own eyes with her apron.

Sunday morning dawned with frigid temperatures. Josie had been up coughing during the night. She sat at the breakfast table, dark circles under her eyes, a forlorn look on her face.

When it was time to leave for the outing, the children bundled into their coats and hats. When Josie went for hers, Amalia held her back.

"No, *piccina,* it is too cold. You cannot go and walk so far."

Josie's eyes widened, her lips trembled. "Mama, I

want to see that big, big Sue . . . Mama, please . . . ."

Her mother shook her head.

"Amalia," Bruno said, "I will carry her. I have this scarf, see. *Mama mia* made it for me. I'll wrap her in the heavy wool and she'll be warm." The two exchanged knowing looks. "She should have a chance to go, too," Bruno said.

Amalia closed her eyes for a moment. She nodded. *"Si."*

"You come, too, Mama," the children chorused.

The woman looked at her thin worn coat and shook her head. "I stay and make the gravy for dinner. I make it with neck bones."

The children jumped and shouted, punching each other and singing. They followed the men down the stairs and into the old car. On the way Bruno held little Josie engulfed in the huge scarf. Yes, she must have a chance as well as the others.

And what about Angelo? Shouldn't he, too, have a chance?

# Chapter 26

The following week the cold spell broke as Emma boarded a plane for Minneapolis. Her sister, Clara, had called gushing over the play. She was certain it would be a huge success. Emma took it all in with a grain of salt. She knew Clara too well. She had asked Nate if he wanted to come with her, but he was rather evasive, said he had an important appointment. It was none of her business, but, she was curious.

She sighed, settled back and looked at the clear blue sky. She took this opportunity to think through a plan of action forming in her mind. It might lead to nothing, then again . . . .

Nate frowned as he dressed for a dinner he both anticipated and dreaded. True to her word, Marsha had called again. She said she was back in Chicago, but only for a short visit and insisted she must see him. It was important.

He held up one tie after another. Then he shook his head and retrieved the first. His fingers clumsily tied the knot after three tries. He scrutinized his reflection in the mirror. *Why am I doing this?* He brushed the few hairs he had left. *I feel as though I'm betraying Emma.*

Did he really love Emma? Yes, he did; she filled a critical need in his life, but the memory of Marsha kept surfacing, no matter what he did. He *had* to make this break, once and for all.

Nate entered the Saddle Bar and Grill. It had been his and Marsha's favorite meeting place. Purposely he never took Emma there.

He spotted her immediately perched on a barstool, an unlit cigarette in one hand and a martini in the other. He stood back and watched her flirting with a man sitting at the other end, her black skirt slit up the side exposing too much of her shapely leg. The neckline plunged to the waist, plump enticing flesh almost spilled out.

Her face was skillfully made up to hide the sagging skin under the eyes and to mask the age lines signaling the relentless passage of time. He slid onto the stool next to her, placing both hands on the bar and gripping it tight.

"Nate," she cooed, "how wonderful to see you." She put her glass down and threw her arms around his neck. Her kiss was a mixture of tobacco and booze.

"You've had too many of those, Marsha," he said extricating himself from her grasp and moving the glass aside. "Let's get some food into you."

"Don't scold," she said in a petulant voice as she slid off the stool and into his arms.

He was forced to put his arm around her waist to keep her from falling. She rubbed her body against him. Nate stiffened, feeling himself begin to respond. He refused to be taken in by this temptress. He pulled her across the room and sat her down roughly at a table in the corner, and seated himself.

"You're angry with me, aren't you?" she asked pouting.

"Marsha, what do you want from me? I thought I made it clear that whatever we had together was over long ago." He folded his hands on the table and frowned. "What happened, did your West Coast gigolo throw you over?"

At that moment the waiter came to the table. "Are you ready to order, Sir?" he asked.

"I'll have a scotch on the rocks and a steak sandwich, medium rare," Nate said. He looked at Marsha.

She frowned. "Greek salad and a vodka martini, with two olives." She looked at Nate, daring him to say anything. "That was not a nice thing to say," she said after the waiter left.

"You haven't answered my question."

"He wasn't like you, Nate. All he wanted was my body." She looked at him through lashes caked with mascara, eyelids heavy from drinking.

"Let's get something straight," Nate said. "There is someone else in my life, someone with depth and intelligence. We have everything in common and I may ask her to marry me." Nate surprised himself. When did he decide that he wanted to spend the rest of his life with Emma?

"Well," she said, startled. "That's a switch. Mr. Party Boy wants to get married. She must really be something special."

"She is — very special, in ways you could never understand."

Marsha gave a coarse laugh and a shrug. "Can't blame a girl for trying. Okay, Nate," she picked up her drink that had just arrived. "To old times and a new life, for both of us."

He nodded and took a sip of his scotch. "What are you planning to do?" he asked against his better judgment.

"I'm off to the Big Apple. My brother lives in Brooklyn. He recently bought a restaurant in Manhattan; says he needs a sexy hostess. I told him I'd take the job." She took a cigarette out of her purse then, realizing there was no ashtray on the table, put it back. "Just stopped here for a couple of days to see old friends. Nothing wrong with that, is there?"

"No, nothing at all." He breathed a sigh of relief.

"Now enjoy your steak sandwich, Lover Boy. I'm not going to try to seduce you. Whoever this gal is, she's got her claws into you, I can see that. She must be some special package. Cheers." She raised her glass and, in one gulp, drained it.

Sunday night Nate waited impatiently at the Northwest Airlines baggage claim area searching for Emma. The plane had landed and the luggage was just beginning to slide precariously down the chute. He paced as he scrutinized the crowd of people walking toward him.

He hadn't told Emma he was coming, but after his meeting with Marsha, he couldn't wait to see her. He felt he had finally broken the spell and was free. When she recognized him, a look of surprise and delight spread across her face. It filled him with warmth.

"Nate," she called starting to run toward him. A child barreled across her path knocking her off balance. Nate just had time to grab her. He held her close and nuzzled her neck.

"Sparrow, I missed you."

"This is a wonderful surprise. I thought you were going to be busy all weekend."

"I finished that business yesterday. It didn't take as long as I thought it would." He held her tighter.

"Come on, I'll take you out for a bite and you can tell me all about the play." She nodded eagerly as they retrieved her suitcase and walked out of the airport arm in arm.

Over egg rolls and Steak Kow, Emma described the theatrical production. "It was *avant garde*, whatever that's supposed to mean. And believe me, it was experimental." She laughed as she dipped an egg roll into a combination of sweet sour sauce and hot mustard.

"So, did it make any sense at all?" Nate asked smiling, content to listen.

"Not as far as I'm concerned. People kept coming on stage uttering phrases I didn't understand. There was no structured plot that I could make out. The main character died at the end, but I don't know why. I think he was supposed to have AIDS, but that was never disclosed."

"Sounds like it could be adapted to a modern opera," Nate said taking a sip of tea.

"Well," she said, "there was a group of college students in one section of the theater who gave it a standing ovation. They must have understood it on an entirely different level.

"I must admit Clara did look striking when she came out for a curtain call with the cast. She wore a top of iridescent green and black diagonal stripes over a long black skirt. A red sash tied around her waist with the ends trailing down the side set it off perfectly. Only Clara could get away with an outfit like that."

"And what did you say to her about the play?" Nate asked, suppressing a grin.

"I told her it was the most unusual production I had ever seen. I said it gave me a great deal to think about." Emma laughed. "She took that as a compliment and we parted with smiles and hugs. I'm glad that's over. The next time any member of my family writes a play, I'll plan to be out of the country."

"And I'll take you there, on a long extended trip." He took her hand and kissed it. "You are so special to me, my dear. Always remember that."

# Chapter 27

The opening night of *The Elixir of Love* at the Lyric was a gala affair. Some patrons appeared in evening dress, others more casual, but everyone was eager to hear the great Marcantonio Speranza. The opera was a light-hearted favorite and the famous tenor was singing the role of Nemorino, the leading man, a rather simple soul who, with the aid of a 'magic elixir,' gets the girl in the end.

James had managed to get Emma and Nate prime seats at the front of the first balcony. Emma looked around at over 3500 people filling the auditorium. She wore a long black skirt topped with a loose purple tunic beaded around the neck. At Sylvia's suggestion, she had found a new hairdresser who cut her hair in a style that complemented her thin face. A saucy curl clung to her cheek. No errant strands stuck out in any direction. Nate's eyes shone with approval.

In Act One, the shy Nemorino, sang to his love, Adina, a chorus of peasants filling the stage. While Speranza sang the aria, '*Quanto e' bella*', Emma raised her opera glasses and noticed a familiar face in the chorus, a man with a malevolent frown. It looked like Bruno Gentile. Goosebumps raised on her arms.

"Look," she whispered to Nate. "Who is that?" A patron from behind angrily shushed her.

Nate put his fingers to his lips and shook his head.

At the intermission, Emma again asked the question. "It was Gentile, wasn't it?"

"I think so. Don't get carried away. He's just a member of the chorus."

Emma could contain herself no longer. She had to tell Nate. Pulling him into a corner, she told him she had discovered the two singers had come from the same town in Sicily. She told him about the letter and her suspicions they might be connected through the boy, Angelo.

Nate gave her a condescending look. "So that's why you were digging in the trash. You certainly have a vivid imagination, I'll grant you that."

"Don't patronize me, Nate Sandler. I know there's history between those two men. I can feel it. This is serious!"

"All right, there may be bad feelings between the two, but that doesn't prove that Gentile is out to harm the tenor. According to rumor, Finelli hates him, too. Does that mean she's trying to do him in?" Nate screwed up his face.

"No, it's more than just bad feelings between the tenor and the bass. And I don't know about Finelli—yet."

Nate shook his head as the bells rang signaling the audience to take their seats.

Emma looked at the envelope again addressed to Bruno in care of Antonio Patano on Taylor Street. She called directory assistance and asked for the phone number. She knew there was a matinee performance today and the two singers would not be at home. Her fingers hesitated for just a moment while she composed her thoughts. Then she punched in the numbers.

"Hallo," a woman's voice answered.

"Hello, Mrs. Patano?"

A hesitation, then the woman said, "Yes."

"I am from the opera chorus. Is Gerard there?" She raised her voice a tone hoping to sound younger.

"No, he and Bruno are at the performance."

"Of course, how silly of me," Emma said. "I couldn't go today because I have a sore throat."

"Make a necklace of garlic and wear it for two days and the soreness will go away," Amalia said with a note of authority.

"Thank you, I will."

"You like my husband's cousin, Gerard?" Amalia asked.

"He's very nice. Tell me, is he married?"

"No, no, they are both bachelors. Maybe we make a match?" Amalia giggled.

Emma laughed in response. If you only knew. "They must have some family back home," she persisted.

"Gerard has a few cousins, no girlfriend."

"And the other one?"

"I think he has a mother living, and a nephew, nobody else, I don't think."

At that moment Emma heard a child coughing. "Mama," a tiny voice called.

"I go now. My little one is sick. What's your name? Maybe you can come over for dinner some time."

"Maybe," Emma said. "Goodbye."

That night when the two men came home, Amalia looked at Gerard with a twinkle in her eye. "I think you got a girlfriend," she said casually setting out the meager supper of beans and greens.

"Eh?" He looked at her, an eager grin on his face.

"A lady called today looking for you."

"A lady? Who? What's her name?"

"She said she was from the chorus. She didn't tell me her name."

"It's Marta. She likes me. I knew it," Gerard said dancing around the table to giggles from the children.

"Fool," Bruno said. "Marta was at the rehearsal, remember?"

"Oh, yes." Gerard made a face, which again sent the children into peals of laughter.

"Sit down and be quiet," Antonio scolded.

"What exactly did she say, Amalia?" Bruno asked.

"She asked if Gerard was married. I told her you were both bachelors." She rubbed her face with both hands and knit her eyebrows together. "Did I say something wrong?"

"No, no," Bruno said, placating the woman. "Did she say anything else?"

"She just asked if you two had family back home." Amalia's face registered fear.

"And she didn't tell you her name?"

"No. Oh *Dio,* did I do wrong?" She wrung her hands and began to cry.

"It's all right," Bruno said. "Forget about it. If she's really after Gerard, she'll call back. Now, let's eat."

Someone is asking questions, he thought. But who? And why?

# Chapter 28

March departed like a lamb; balmy spring breezes and warm temperatures coaxed the leaves from the trees and encouraged the bulbs to poke their heads out of the ground.

Emma tried to put all thoughts of Speranza out of her mind, but they kept surfacing. She thought a trip to the Brookfield Zoo, before the warm weather made the animals sluggish, might help to distract her from the dilemma. The zoo sprawled over two hundred acres of well-tended natural habitats, a collection ranging from powerful polar bears to tiny venomous spiders.

Emma and Nate went through the main gate, down the wide walk to a fountain spilling water into the air in the center of a clear pool. Early tulips, planted around the periphery, were just beginning to open.

They walked arm in arm along the paths from one exhibit to the next. The monkeys ran among the rocks and copulated with abandon.

"Mommy, what are they doing?" a little girl asked her mother. "He's hurting him!" The child looked distraught.

"They're just playing. Come on," the mother said, quickly pulling her away, "let's get a hot dog."

"Do they put you in the mood?" Nate asked sliding his hand down Emma's back.

"Behave yourself, Nate Sandler," she scolded, frowning, but suppressing a smile. "They don't have a Jacuzzi," she whispered.

He threw his head back and laughed, then gave her an enticing squeeze.

As they stood in line for the Dolphin Show, Emma noticed a family ahead of them. One man in particular drew her attention. She knew she had seen him before, but couldn't remember where. He held a small girl on his shoulders. She was laughing and clapping her hands until, suddenly, she began coughing spasmodically. The man took her down from his shoulders and held her gently in his arms as her tiny body convulsed with each cough. He patted her back until the attack subsided.

"Do you recognize that man?" Emma asked Nate.

He screwed up his face. "He does look familiar, but I can't place him."

Emma suddenly realized who he was. "Oh my God, it's Bruno Gentile." She instinctively pulled back. He looked different without makeup.

"Might be," Nate said. "It sure looks like him."

As they took their seats around the large pool, Emma watched the man. He was so gentle with the child, who seemed so frail. Bruno never took his eyes off her, holding her securely on his lap. She remembered the call to the Patano residence, the sick child calling her mother.

Emma could feel the love he bore the little girl. He wasn't an evil man; he couldn't be if he cared so much for another human being. But why did he seem to harbor so much hatred for Speranza, hatred she could feel? Was she overreacting? No, she didn't think so. Was he behind the accidents that had happened? Emma knew Speranza was in danger. She had always known such things. She felt a chill run through her though the day was warm.

That night an early spring storm hit the Chicago area with a vengeance. Emma stood in her living room looking out the window. The smaller trees bent nearly to the ground under the force of the wind. Some larger branches resisted and cracked, crashing down. The heavy rain slanted sideways beating against the windows with such force that Emma instinctively backed away. Lightning lit up the street followed by booming thunder.

Nate called, anxiety echoed in his voice. "Are you all right, Sparrow? I hear the storm is worse in the western suburbs."

"I'm fine, so far. Some tree branches have fallen, but none has hit my house."

A sudden loud crash plunged the entire area into darkness. "Oh oh, there go the lights. I'll talk to you later. Try not to worry." Emma pulled her sweater tight and grabbed the flashlight she had left lying on the kitchen counter.

She lit the candles that lay in readiness around the living room, giving it an eerie feeling. Then curled in a lounge chair away from the windows and opened a new murder mystery. It would be a long night.

In the house on Taylor Street, Amalia also lit candles. But their purpose was more than illumination. Her fingers shook as she held the match to the wick. Josie lay on the bed, covered with a frayed blanket, struggling for breath, her pinched face and thin fingers cold and blue. The mother placed the candles around the little girl and in front of a statue of the Virgin Mary. She knelt beside her daughter, bowed her head, and, with a heavy heart, began to recite the rosary.

A neighborhood healer, a *maga,* had come that afternoon to pray and recite magic intonations, but nothing helped. Amalia knew what the outcome would be. For three nights she had had the same dream. She saw a falling star over a stormy sea. That could mean only one thing. Tears mingled with her prayers.

Outside the bedroom Antonio and Gerard sat, heads also bowed, their hands folded in acceptance. Bruno paced, mumbling and shaking his head. "We should take her to the hospital," he said, rubbing his hand across his face.

"You heard what the doctor said when we took her to the clinic," Antonio said. "They can do nothing. She needs new lungs, a double transplant, and there are so many people on the list that . . ." Tears rolled down his cheeks as he acknowledged that his daughter was dying.

"No!" Bruno insisted. "There must be something, more medicine, more treatments. Please, Antonio, let's take her to that County Hospital. What do they call it? Stroger?" He was like a madman, pacing from one end of the small room to the other.

Antonio went into the bedroom and talked with his wife. When he came out he was nodding. "*Si,* Amalia will wrap her up warm and we take her."

The mother held out no hope. She had seen too

many unfortunate children die before their time. She wrapped her child in the frayed blanket, made the sign of the cross on her daughter's forehead, kissed her for what might be the last time, and said goodbye. She stayed behind with the other children as Antonio, Gerard, and Bruno bundled Josie in the back seat of the car.

Antonio drove through the flooded streets as fast as he was able. Bruno held Josie close talking to her in a gentle singsong tone. Gerard clutched her favorite book, *The Cat in the Hat.* The sound of her labored breathing filled them with dread.

Outside nature pummeled the machine with all its might. Antonio's white knuckles clutched the wheel as he tried to keep the car under control sloshing through flooded streets that threatened to wash them all away. He turned the steering wheel from side to side attempting to avoid the deeper water. At times the car stalled, but Antonio was able to coax it into motion. When he finally pulled up to the Emergency Room, Bruno jumped out, and clutching Josie, ran inside with Gerard close behind.

The two men looked at the waiting room filled with people; some moaning in pain; others with dirty bandages seeping blood; some crying; some just sleeping in a corner.

"Please," Bruno said to a harried nurse. "This child needs help."

"You'll have to fill out papers and wait your turn," she said in an exhausted voice. Then she looked at Josie, shook her head, and beckoned. "Come this way."

Bruno laid the child on the designated cart, tucked a blanket around her tiny body, and lovingly placed an extra pillow under her head in a vain attempt to ease her breathing. Josie opened her eyes and smiled. She tried to raise her arms, but they fell to her sides.

"*Zio* Bruno," she whispered. He bent down and put his ear to her lips. "*Ti amo,*" she said.

"Oh little Josie," he sobbed. "*Ti amo, sempre, sempre.*"

Inside the examination room, the nurse adjusted oxygen through tiny prongs in the child's nose, but her blue face didn't change color. Her respirations became shallower. A young doctor listened to Josie's chest with a stethoscope, trying to hide the look of helplessness on his face. He whispered some orders to the nurse, patted the child's hand, smiled at her and went to the next patient. The nurse hooked up an electrocardiogram and the three men watched the blips on the screen. At first they were rapid as the little heart tried to compensate for the lack of oxygen taken in by the failing lungs, but after a while the pump began to tire.

Bruno, Antonio, and Gerard sat at the bedside watching an intravenous drip slowly into the tiny blue vein. They watched the blips on the screen become slower and farther apart, until they stopped. An alarm sounded. Nurses and doctors ran to the bedside and began an attempt to bring life back to the tiny body.

Antonio cried out, sobbing for his child. Gerard tried to comfort him.

Bruno stood transfixed, as if in a dream. He refused to believe what was happening. He heard orders called out, saw people running in and out of the room. In a daze he walked outside into the storm, the rain streaming down his face mingling with tears. He raised his fist to heaven. "No!" he cried out. He cursed a God who would allow the innocent to die like this; little Josie, who never had a chance to live; his beautiful sister stripped of life giving birth to that bastard, Angelo, while the guilty went on living and became famous.

Two days later as Emma read the morning paper, she glanced at the obituaries. She wasn't in the habit of reading them, but this morning she seemed compelled to do so. As she looked down the list of names, her eyes rested on Patano. She read the notice. Josephine, age eight, beloved daughter of Antonio and Amalia . . . She remembered her phone conversation with Mrs. Patano, the child coughing in the background, the child she had seen at the zoo. The poor little thing.

Emma clipped the notice out of the paper and looked at the address of the funeral parlor. She could take the Metra train and a bus. Am I crazy? What am I thinking? I don't even know these people. But, for some reason, she had to go. On her way, she stopped at a store, bought an appropriate card, signed it 'a friend', and slipped two twenty dollar bills inside.

A damp wind blew, warning of another approaching storm as Bruno followed Gerard to the Capano Brothers Funeral Home. He hesitated at the door examining the ancient building. In its early days it had been an opulent residence. Such irony, probably filled with rich people laughing and dancing. Now everyone who walks in is in mourning. He looked at the decaying stone lions standing on either side of the entrance. Half of the face of one had been eaten away by time and the elements.

It seemed to say to Bruno this was the fate of all living things. He shivered. Under his arm he carried the old copy of *The Cat in the Hat.* Josie would be lonely without it.

Gerard turned and looked at his friend. "Are you coming in?"

*"Si."* Bruno gave a deep sigh and followed Gerard. Only one of the three parlors was occupied. Bruno looked at the notification on the side:

Josephine Patano
Service 9AM
Mass 10AM
Internment: St. Joseph Cemetery

It was so final. Was there nothing more? Was there a God? How could He let this happen? Josie . . . his sister, Angela . . . both too young and innocent. With stooped shoulders and a heavy heart, he followed Gerard.

The two men stood at the back observing the time honored ritual. Three Italian women clad in black stood around the small white casket, wailing. Amalia sat dry eyed, in a trance-like state, in the front row flanked by her other children. Antonio stood to the side greeting the visitors as they entered, shaking his head and mumbling.

Gerard took Bruno's arm and walked slowly to the casket. They looked down at the pitifully small body lying there. She looked like a porcelain doll, her hair curled around the thin face, a pink dress ruffled around her neck. She wore an expression of peace and contentment.

Gerard crossed himself, kissed his fingers and touched them to the cold cheek. Bruno let out a low moan. He picked up the cold stiff hand and placed the book on Josie's chest. Then he turned and walked out of the room, past the mourners, out the door, past the silent lions, and into the driving rain.

He fell to his knees on the wet pavement, buried his head in his hands and wept bitter tears, of grief, regret, and … determination.

Emma stood hidden by a huge umbrella a few doors away. She saw Bruno kneeling on the pavement, weeping. Her heart went out to him. She could feel his pain. He needs help, she thought, but she was powerless to be of any assistance.

She walked unobtrusively into the funeral parlor and knelt at the casket. No one seemed to notice her. She was not one of them. The sight of the book in the alabaster-like hands clutched at her heart. She said a prayer for the tiny soul on its way to a better life, placed the card on the rack, looked at the grieving mother surrounded by the women in black, turned, and left as quietly as she had come.

# Chapter 29

Should I or shouldn't I? Emma asked herself as she paced the floor. I swear I'm going to wear out this tile if I keep this up. She brewed a cup of tea then sat in her favorite lounge chair.

"All right, Guardian Angel, tell me what to do. I sense that Gentile is not truly an evil man, but for some reason he hates Speranza. How can I stop him from ruining his life? From that letter it certainly sounds like his family needs him, and, if he's in jail for injuring the tenor, he can't care for them."

*Do it,* her inner voice said.

She sighed, took out a pen and paper as well as her English□ Italian dictionary and began to write two letters.

A two-week break between the last performance of the Lyric and the beginning of rehearsals for *A Masked Ball* gave the performers a chance for some much needed rest and relaxation. Some of them flew home, wherever that might be, but most decided to take advantage of the many amusements Chicago had to offer; fine restaurants, museums, plays, shopping.

Marcantonio Speranza sat back in his suite at a downtown hotel. A new member of the chorus had caught his eye. She was due to arrive at any moment to sing for him, and perhaps, something more. Her contralto voice was provocative as well as her shapely body. He looked forward to an enjoyable afternoon.

The only thing that interfered with his anticipation was a letter he had received the previous day. He picked it up and read it for the third time.

*Dear Mr. Speranza,*

*This letter may sound strange and I don't blame you if you throw it away without giving it a second thought. But please believe me. I frequently have premonitions which usually turn out to be accurate. I feel someone is trying to harm you. Please be extra cautious for the remainder of your stay in Chicago.*

*A Friend and Admirer*

"Ah," he said aloud tossing the letter aside. "There are crazy people everywhere. Why should anybody want to hurt me? I am the most famous and beloved tenor in the world."

He felt a sudden chill. There were jealous people, and he did believe in the *malocchio*. He remembered unexplained events in his home town; the backdrop in Milan, and the railing that had mysteriously come lose at the Lyric; he envisioned the face of the man in Sicily the previous summer, filled with hate, his hand making the sign of the horns. Maybe I will take this advice and be extra careful.

A knock on the door followed by a melodious voice pushed all thoughts of harm and curses out of his mind.

In the house on Taylor Street, the occupants went

about their daily routine with heavy hearts. A light had gone out, as if someone had turned off the sun.

"So," Gerard said, "what's wrong with your mother?"

"Padre Martino didn't say. For once I think it might be true. Maybe she is really sick," Bruno said as he packed a suitcase.

"You'll be back in time for rehearsal, right? You have an important part," Gerard said.

"*Si,* I'll be back. Nothing will make me miss this chance to be close to the great Speranza." He looked at his friend. "Why don't you come with me and get out of this house of tears?"

Gerard shook his head. "No, Antonio needs me. I stay here."

As the plane prepared to land in Palermo, Bruno had mixed feelings about coming home. He felt this was where his roots were tangled firmly in the soil, but the opportunity to become famous lay in America. He would probably have to see Francesca. What would he say to her? Would he ask her to come with him? No, not now. His plan might be dangerous, and this was his only chance for revenge.

The bus ride from Palermo to his home-town was long and uncomfortable. He looked out at the barren landscape, felt the searing heat. And it was only March. Maybe he could convince his mother to come back with him to America. He had tried that before, but she wouldn't hear of it. She told him this was where she was born and this was where she would die. He knew how stubborn these Sicilian women were. That would never change.

And there was Angelo, always Angelo. Why do I have to have this responsibility? Bruno asked himself for the one hundredth time. The answer was always the same, because there was no one else. He was family, whether Bruno liked it or not. "*Io promesso*," he muttered.

Padre Martino stood at the bus stop. His shoulders drooped, his balding head brown from the sun, his cassock covered with dust. When he saw Bruno, a smile brightened his lined and weathered face.

"Ah, my son, I am so happy to see you." He shook Bruno's hand with a strength that belied his appearance.

"How is my mother?" Bruno asked.

"Eh, some days good; some days not so good. She will be better now that you are here. Come, my car is over there."

The priest led Bruno to a battered vehicle of unknown vintage. It looked like it belonged in a museum, or a junkyard. Never in America would anyone drive a car like that.

After much coaxing and a few prayers, the tired engine coughed and groaned as it began moving slowly ahead. While the car bumped along the road, Padre Martino said, "I think you should come home, my son."

"Why? I send money. There is nothing here for me. In America maybe I can make a name for myself. No, I'll never come back." Bruno saw the priest grimace. "What is it Padre? Is there something you're not telling me?"

The priest stopped the car and turned toward Bruno. "I got a letter, from America."

"Who sent it?"

"I don't know. It was signed 'a friend'. No return address on the envelope."

Bruno felt uncomfortable. Someone knew too much about his affairs. But who? "What did the letter say?"

The priest sighed. "It said you might be in much trouble if you stay in America. You should come home." He turned toward Bruno. "What kind of trouble are you in? Is it drugs?" He said the last words in a whisper.

"Padre," Bruno said, gripping the older man's shoulder. "I have nothing to do with drugs. What I do in America is sing, that's all. Somebody is telling lies about me and I'm going to find out who it is. Don't worry, and don't tell my mother about the letter."

The priest nodded. "But I will say three special masses for you. Your mother had three dreams about water and she, too, is afraid."

"Bah, superstition. I don't believe in dreams. But say the masses if it makes her feel better." He took a wad of Euros from his pocket and handed them to the priest.

"You are a good son," the Padre said shoving the bills in his pocket.

Without another word, he started up the old car and jostled over the rutted dirt road until Bruno thought he would rather walk. When he saw the house up ahead, it looked tired and worn like an old man who had walked the earth too long.

"I leave you now," the priest said. "We have choir practice in an hour. I hope you will come."

Bruno didn't answer. He took his bag from the back seat, thanked the priest and walked slowly to the front door. He noticed the broken latch and the cracked front window. He would see that they were repaired. The house needed a coat of paint. He blew out a deep breath as he looked at a potted geranium on the windowsill struggling to survive. A few tomato and pepper plants tied to rigid stakes and mulched with straw, thrived in the side garden. His mother might be in failing health, but she would tend to her garden with her last breath.

"Mama," Bruno called, pushing open the door.

*"Figghiu miu,"* a weak voice answered. Giovanna Gentile hobbled in from the kitchen leaning heavily on a cane.

Bruno noticed how frail she looked. She seemed to be shrinking away. "Mama." He held her in his arms feeling her body tremble.

"Oh my son, I am so happy to see you once more. I was afraid the good *Diu* would take me before you came home." A tear trickled down the withered cheek.

He held her face in his hands, pushed back the few fine hairs escaping from the bun atop her head. "Don't talk like that, *Mama mia.* He has enough angels in heaven right now." He tried to laugh at the absurdity of his words.

"Come, have coffee," she said leading him into the kitchen.

The room took him back to his childhood. Nothing had changed. The dark patch on the ceiling where the roof leaked was larger as well as new areas of paint peeling off the walls. A bare light bulb hung over the same kitchen table covered with a piece of cracked stained oil cloth.

Bruno promised himself to make arrangements to

have everything repaired and repainted.

Giovanna took two chipped cups off the shelf and placed them on the table next to a plate of pine nut cookies that Francesca had brought from the bakery. They were Bruno's favorite.

"I pour, Mama," Bruno said grasping the ancient coffeepot with a worn towel. He marveled that the old wood burning stove still functioned.

Mother and son sat sipping the bitter coffee. Her hands shook as she steadied the cup.

"Mama, come with me to America," Bruno said. "I make a good life for you."

The old woman shook her head. "No. What would I do in America? I don't speak the language. I have no friends there. This is my home. This is where I was born and this is where I die."

He knew he couldn't change her mind. He had tried many times before. "What did the doctor say?" he asked.

"He said I am old and worn out." She pushed the plate of cookies closer to her son. "Eat."

"In America there are special doctors, new medicines. Many people older than you go to nice restaurants, to the opera, even drive cars."

"Eh Bruno, you were always a dreamer. I would be lost. No, I die here. I want to lay in the ground next to your papa." She clasped her hands, raised her eyes to heaven, and made the sign of the cross.

Bruno heaved a sigh of frustration. He knew it was useless.

She looked up at him with a shrewd expression on her face. "Why don't you take Francesca to America?"

"Eh, I have no time for a woman now, Mama."

"But she loves you, Bruno, so much. I see her walking by the house with her young sisters. She will make a good wife and mother."

He nodded. "Maybe someday."

The old woman shook her head then glanced at the ticking clock on the sideboard. She stood up, taller and straighter than before.

"We go to church." She picked up an old black shawl hanging on a hook.

Bruno placed the shawl around his mother's shoulders and followed her out the door. She had little difficulty walking the five blocks to the church and Bruno knew that, for Angelo, all her complaints disappeared.

A number of women, clad in black, tended the altar. He knew only too well that when women in this part of Italy went into mourning, they wore black for the rest of their lives. They dusted the statues of the saints and arranged flowers for the following day, a feast day. Bruno didn't know which one nor did he care.

Leaning heavily on the rail, Giovanna genuflected and slowly knelt on the splintered wooden kneeler. She refused any help from her son. Bruno knelt next to her, made the sign of the cross, and tried to pray, but no words came. No visions of piety nor sainthood, only thoughts of indecision and the promise he had made.

Someone slid into the pew next to him. Bruno turned to see Francesca, smiling. She had changed, looked thinner and prettier than he remembered. She squeezed his hand, made the sign of the cross, and began saying the rosary.

A few moments later, the old organ issued a few

apologetic squeaks. After some vigorous pumping, the organist was able to produce a recognizable facsimile of a hymn and the choir began to sing.

Bruno couldn't believe the improvement over the last time he had heard them. Then a single sweet voice rose above the others, the tone pure, the notes true. Bruno felt a chill as he listened to the heavenly sound. The singer was truly gifted. He didn't have to wonder whose voice it was. He turned to look and saw the beautiful face of his sister, Angela, on the nine-year old boy standing straight and tall, his voice praising a God who had deprived him of both mother and father. Unshed tears burned Bruno's eyes as he stared at the boy, could almost see his sister standing beside him.

After the practice, Bruno felt uncomfortable as he waited with his mother and Francesca for Angelo to come down from the choir loft.

"Tell me about America, Bruno," Francesca begged.

"It's a big country. Everybody is in a hurry. They drive fast cars and eat in fancy restaurants. Some are rich and live in big houses with servants, but many, like Gerard's cousin Antonio, are poor and live in crowded buildings with rats in the alleys." He saw the women cringe at these words.

He continued, "There's room in America for all kinds of people. Some are black, some are brown, and some are yellow. They all live together."

Francesca looked at him in amazement.

Giovanna grunted. "I would get lost in such a place."

"Yes," Bruno said. "People can get lost there, but sometimes that's not a bad thing. Nobody knows who you are and nobody cares."

Giovanna looked at her son and frowned. "What do you mean? Are you doing something that you don't want anybody to know about?"

"Why do you say that, Mama? I am a singer, that's all. I'm getting bigger roles. Someday, I'll be more than just a member of the chorus." He wondered just how much his shrewd mother had surmised.

"Bruno, talk to him," his mother said as she sliced crusty country bread and cut chunks of rich cheese. A bottle of wine accompanied the Spartan meal. "He is so proud of you. He tells the other boys his uncle is a famous opera singer. You should see how he pushes out his chest and stands tall. But he is afraid of you. You are always frowning and say nothing to the boy. He feels guilty that his mother died bringing him into the world. He thinks you blame him. My poor *Angelinu*." She raised her eyes to heaven and made the sign of the cross.

Bruno said nothing, his mind in turmoil. He knew it wasn't the boy's fault that fate had dealt them all a cruel blow. He had failed to protect his family, to shield his sister from temptation. It was his fault. And now he had forsaken Francesca, too. He was ridden with guilt.

At that moment, Angelo crept into the kitchen and took his place at the table. "*Buon giorno, Zio* Bruno," he said, barely above a whisper.

Bruno felt his chest constrict at the words, *Zio* Bruno, just what little Josie used to call him. "*Buon giorno,* Angelo." He forced himself to smile at his beautiful nephew. "I see you are speaking Italian and not dialect."

The boy grinned. "We learn Italian in school," he said puffing out his chest.

Bruno nodded his approval.

"And," the boy continued, "my singing teacher said that all good singers sing in Italian, not dialect. *Nonna* still talks to me in dialect, but I talk only in Italian."

"That's a good start, something to be proud of," Bruno said.

Mama Gentile smiled; her color improved; she poured herself a large glass of wine. "He sang well, no?" she asked.

"*Si,* very well. How are the lessons going?" Bruno asked.

"It is very hard, *Zio,* but I practice every day. Someday I want to be just like you."

It was impossible for Bruno to look at the angelic face with rancor. "Good. You practice and someday you will be better than me. You will be the best."

Giovanna rose from her chair and left the room.

Angelo looked at Bruno with frightened eyes.

The older man sighed and held out his arms. "Come here, Angelo." He held his trembling nephew close and stroked the thick black curls.

"You must not worry. Never be afraid, not of me or anyone, understand?"

"*Si,*" the boy whispered.

"I promised your mother I would take care of you," Bruno said looking into the black eyes, "and I will!"

"Tell me about my mother," Angelo said.

Bruno closed his eyes a moment picturing the sylph-like creature who had been his sister. "She was the most beautiful woman *Dio* ever created, with long curly black hair, big dark eyes, always smiling and laughing. She didn't walk. She danced, everywhere."

Angelo laughed and clasped his hands together. "I like to dance, too."

"She made beautiful drawings. You see that one up there on the wall?" He pointed to a crude landscape, elegant in its simplicity.

"I draw, too," Angelo said jumping with excitement.

Bruno nodded. "Later you must show me some of your work."

"Was my mother smart?" the boy asked.

"Oh yes, always the best." Bruno remembered how she had struggled with her studies, the long hours he spent helping her, the perplexed look on her face when she failed to understand.

Angelo began to shuffle from one foot to the other. "*Zio,* tell me about my father."

Bruno stiffened. "What did *Nonna* tell you about him?"

"Only that he died in a war."

"Hmm," Bruno said. "Yes." He paused for a moment. It was not a lie. The man was 'dead' to his son.

"Was he a hero?" Angelo asked, his eyes gleaming.

Bruno snorted. "Many people thought he was a great man."

"Angelo," called Giovanna. "Come here."

"Go," Bruno said. "We talk again later."

The boy ran out of the room, smiling and singing.

Bruno poured himself a glass of wine, stood by the window, and stared out at the arid landscape. His thoughts transported him back to the past.

He had been the man of the family since their father died in a boating accident when Bruno was twelve. Pasquale Gentile had a fine baritone voice, untrained because of poverty and lack of opportunity, but had passed that talent on to his son. He was a humble fisherman, barely able to eke out a living for his family. He went out every morning and cast his nets in the water with the other fishermen. Some days they came back with their boats filled; other days they came back with nothing; some never came back.

Although Bruno had to assume the responsibility of his family at a tender age, he was determined not to follow in his father's footsteps. He kept up his studies and took every menial job he could find. His mother wanted him to join the fishing fleet, but he had other ideas. He knew he had inherited his father's voice and intended to become someone great. He had shared these thoughts with Francesca from the time they were children.

"Bruno, when you are a famous singer, will you still love me?" she had asked.

"Of course, I will always love you," he answered as he explored her growing body.

He sang in the church choir and took lessons from the priest. Some nights he slept only three or four hours, but he didn't care.

One day a teacher passing through heard him sing. That was the beginning of his career. He was taken on as a protégé by the teacher and eventually became a member of the chorus of the Palermo Opera. All this time he sent money home to his mother and sister, but he wasn't there to protect them. He had failed in his duty.

Another memory surfaced, one that caused him

great pain. He remembered Angela's screams — cries for help — his mother and the midwife running in and out of the room — a storm raging outside as if a demon from hell had come to punish her for her sin. Finally the cry of the newborn. Then his mother's scream. He ran into the room — blood everywhere. He looked down at his sister's ashen face.

"Angela! Angela!" he cried.

She opened her eyes and smiled at him. "Bruno, take care of my son, *promettimi?*"

*"Si, prometto,"* he said through streaming tears.

Her eyes closed; her limp hand slipped from his.

He made another promise that night.

# Chapter 30

Emma began having a new type of dream. These frightened her more than the previous ones. The first was most disturbing, but she explained it away by the fact that she was reading a biography of Maria Callas and *Norma* was one of her favorite roles.

*Emma is dressed in the stark white robe of the Druid priestess, Norma. Her blond wig hangs gracefully down her back. She is standing over her illegitimate children, offspring of her illicit love affair with the Roman proconsul Pollione. Norma sings of her heartbreak with the realization that her lover has turned to another.*

*Norma has broken her vows and desecrated the virginity of the temple. As she sings with a voice inspired by the angels, she looks at the dagger she holds in her hand. She will kill the children, then herself, in a ritual of cleansing sacrifice.*

*But she is puzzled. The dagger is made of glass, both the sharp pointed blade and the thin handle. As she raises it in her hand, she wakes.*

Emma shook her head to clear away the troubling vision. She swung her legs out of bed, plunged her feet into bright pink fuzzy slippers, stretched and shivered.

Now, what was that dream? She was singing the

role of *Norma*, one requiring a soprano of tremendous stamina. Of course in her dreams, and daydreams, Emma was versed in every operatic role. But the dagger confused her. She had never seen one like it before. She thought about it for a moment then shrugged it off as merely a figment of her vivid imagination. But for a long time her dreams had been of shiny glass objects. Could they be daggers?

Throughout the day the memory surfaced. Something about it bothered her. The next night Emma again dreamed of a tragic operatic role.

*She is the mad Lucia of Lammermoor, forced to marry a man she does not love. It is her wedding night. Lucia stands at the head of a staircase, her nightdress covered in the blood of the husband she has just stabbed to death.*

*The famous mad scene requires the skill of a vocal technician of the highest order. Of course, in her dreams, Emma is this, and more.*

*But what does Lucia hold in her hand? As her voice reaches heights of tone and clarity, she stares at the dagger she holds. It is not made of gleaming metal, but of shimmering glass.*

Emma woke, shaking off the reality of the dream. She squeezed her eyes shut and wiped her hand across her face. As she reached for her glasses, Emma spotted the book she was reading the previous night, *Operatic Tragedies and Their Heroines.* With a shiver she ran the water in the shower to wash away Lucia's imaginary blood.

She phoned Gladys later that day. "Boy, have I been having strange dreams."

"So what's new about that?" her friend asked. "I

love hearing about your fantasies."

"Well, last night I was singing *Lucia* and the night before it was *Norma.* But the weird thing was they both held daggers made of glass. Did you ever hear of such a thing?" Emma frowned and bit down on her lip.

"Can't say that I have, but nothing that you come up with surprises me anymore, my friend. You've always been a bit out of the ordinary." The women laughed and turned the conversation to the banalities of life. Emma was relieved that Gladys didn't mention the book. She had other things on her mind right now.

The third night Emma again dreamed of tragedy.

*She is Cho Cho San, Madame Butterfly, deserted by her American husband and left in shame.*

*Butterfly is determined to die with honor. She raises a ceremonial dagger, about to plunge it into her breast as she sings a heart-rending goodbye to her small son.*

*But what is that light reflecting off the dagger? It is not metal, but glass. Suddenly it explodes into shards of radiating color.*

Emma sat up in bed, her breathing labored, her heart beating erratically. Another dream about a glass dagger. Where did the image come from? She didn't remember ever seeing anything like it before, nor had she read about such a thing. She went to the window pulling her robe tight. Everything looked the same, birds flitted around building nests and twittering, squirrels chased one another. But what was the meaning of these dreams?

It's a portent of evil, a warning from the spirit

world. She felt certain of it.

"Sylvia, I need some information," Emma said holding the phone a little too tight.

"What kind of information, Mom?"

"Did you ever hear of a glass dagger?"

"Oh lord, what have you been reading? A historical novel, or a horror story?" Sylvia asked.

"Bear with me. I've been having strange dreams again. I'm sorry but I take these things seriously even if you don't. I think they may be some kind of warning." Emma knew how ridiculous this sounded to her practical daughter, but she felt compelled to investigate.

"Do you think you're in some kind of danger?" Sylvia asked, a note of concern in her voice.

"Not me, but someone. I'm not sure who," Emma answered.

"All right. I'll ask my friend Fran, the research librarian at school. She may be able to give you some insight. Now tell me more, just what is this glass dagger?"

"Three nights in a row I dreamed that I was singing a tragic scene in an opera, first *Norma*, then *Lucia*, then *Butterfly*. In each dream I had a dagger in my hand. It was very beautiful, all glass, both the blade and the hilt. Now, I want to know if there is such a thing and where it might be obtained."

"And, what do you intend to do with this information?"

"I'm not sure. I'll decide that later. But I need to know, for my own peace of mind, if for nothing else."

"Okay, Mother. I know how persistent you can be.

I'll see what I can find out and call you back."

"My daughter thinks I've lost it," Emma said. She and Nate were clearing the table after a pleasant Sunday dinner. The late afternoon light streamed into the dining room window, shedding a soft glow about the room.

"And why should she think that?" Nate asked.

"I've been having strange dreams about glass daggers. See, I can tell by your face that you agree with her. Do you want another glass of wine?"

He rolled his eyes. "I think I may need one."

She poured the burgundy colored Merlot into their glasses. It reminded her of blood pooling in a corner. She shivered.

"Tell me," Nate said. "What kind of novels have you been reading, my dear?"

"Don't patronize me, Nate. It's a warning. I feel it. Something bad is going to happen."

"And, may I ask, to whom?"

"I'm not sure, but I think it may be Speranza." She walked to the window and looked out at the early spring evening. A golden hue lingered in the atmosphere. She turned toward Nate, her hands clenched into tight fists. "I can't explain it. I just know."

"All right," he said. "I want to help you, but what can I do?"

"I don't know … yet."

# Chapter 31

Emma sat in a room at the local library waiting for a lecture on twentieth century opera sponsored by the West Suburban Opera Chapter. She was busy reading the information, but couldn't help overhearing a conversation between two women sitting behind her.

"Well, I heard he was having an affair with a girl from the chorus."

"Really."

"You know what a womanizer he is; with his good looks and gorgeous voice he can get any woman he wants."

"Doesn't he have a wife and family somewhere?"

"When did that ever stop a man? I wouldn't want to be married to a man like that. You could never trust him. No, I tell you some jealous husband is going to get even someday. I wouldn't be surprised to see the headline: 'Famous tenor, Marcantonio Speranza, shot by husband while climbing out of bedroom window.'"

Emma's eyes widened as the two women began smirking. It just might be the motive, the warnings, the meaning of her dreams. She had heard those rumors, too. Women certainly did throw themselves at famous men. Maybe he wasn't altogether to blame. She didn't want to think ill of such a man. It might only be idle gossip. She would ask Nate's opinion.

"Do you think a man like Marcantonio Speranza is unfaithful to his wife? I mean with all the women throwing themselves at his feet?" Emma asked Nate.

They sat in a small sandwich shop downtown, drinking latte and eating avocado and cream cheese sandwiches with alfalfa sprouts peeking out from the bread.

"How do you know women are throwing themselves at him?" Nate asked, taking a generous bite.

"I overheard two women talking before the lecture yesterday. That could be the reason, you know, someone hates him and wants to get even." She reached over and wiped a drip of mayonnaise from Nate's chin and received a frown in return.

"So you're listening to gossip and using that to justify your suspicions. None of this has any basis in fact."

"I know, but it's so frustrating. I know Finelli dislikes him, but that has nothing to do with infidelity, I'm sure. I saw the way Gentile looked at him. I can feel the danger and yet I can't prove a thing." She shook her head and let out a deep sigh.

"Emma," Nate said. "Let it go, please?"

She shrugged, and let out a long breath. "I'll think about it." But she knew she could never let go of her suspicions. This went deeper than mere infidelity. Gentile didn't have a wife. He did have a nephew. And what of the boy's mother? Had she run off with the famous tenor? If so, where was she?

# Chapter 32
# A Village in Sicily

Wearing a large straw hat to protect her from the baking Sicilian sun, Giovanna Gentile watered her tomato plants, and from the corner of her eye, watched her grandson skulking through the narrow alley. He stopped every few moments and looked around, then went quietly to the back door. He grimaced at the squeak as he tried to flatten himself against the wall.

"Angelo. Come here," his grandmother commanded, walking in the front door.

"*Pronto*," he said.

"*Matri di diu!* What happened?" She hurried to the boy grabbing his chin and turning his face up to hers. "Fighting! I told you not to play with those boys. They're too rough and they're bigger than you."

She busied herself putting cold cloths on his blackening eye and on his swelling lip, gently wiping the blood from his nose. She fingered the torn shirt and shook her head. She could fix it so it would hardly show.

"*Nonna*," he said slowly clenching and unclenching his fists, "Am I a bastard?"

He looked at Giovanna with so much pain in his eyes she clasped him to her heart. "Who said such a thing?"

"Edwardo and Carlo. They say I have no father — *Bastardo* they called me!" He began to sob, the sounds coming in heart-rending gasps.

Giovanna shook her head. She held the boy at arm's length and pushed back the curls matted against his sweaty forehead. "Listen to me! You had a father. He was a great man — but he is dead. You are not a bastard!"

But the boy was not satisfied. "Then why is my name Angelo Gentile? That was my mother's name."

She hesitated for a moment. "Eh, that's just the way it was done. Ah *Angelinu miu*," she said clutching the boy to her heart.

"No Angelinu! I'm not a baby! My name is Angelo and I want to know my father's name." He pursed his lips and stamped his foot on the floor.

"Enough!" his grandmother commanded. "Now, go wash your face and get ready for supper. I made your favorite, pasta e fagioli and give me that shirt so I can mend it."

Questions, questions, what was she to tell this boy? The truth?

That afternoon Francesca stopped on her way home from work.

"*Comare,* are you home?"

"Oh Francesca, come in," Giovanna called out. She lay on the worn sofa, an old shawl covering her head to keep out the draft.

"What's the matter, are you sick?" Francesca ran to her and knelt beside the woman.

"Ah, *Figghia mia*, I am old and I cannot carry this

burden any longer." She groaned.

"Has Angelo done something wrong?"

"He came home from school beaten up. The boys called him bastard. He's asking about his father." Bitter tears sneaked out of the corners of her eyes and snaked down the creases in her cheeks.

"Oh *Diu*," Francesca said folding her hands under her chin and raising her eyes to heaven.

"Bruno must come home," the old woman said with bitter determination. "I will talk to Padre Martino. He will write another letter. Now let us say the rosary."

The two women knelt down, and with bowed heads, crossed themselves and began to pray.

# Chapter 33

In the house on Taylor Street Bruno and Gerard sat in the kitchen drinking bitter espresso and eating stale rolls.

"What do you mean you're going back to Italy? You're not signing the contract for next year?" Gerard almost spilled his coffee.

"Just what I said. My mother is sick and I have to take care of her. Padre Martino wrote me another letter." Bruno didn't meet his friend's gaze, didn't tell him about the mysterious letter of warning the priest had received. Someone was watching him and he was beginning to doubt himself.

"That is not the reason," Gerard said. "There is something else."

"I miss Fancesca, and the people here are not so friendly," Bruno lied. "I don't belong."

"Eh!" Gerard threw up his hands. "A few months ago you couldn't wait to come here, the land of opportunity, a chance to become famous. And you said there was no place in your life for a woman. That's just what you said. Besides, how do you know your mother is really sick? *Mia Mama* used to have fits every time she didn't get her way, but she's still strong as an ox." Gerard shook his head. "What's the real reason? Angelo?"

Bruno shook his head, his face a mask of indecision. "The boy has talent, a gift from God. If the voice is trained right, he can be the greatest singer in the world," Bruno answered.

"And how do you know that? You got, what you call it, ESP?"

"I heard him sing. It was like a sound from heaven. But he needs training to bring out the full measure of the voice. He can be great. I know it." Bruno pursed his lips and stared at his friend.

"But he's just a kid. What happens when the voice changes? That might be the end of it," Gerard argued.

"And it might not." Bruno's eyes narrowed as he pictured Angelo Gentile's name on the front page of the newspapers, acclaiming him the wonder of the century.

"So, you're giving up your own career for a nephew you resent?"

"I'm not giving up anything. And I don't feel resentful toward the boy anymore. It isn't his fault. I'll sing in the Naples Opera, or in Milan. They still want me. And Angelo can study there. I'll see that the voice is trained right, and someday, he will surpass Speranza." He spat out the name.

"So that's why you're doing this? To get back at Speranza?" Gerard looked at his friend in disbelief.

"Because of him my beautiful sister lies in the grave. She was sweet and innocent until he put his filthy hands on her. I do not rest until he gets what he deserves."

"Bruno," Gerard said. "I think you should talk to a priest. You're confused about Angelo and his father." He put his hand on his friend's shoulder. Bruno didn't shrug it off.

"Come with me," Bruno said. "We always sing good together. We don't belong here."

"No, I stay here with my cousin for a while, and then, maybe, get a place of my own. I already signed for next year. I sing again with the Lyric and with Midwest, and that girl in the chorus, Marta, she's pretty nice. I think she likes me. Maybe I become a citizen." He grabbed Bruno's arm and gave him a glaring look. "Think, my friend, before you make a big mistake."

# Chapter 34

Emma searched her wardrobe for just the right outfit, something fashionable but comfortable. She pulled out three skirts and finally decided on a brown tweed. When she slipped into it she struggled with the zipper and felt the button at the waist a little tight.

"Hmm," she said standing in front of the full-length mirror and looking at herself from every angle. "It must be the effect of the padded panties, or maybe the few pounds I gained." Either way, she liked what she saw.

She chose a loose pebble weave cotton sweater. The opera house tended to be warm on these back-stage tours. She grabbed a pair of comfortable brown walking shoes and a brown purse to complete the outfit.

The Lyric Opera Westside Chapter had scheduled a backstage tour that afternoon for its members. It had been a few years since Emma went on a tour of the Met with Gladys. Now she would see how the Lyric compared.

This year she had a purpose in mind. Sylvia's friend had found a vague reference to glass daggers used in assassinations in Venice in the fourteenth century, but Emma wanted more information and was determined to continue the search. Perhaps she could ask someone at the opera house.

The tour was supposed to start at three-thirty, the last one of the day lasting about two hours. Afterwards she planned to meet Nate for dinner. She remembered their phone conversation with a little annoyance.

"What time will the tour be over?" he had asked.

"About five or five-thirty. I'll call you as I'm leaving the opera house and we can meet at the restaurant."

"Sounds good. And, Emma, please don't get into any trouble."

"Trouble? What kind of trouble could I possibly get into? I'll be with a group of people." What did he think she was, a total flake, another helpless woman?

She took the Metra train to Union Station and walked the two blocks to the opera house. There was little traffic on a Sunday afternoon.

As she walked across the bridge spanning the Chicago River, she looked down at the water reflecting fluffy clouds. She noted a new restaurant along the waterfront. She would ask Nate about it.

At the opera house Emma met up with her group in the foyer and exchanged pleasantries and small talk. The previous groups were running late so there was a long wait. They sat at tables set up for the occasion and drank too much soda and bottled water. By the time their tour started, it was after four and Emma's bladder was sending out signals, but there wasn't time to make a pit stop.

They listened to a brief history of the building, built in the late 1920s by Samuel Insull at a cost of twenty million dollars. He was determined to make the stage visible and the sound audible to every patron. He deliberately avoided the horseshoe design and the pillars found in many of the European houses.

The tour guide discussed the general managers throughout the years and their contributions, emphasizing the fact that Maria Callas had made her American debut here in 1954.

Next stop was the property room, a cavernous space filled with furniture and props, some specific to certain operas and some generic. The fake snow was especially interesting. It was made of small pieces of waxed plastic which fell through holes in a trough suspended across the top of the stage. When the scene was over, the stagehands swept it up and stored it for future use. Emma remembered how real it looked from the auditorium when she had seen certain productions set in the winter.

The Opera Company owned a warehouse a few miles away where scenery, costumes, and more props were easily accessible as needed. Some productions were owned in conjunction with other opera companies; some loaned out, and some borrowed. They all included scenery, costumes, and stage directions.

The tour guide led them in and out of freight elevators, up and down stairways, down long hallways, and huge rehearsal rooms.

"This is the catwalk," he said as they got off the elevator on the sixth floor. Emma hesitated, had always been afraid of heights, became woozy, and sometimes, nauseated. Now she pulled back as the group began to make its way across the walkway suspended high above the stage area.

". . . miles of rope and cables holding up the backdrops that weigh about two thousand pounds each," the guide's voice droned on.

Emma took a deep breath and ventured out taking mincing steps. She clung to the five foot high supporting railing on the sides. A wash of vertigo gripped her as she looked down. She forced herself to look up, but that wasn't much better. The backdrops rose another four stories into the air.

"Come on, folks, we're running late. Don't fall behind," the guide called from a distance.

Emma gritted her teeth, gripped the rails, and plunged ahead. She let out a sigh of relief as she stepped off and saw her group heading down a flight of stairs. She was tempted to stop in a ladies' room next to the staircase, but feared she wouldn't find them again.

Next they went through the wardrobe room where rows of costumes hung on racks. Some were made to the specifications of the lead singers. The Wardrobe Mistress showed them a bodice with hooks and laces that adjusted to a four-inch difference in size.

"Why don't you use Velcro?" someone asked.

"Can you visualize a singer taking a deep breath and the Velcro coming apart with a loud ripping sound?" The woman smiled. "We tried it."

In the wig room a mesh cap sat on a model. The guide explained that real hair was painstakingly hooked into the mesh from the back to the front. Each wig took forty to fifty hours to make. The stylist then cut, washed and coifed each wig to detailed specifications.

Emma shook her head. She never realized how much work went into the details of production of an opera.

Finally they came to the armory. The Weapons Master was waiting to give them an overview. He showed them some pieces that were more than one hundred years old. He said there were over four thousand assorted crowns, weapons, and metal ornaments in their collection.

The blades of the swords were all dull to avoid injury. Emma was especially interested in the daggers. Most of the blades retracted on impact. She saw nothing that resembled the daggers in her dreams. When the talk came to an end, Emma moved closer.

"Do you have any glass daggers in your collection?" she asked.

"Glass daggers? No, they would be too dangerous and impossible to modify for safety. Why do you ask?" He looked at her quizzically.

"I read someplace about such weapons used for assassinations," Emma stammered.

"Are you referring to the Venetian daggers crafted in the fourteenth century?"

"I believe so. Can they make such things today?"

"Well, I suppose. There was a special formula known only to a few glassmakers. The dagger was supposed to shatter on impact. I don't think anyone would make them today. Still, you never can tell."

Emma thought for a moment. It sounds pretty gruesome, but somebody must be able to make such a thing, otherwise why would I dream about it?

"Now you had better catch up to your group. I'm sure they're down in the orchestra pit by now."

"Which way do I go?" Emma asked.

"Just follow the signs." He walked over to her and pointed. "Turn left and down that flight of stairs. Follow the signs from there and you'll be all right."

"Okay." Emma hurried toward the stairwell. When she spotted a men's room, she stopped. Her bladder was now sending out serious signals. She was tempted to go in.

"There must be a ladies' room here, too," she muttered turning a corner. She saw it and ran inside, locked herself in a stall and just managed to pull her underwear down and sit. The relief was heavenly. She didn't think her bladder could hold that much. She finished, quickly washed her hands and hurried down the stairs.

The signs led down a hallway of closed doors labeled with the names of the lead singers. Sounds issued from behind a door.

"Someone's in there," she muttered. "I'll ask for directions." Hesitantly she knocked.

"*Pronto*," a voice called.

Just at that moment Emma noticed the name on the door—Rosa Finelli. Oh my God, she thought.

The door opened to reveal the statuesque soprano, her face a mask. "Who are you?" she demanded.

Emma found herself in a very awkward position. "Signora, please forgive me for disturbing you. I—I was with the tour and I'm lost. Can you show me the way out, please?"

"I am not a guide," Finelli said. "I am personally escorted out of the opera house. Now go away. I have work to do." She slammed the door in Emma's face.

What a rude woman Emma thought as she turned down another hallway and found herself back in the property room.

I must have turned around. I'd better retrace my steps. She turned back, but didn't see any signs and arrows designating the tour route. She felt the perspiration begin to run under her arms and down her back.

"Guardian Angel," she said aloud. "Please point me in the right direction." She decided to go back upstairs and look for the armory. Someone might still be there.

Her watch said five forty-five. The last tour would be finished by now. She began to hyperventilate, became light headed and weak. She had visions of being trapped in the opera house all night. No, Finelli was still there. There were probably others as well. Then she remembered Nate's warning and was angry with herself for falling behind. She roamed through hallway after hallway, up and down stairs until she finally saw one of the tour signs pointing to the right.

Were those footsteps behind her? Oh, thank God, somebody's here. "Hello," she called. "Is anyone there? I need directions." No answer. She frowned. Must have been my imagination. She started walking, and again, heard footsteps.

"Hello, who's there?" Again no answer. Her hands grew cold; a chill ran through her. Perhaps it was better if she didn't know who was there. She hurried along, almost running now. She turned another corner and reached□ the catwalk.

"Oh God, not this thing again!" she moaned. She inched her way onto the bridge then felt the hairs rise on the back of her neck. Someone was behind her. She turned and saw a cloaked figure standing there, barring her way back. She grabbed the railing, her breath coming in gulping rasps. Her heart raced, much too fast. Her vision blurred. I can't have an anxiety attack now. She commanded herself to take control, slowed her breathing, closed her eyes for just a moment. Better.

She remembered the pepper spray she carried in her purse, fumbled around through keys and all the unnecessary things women carry in their purses. Her hand grasped the hard cold metal can.

"Get away from me," she shouted. "I have a weapon." With trembling hands she pointed the can at the man.

"Who are you?" he asked. He stood in shadow that obscured his face, but his voice was deep and resonant.

"I was on the tour and got lost. I just want to get out of here."

He started toward her, holding out his hand. Was it to help her or did he mean her harm? Instinctively she backed away. When he came closer she got a glimpse of his face … Bruno Gentile.

"I know who you are. I know all about you. Don't come any closer or I'll use this." She pointed the can toward his face.

He came closer; she backed away.

"I know about you and Speranza," she hesitated for a moment, "and Angelo."

"What do you know about me? Are you the one who has been asking questions, writing letters? You're a *Strega,*" he shouted and rushed toward her.

She depressed the button on the spray can just as the lights went out.

# Chapter 35

"Help!" Emma yelled as loud as she could. She was still inching backwards when she tripped over something on the floor, fell back and hit her head on the railing. She heard the can of pepper spray hit the cables, and after a long interval, bounce on the floor six stories below. She screamed again and again. Almost immediately the lights came on.

Emma looked around in terror, but Gentile was gone. She breathed a sigh of relief.

"Help," she yelled louder. "I'm up here . . . on the catwalk . . . someone's threatening me . . . hurry!"

"Stay where you are, lady. We'll be right up to get you."

*Oh thank you, Guardian Angel. They know I'm here and they're coming for me.* She sat up, and unable to control her shaking limbs, crawled off the catwalk. She sank down to the floor resting her aching head against the wall. Stars danced before her eyes. She closed them and relaxed.

"Lady, are you okay? Do you need a doctor?"

A man handed her a glass of water. She drank too fast, sputtering and coughing. "I think I'm all right." She reached for his hand and stood up.

"I fell behind the group, then got turned around. I found Signora Finelli's dressing room, but she was no help."

The man pursed his lips and nodded.

"I walked and walked . . . and then there was a man . . ." She couldn't say another word.

"When there are only a few lights on, this place can get pretty spooky. You can imagine all sorts of things," the guard said.

"I didn't imagine it. He was here and he threatened me. I suggest you search the opera house." She could tell by his look that he didn't believe her.

"The chorus was rehearsing. I just saw the last one leave a few minutes ago, and one of the guards just went up to escort La Finelli to her limo," he said. "Can you walk?"

"I think so." He took her arm and slowly escorted her to the lobby.

"Can I call somebody for you?"

"Just get me a cab." Emma was on the verge of tears but desperately controlled herself. She just wanted Nate. She forgot all about the restaurant. When the cab deposited her at his condo, she leaned on the bell.

"Hello?" he answered.

"Nate, let me in, hurry." The fear in her voice apparently alerted him. The buzzer sounded immediately.

He was waiting as the elevator doors opened. Emma flew into his arms, trembling and sobbing.

"All right. You're safe," he said cradling her head. "Come in and tell me what happened."

When Emma had calmed down and was sipping a glass of brandy, she told him the story.

"They didn't believe me," she said shaking her head.

"You have to admit, it does sound rather far fetched."

"See, you don't believe me either." She turned her head away.

"I do believe you, Sparrow. There's something suspicious going on." He put his arms around her. "And from now on, I'm not letting you out of my sight."

# Chapter 36

For the next two weeks Emma worried and fretted. Her dreams about glass daggers intensified. She always woke in a cold sweat. It would soon be time for rehearsals of *A Masked Ball.* In the early ones, the performers wore street clothes. Would Gentile recognize her? Of course, he had seen her on the catwalk. The thought terrified her. She promised herself to stay close to Nate.

"Sylvia, did you find any more information on those glass daggers?" Emma gripped the phone as she looked out the window at the approaching spring storm.

"I was going to call you," Sylvia answered. "Fran did a lot of digging and could only come up with one more reference. That was back in Venice, in about the thirteenth or fourteenth centuries, when the island of Murano was the glass production capital of the world. Apparently there existed a secret group who crafted glass daggers. The blades were made so paper-thin that when someone was stabbed with the weapon, it snapped off at the handle. There was very little external bleeding. But, of course, the person died of infection and whatever internal damage the dagger inflicted. But by that time, the assassin was long gone. It sounds pretty awful. That's it, all she could find." Sylvia took a deep breath.

Emma looked at the black clouds roiling overhead as thunder rumbled like a waking beast. "Hm," she muttered.

"Mom, are you still there?"

"I'm thinking. I'm still having dreams about shiny pointed objects. I wish I knew what they meant. I'll have to ponder this a while. Bye now."

As Emma hung up the phone, lightning streaked across the sky followed by a crash of thunder that made her jump.

"I don't know what to do, Gladys. I know instinctively that someone is planning to harm Speranza, and I'm reasonably sure it's the bass, Bruno Gentile, but I have no proof." Emma walked back and forth clutching the phone. Should she confide in Gladys about her research and her meeting with Gentile? Better not, she might call Sylvia.

"Try to calm down," her friend said. "Let's see if I have this right. You've been dreaming about glass daggers. Sylvia says she found a reference to them used in Venice a couple of hundred years ago, and the Weapons Master at Lyric said he had heard about them, too. And you're afraid that someone will actually try to stab Speranza with one of these in the last scene. Is that it?"

"That's it." It sounded fantastic when she heard Gladys putting forth the facts in an unemotional manner.

"Let me ask you this," Gladys continued. "Aren't

there two different endings to that opera? In some productions Renato shoots the king instead of stabbing him, doesn't he?"

"That's right," Emma said, amazed that she hadn't thought of that herself.

"Well, which one is Midwest using?"

"I'm not sure."

"If they use the gun, you're worrying for nothing."

"You're right. I'm such a fool," Emma said, plopping down in a chair.

"Check it out, my friend, and let me know."

"I will. Thanks. Bye."

Why didn't I think of that? The videotape she had portrayed the assassination by stabbing, which was the more popular version. But in reality it was a gunshot, and some productions used that version. She asked Nate about it, but he wasn't sure either.

But why the dreams about the dagger? She shook her head. Life would be so much simpler if I didn't have these premonitions. She could ask James, but rehearsals would start in a few days; then she would find out. Would the famous tenor still be alive for the rehearsals?

# Chapter 37

The first afternoon of rehearsal, Emma and Nate sat in the community room drinking herbal tea. The supers appeared only in the third act, during the masked ball in the palace of the king. Emma fidgeted and fussed.

"What's wrong? You're worried about seeing Gentile, aren't you?" Nate asked.

"I suppose. Do you think he'll recognize me?"

Nate shrugged. "And if he does, exactly what do you think he'll do? I'll be right beside you." He gave her a reassuring hug.

She smiled. She could always depend on Nate. "Since we're not in costume, I think I'll slip out front and watch for a while. I want to see Speranza in action."

"I'll come with you." Nate picked up the teacups, put them down on the table in the corner, and followed Emma out into the auditorium. They sat down in an inconspicuous area and watched.

Since many of the singers did not sing with full voice during rehearsal, she could understand most of the dialogue in Italian.

*The opera is loosely modeled after a political assassination of the king of Sweden in 1792. In Verdi's opera, the king,*

*Riccardo, is killed by his best friend, Renato, in a fit of jealous rage after he finds the king in a compromising situation with his own wife, Amelia. In the first act two conspirators, Samuele and Tommaso, are planning to kill the king to revenge the executions of members of their families. Renato learns of the plan and tries to warn Riccardo.*

Emma listened as the plot unfolded and watched, fascinated by the interplay of characters. She froze when she recognized one of the conspirators, the one named Tommaso.

"Isn't that Bruno Gentile?" she asked Nate.

"Hm? Where?"

"One of the conspirators. See? In the corner, those two whispering to each other."

"Yes, it's him. Try to relax." He slipped his arm around her and held her close.

Fear crept up Emma's spine. She could feel the malevolence emanating from the man. For a moment she felt light-headed, but with a few deep breaths, it passed.

At the end of act one, the cast took a break. Emma and Nate decided to walk outside. It was a balmy spring day; people walked and jogged along the lakefront; young children ran after each other laughing and tumbling in the grass; teenagers sped past them on roller blades; a few sailboats doted the lake.

"What a romantic time," Nate said taking Emma's hand.

"Huh?" she asked, almost as if she didn't know he was there.

"Here we are on this gorgeous afternoon walking by the lakefront, and you're a million miles away. Do I have a rival? Who is he? I demand to know his name so I can challenge him to a duel," Nate said with as much theatricality as he could muster.

"Oh Nate, I'm sorry. I can't concentrate on anything but this dilemma. Gentile harbors a vendetta against the tenor. I think it has something to do with their past. We know they came from the same town and Gentile has a nephew with a promising voice. Speranza fits into this puzzle, somewhere."

Nate sighed. "Okay, the fact that it's spring and the tulips are blooming and romance is in the air doesn't matter to you. Come on, let's go back. It's probably time for the second act."

Emma and Nate were supposed to stand behind the chorus with the other supers and move about the stage as if they were socializing at the ball. The first rehearsal was with piano accompaniment and no one was in costume, so the fairy-tale atmosphere was missing.

*In the beginning of the final scene, Gentile and the other conspirator talk with Renato, the cuckold husband, discussing the planned murder of the king. The conspirators then retreat to the rear of the stage on the left as Renato quizzes the page as to the costume the king is wearing.*

*The king, Riccardo, talks with Amelia, Renato's wife, and tells her he plans to send her and her husband away. As long as she is near, he cannot contain his love. The husband comes up from behind and stabs the king.*

*There is much commotion as the chorus sings of such infamy. During this time, the conspirators remain in the background. As Riccardo dies, he forgives Renato and the chorus and principals sing their farewell.*

Assassination by stabbing — so that *was* the version Midwest chose. Emma was more convinced than ever but there was no interaction between Gentile and Speranza that Emma could see. Even though the conspirator remained in the background, she still felt something amiss. Was the bass planning some violence with a glass dagger? It was *not* just her wild imagination. She decided to warn Speranza herself. If he thought she was crazy and laughed it off, she could live with that. But at least her conscience would be clear.

Before going to the dressing room to pick up her things, Emma made her way through the crowd to the stars' dressing rooms.

*Guardian Angel, help me to say the right things, to convince this man he may be in danger.*

She saw Speranza in the hallway talking to Rosa Finelli who sang the role of Amelia. Finelli's voice was raised. "You cannot occupy the same space on the stage that I do!" she almost shouted as she stomped away.

Emma boldly walked toward them. A security guard blocked her way, crossed his arms, and shook his head. "Mr. Speranza can't be disturbed."

"But I must speak to him, just for a minute. It's urgent!" she said trying to attract the tenor's attention.

"Please," the guard said, "go away!"

"Signore Speranza," Emma called. "I must speak with you."

The singer gave Emma a condescending look. *"Un momento,"* he said beckoning to Emma. He seemed relieved to leave the complaining soprano.

"I know you're a busy man, but I came to warn

you. You're in danger. You see, I can see things, and I've been having strange dreams about glass daggers and I think someone wants to hurt you. I sent you a message. Please be careful."

Speranza smiled then shook his head and motioned to the guard. "*Grazie,*" he said, as he turned away and entered his dressing room.

Finelli gave Emma a look of disdain as she turned and marched toward her dressing room.

The guard scowled at Emma as she hung her head, sighed, and slowly walked away. She had botched it up. Said all the wrong things. He would never believe her now.

# Chapter 38

The dress rehearsal was scheduled for the following Thursday afternoon with the first performance on Friday night. Emma's apprehension grew stronger with each passing day, her fretful sleep filled with disturbing dreams.

The phone rang two, three, four times. Where was the darned thing? It wasn't on the charger where it belonged. As Emma ran from room to room trying to pinpoint the sound, it stopped.

"Modern technology," she grumbled. "Where is that damned phone? Sylvia was supposed to call me back." She had left an urgent message on her daughter's answering machine early that morning.

After a few minutes the phone began ringing again. Emma ran to pick up the phone in the living room, but it had stopped ringing, too. A few minutes later the doorbell rang. She hurried to the front door and opened it to a distraught Maria.

"Emma, why you no answer the phone? I try to call you. When I saw the light on in the kitchen I knew you were home and thought something happened. Are you all right?"

Emma shook her head. "You're such an alarmist."

Maria made the sign of the cross as she came into the living room and closed the door behind her.

"Maybe you fell down the stairs; maybe somebody put the *malocchio* on you?"

"I simply can't find my new phone," Emma said in exasperation. "I've looked all over the house."

"Eh, if you have a phone on the wall, like me, you always know where it is. It don't walk away." Maria folded her arms across her breasts and raised her eyebrows.

"I know," Emma answered, "but the kids gave me this fancy phone for my birthday. I swear it's supposed to do everything but cook dinner. It took me two weeks to learn how to use it and to program in all their numbers. Maybe I'll let it stay lost and pull out the old one that I put up in the closet." She began making a pot of coffee.

"Sit down. What did you call me about?"

"I want to see the opera Friday night. Can you get me a ticket?"

"Why do you wait 'till the last minute?" Emma was aggravated enough over the missing phone; now Maria added to her annoyance.

"Eh, I was supposed to go to the church raffle with Mrs. Simonelli. But now she can't go and I don't want to go by myself. So I go to the opera." Maria reached for a chocolate chip cookie from a plate on the counter.

"Put them on the table," Emma said. "We might as well eat. Oh, there goes that phone again."

"Sound like from the bathroom," Maria said tilting her head.

Emma hurried into the powder room off the kitchen and came out clutching the phone, a triumphant look on her face.

She quickly dialed her daughter's number. "Hello,

Sylvia? I've been trying to reach you. Did you tell James about my dreams? Did he warn Speranza?" Emma took two mugs from the shelf and motioned Maria to pour the coffee. She didn't tell her daughter about her failed attempt to warn the tenor herself.

"Mother, he can't just go up to the man and tell him someone may have put the evil eye on him. There's no proof of any danger."

"I suppose it does sound foolish when you put it that way, but I can't help it. Will he at least tell him that there have been problems in the area and to be careful?"

"I suppose he can say that."

"Good, and can you get a ticket for Maria for Friday night? I know it's short notice."

A sigh from the other end. "I'll try, but it's a nearly impossible."

"I know. Thanks, bye." Emma plopped down in her chair and shook her head.

"What's this all about? Dreams? Warnings?" Maria asked a look of alarm on her face.

Emma explained her dreams and vague premonitions to her friend, the nagging fear that Speranza was in danger.

"Sounds like the *malocchio* to me," Maria said again making the sign of the cross and dunking a cookie in her coffee. "So what are you gonna do?"

"There's not much I can do. I sent him a letter, but I didn't sign it. He probably threw it in the wastebasket. I tried to talk to him after the rehearsal yesterday, but that didn't work, either." She recalled the look on the tenor's face. He certainly must have thought she was just another nut case. She said nothing about her own close call on the backstage tour.

Maria would surely get out the oil and water and perform an exorcism.

"I've watched Gentile carefully at all the rehearsals. There's no scene where he gets close enough to the king to do anything, but still . . ." She shook her head. Maybe it wouldn't happen during a performance, but she knew something was wrong and she felt helpless to stop it.

"What did Sylvia say about the ticket?" Maria asked.

"She said she'll try, but don't wait 'till the last minute next time."

# Chapter 39

Emma woke to the patter of rain against the window. She stretched then rubbed her eyes. They itched. As soon as I shower I'll be okay. She shuffled into the bathroom and glanced at her reflection in the mirror. She got as close as she could to see inflamed eyes peering back at her under swollen lids. She had been reading for over two hours the night before, so she thought nothing of it as she adjusted the water in the shower.

I must have soap in my eyes. She dried herself and squeezed her eyes shut. They didn't burn, they itched. She brought her face close to the mirror and looked again, eyelids puffy, sclera flaming, a yellowish discharge in the corners.

"Oh God, now what," she wailed. She bathed her eyes in a weak boric acid solution, her mother's remedy for all inflammations. She put a cold compress on her eyes and lay down again.

Two hours later, after more ablutions and compresses, she was no better. She reached for the phone, dialed, and heard the recorded message: "Dr. Strong is not in today. For emergencies call the hospital at..."

It's Wednesday, they're all on the golf course. The driving rain outside dispelled that thought.

Emma squeezed her eyes to shut out the light. She

couldn't possibly put in her contacts; had put off repairing the broken ear-piece on her spectacles, so she reached for her prescription sunglasses. At least she could see enough to get around. The dress rehearsal was in two days. This was bound to be gone by then.

She put on a jacket, took her umbrella and walked the two blocks to the drug store, pummeled by rain, sloshing through puddles of water. She had known the pharmacist for years.

"Hello, Mrs. Winberry," he said. "What can I do for you this soggy morning?"

"Soggy is right. Look at my eyes." Emma said taking off her glasses. "They itch like crazy."

"Well don't rub them." He looked closely at her face. "You have a dandy case of conjunctivitis. I think you should see your doctor."

"So do I, but he's not in today."

"Hmm," the pharmacist muttered searching the shelves.

"Try these drops. They're just a salt solution, but they might provide a little relief. This is all I can give you without a prescription, but see your doctor tomorrow if you're not better. You might need some steroids and antibiotics."

"Thanks," Emma said as she paid for the medication. What a time to get sick. She was supposed to be watching the performance with an eagle eye. Now she would be lucky to see the stage. If she couldn't put in her contacts, she would be practically blind, but she couldn't worry about that now. She simply had to get over this.

"Oh Nate, I can't go to dinner with you tonight. I

have severe conjunctivitis." Her voice reflected self pity as she moaned into the phone.

"Maybe I should come over," he said, "and take care of you."

"That's very sweet, but it may be contagious. I don't want you to catch it." She would need him to be vigilant at the dress rehearsal as well as the performance, but she didn't say that.

"All right. But you will see the doctor if it's not better by tomorrow."

"I will, promise."

"Call you later, Sparrow. Bye."

Now what could she do that didn't require vision? She couldn't read; hated banal television; early gardening was out of the question because of the downpour.

She decided on the CD of *A Masked Ball* with Marcantonio Speranza. She would listen closely to the words and try again to identify any place in the opera that was particularly suspicious.

The next morning Emma woke with her eyes "glued" shut. She had to bathe them with warm water before she could even open them.

When she pushed her face up to the mirror, they appeared worse, if that was possible. She went directly to the phone and called the doctor's answering service.

"Please have Dr. Strong call me as soon as possible. I *must* speak to him." That sounded emphatic enough. I've given that old coot plenty of my money through the years, especially when the children were young. I deserve special consideration.

About a half-hour later, the phone rang.

"Hello."

"Mrs. Winberry, this is Dr. Strong. What's the problem?"

"Oh, I'm so glad you called. I have a terrible case of conjunctivitis. My eyes are red and swollen and I can barely see, and they itch like crazy, I am a supernumerary at the opera, and tomorrow is the dress rehearsal." She took a deep breath.

"Whoa," he said. "Slow down. Let me think a minute. I want you to see Dr. Ambrose. He's an ophthalmologist friend of mine and can patch you up a lot faster than I can."

"That's great. I need instant results."

"I'll call him and tell him you need to be seen today. He owes me a favor. His office is downtown. If you call about ten, I'll have contacted him by then. Here's the number. Let me know if there's anything else I can do."

"Thanks loads." Emma wrote down the address and phone number and squinted at the clock. She couldn't call for another two hours. So she lay down with a cold compress over her eyes and listened to the CD of *A Masked Ball* again.

# Chapter 40

At noon Emma stood on the platform waiting for the Metra train that would take her into Union Station in downtown Chicago. From there she could take a taxi to the doctor's office. The rain had stopped, that was a blessing, but when the sky cleared, the bright sunshine hurt her eyes and made her squint even more. Thank God for prescription sunglasses, she thought.

When the train came, Emma bought a round trip ticket and slipped the return in the pocket of her slacks. She sat back, closed her eyes, and tried to concentrate on the opera.

In the second act, Riccardo, the king, and Amelia, the wife of Renato, meet at midnight in a lonely spot where criminals are hanged. The conspirators appear in that scene, but it wasn't the right time for an assassination. No, she decided, the opportune moment was in the last act when Renato, the jealous husband, stabs the king. She was convinced that was Bruno Gentile's best chance to accomplish the deed.

From time to time she took off her glasses and gently dabbed her eyes with a tissue. She would love to rub them as hard as she could, but didn't dare.

About twenty minutes later the train arrived at Union Station, the end of the line. Emma moved with the flow of people hurrying along the platform. She was hesitant to walk too fast, because everything was a blur even with her sunglasses. She grabbed one of the pillars for balance.

"Lady," a voice said, "you look kinda unsteady. Can I help you?"

"That would be wonderful. I have an eye infection and I can't see very well. If you take me to the cab stand, I would be very grateful."

"Sure." The young man took her arm and led her along.

Emma was thankful for the help. She could just make out that he was a young man with rather long hair and a shabby jacket, but it didn't ring a bell.

At that moment a crowd of teenagers heading for the exit jostled Emma. The young man tightened his grip on her arm.

"Thanks," she said.

"Can you see that doorway over there?" he asked.

"Yes, I can make that out."

"Cabs are lined up out there."

Emma turned to thank him again, but he was gone. Oh, I was going to give some money to that nice fellow. She reached for her purse—gone! Oh God, what a fool I am! She leaned against the wall and held her head. I was a sitting duck just waiting to be plucked.

"Are you okay, Ma'am?"

She saw a man in a blue uniform standing in front of her. "My purse was stolen."

He led her to a chair where she told him the whole story.

"How much money did you have?" he asked.

"About fifty dollars. But it's all my identification that I'm concerned about, and my keys. I have to get to the doctor. What time is it?"

"It's twelve forty-five, Ma'am. Come to the office and we'll fill out a report. Can I call somebody for you?"

"No, there isn't time. Just point me in the right direction and I'll be fine," she lied. "I must make my appointment. I'll fill out the report on my way back."

The guard shook his head and escorted Emma outside. "Walk two blocks straight ahead, then turn right, and walk another two blocks. Are you sure you can make it? I should get you a cab."

"That would be great, but I have no money and no credit cards. I'll be all right. Thank you."

She began to walk with more confidence than she felt, keeping close to the buildings. At that point she almost wished for a white cane.

*All right, Guardian Angel, you haven't been doing much of a job lately, so get me to the doctor's office. Where were you when that fellow stole my purse? Goofing off, I suppose.*

"Do you need some help?" a voice asked.

He must have seen me muttering to myself. "No thank you, I'm fine." Of course, she didn't have anything else to steal, but she wasn't taking any more chances.

Her Guardian Angel made up for neglecting her welfare and got her to the doctor's office without further incident.

"I have an appointment with Dr. Ambrose, Emma Winberry," she said to the woman behind the desk.

"Fill out this form and I'll need your insurance card."

"First of all," Emma said, "I can't see to fill out the form, and secondly, my purse was just stolen at Union Station with all my identification, insurance, and credit cards." At this point Emma wanted to sit down and cry.

The woman looked up and shook her head. "We have to have payment at the time of your appointment. That's our policy." She folded her hands and looked directly at Emma.

"But these are extenuating circumstances," Emma insisted. "I must see Dr. Ambrose, today."

"I'm sorry," the woman said. "I can give you another appointment." The woman began turning the pages of a huge ledger.

"No!" Emma stamped her foot. "Ask Dr. Ambrose. He spoke to my physician, Dr. Strong, this morning. I insist!"

The other patients in the waiting room were staring and whispering. Emma didn't care. She stood firm.

The woman frowned and picked up the phone. She spoke to the doctor explaining the situation, then turned to Emma. "He said we can send you a bill. Give me your name and address." Her attitude told Emma she was in the wrong line of work. "Have a seat over there."

Emma turned toward the waiting area filled with people, some wearing eye patches, others with dressings over their eyes. Emma hoped that more than one doctor shared this waiting room.

After an hour and a half, she was called into an examining room. "Mrs. Winberry, Dr. Strong told me you are appearing in the opera and have a serious problem," a rotund, short, bald-headed man said entering the room. "I'm Dr. Ambrose. I'm sorry if my receptionist gave you a hard time. She sometimes gets carried away."

"Thank you for seeing me on such short notice, Doctor. I'm a supernumerary, an extra, in the opera. Tomorrow is the dress rehearsal and my eyes are in terrible condition."

"Let's take a look. Please take off your glasses."

He turned an examining light to Emma's face. The glare made her flinch.

"Hm, you have a bad case of conjunctivitis. Let me culture some of this exudate." He took a swab, touched it to the inner aspect of Emma's eye, and pushed it down into a test tube.

"What have you been doing for this?"

"Bathing with boric acid solution, wet compresses, and using some drops the pharmacist gave me, a salt solution. Oh dear, it was in my purse that was stolen."

"You are having a rough time. No matter. I'll give you something to fix this. First I'll put some corticosteroid drops in your eyes to decrease the inflammation. Hold still, these may burn."

He put two drops in each eye. Emma jumped at the sensation, but the relief was almost immediate.

"That does help the itching," she said.

"Yes. I'll give you a prescription for the drops. Use them four times a day for two days, then twice a day. I'll also give you a prescription for one of the new antibiotics in ointment form to use. Are you allergic to anything?"

"Not to my knowledge," Emma answered. "When can I wear my contacts?"

"Not until I see you again. Come back on Monday. Here are your prescriptions, and good luck at the opera." With that he walked out the door.

Emma's eyes did feel better and her vision was clearer, but without her contacts, she would be virtually blind onstage. What could she do? Depend on Nate. He did seem a little more suspicious of Gentile. She made another appointment, put on her sunglasses, and left.

She walked to Union Station as quickly as she could; at least she had her return ticket in her pocket. It was getting late and the trains would be filled with commuters.

Emma waited impatiently with the weary crowd. Anxious to get home, they pushed and jostled her onto the train. She flopped into the first seat she saw, but she couldn't relax. Now what all did I have in my wallet? Two credit cards, drivers license, insurance cards. What else? Oh yes, and my checkbook.

She had recently read an article about identity theft. Did she have her social security card in her purse? She thought she took it out, but wasn't sure. With her social security card and all that other information a thief could easily become Emma Winberry. She held her head in her hands wallowing in self-pity.

By the time she finally got off the train in Brookfield, it was after five. She went directly to the drug store and left the prescriptions and trudged home, exhausted. The pharmacist promised to have the medications delivered as soon as possible. Emma remembered she was supposed to fill out a report at the security desk at Union Station. She would call them and give them the information over the phone.

She was completely deflated as she rang Maria's doorbell. When the motherly woman answered, Emma practically fell inside.

"What's the matter?" Maria asked with a look of alarm.

"Don't get too close to me, I have an eye infection." She plopped into a plastic covered armchair, listening to the slow squish as the air was displaced. Then she told her friend the whole sad story.

Maria sat on the sofa shaking her head, slapping her face with her hands, and making the sign of the cross. "The *malocchio*," she said with authority when Emma finished the story.

Emma nodded. Who was she to disagree? "I'll need my extra set of keys. It's a good thing I gave them to you in case of an emergency."

"Now you gotta have all the locks changed," Maria said.

"Yes, and I have to call the credit card company, the license bureau, the insurance company—all those places." Emma shook her head and wailed. It was too much.

When she opened her own door, she could just make out the blinking light on her answering machine. She depressed the button and heard Nate's voice.

"Emma, where are you? How are your eyes? Call me as soon as you get in."

The next message was also from Nate, a repeat of the first. But the third was from the security office at Union Station. They had recovered her purse in a trashcan right outside. The money, of course, was gone, but all the identification and credit cards were intact. She called and thanked them profusely and said she would pick it up the next day at the security desk.

*Oh Guardian Angel, thank you. That saves me all kinds of grief.* She threw herself on the bed and cried with relief.

# Chapter 41

"So, are your eyes any better?" Nate asked.

"A little," she said, holding the phone in one hand and pouring coffee with the other. "They're not itching as much and the redness is beginning to clear up. I can't wear my contacts yet. That means I'm practically blind."

It was the morning of the dress rehearsal. The dancers and chorus members were supposed to be at the Performing Arts Center by one. The performance started at two, but since Emma and Nate were not on stage until the last act, they were not required to be there that early.

"Don't worry," he said. "I'll take care of you, won't let you walk off the stage."

His laughter irritated her. "Listen," she said. "You're going to have to watch Gentile for any suspicious moves."

He hesitated a moment then blew out his breath. "Nothing is going to happen, Mrs. Sleuth, but I will watch him."

"If nothing happens, that's fine. But what if something does? What if, when Renato stabs the king, Gentile also stabs him, with some sort of glass dagger? Those dreams mean something, I'm certain of that. I know you think I'm crazy, but humor me, please. What harm can it do?" Emma realized how theatrical she sounded. Silence from the other end of the line. "Nate, are you still there?"

"I'm here."

"Promise you'll watch, please."

"I said I would," he sighed. "Now, do you want me to pick you up?"

"No, I'll take the train. I have to stop at the security office at Union Station to pick up my purse."

"What about the locksmith?" Nate asked.

"He just left. That cost me a bundle."

"It could have cost your life. I'll see you later, and, be careful."

Emma decided to soak in the tub for a while. She wished she were in Nate's Jacuzzi, but she would have to make do with her old fashioned tub. She poured in some herbal salts guaranteed to promote relaxation, then leaned back in the warm water and thought about last night's dream. She hadn't mentioned it to Nate. He would think she had really gone round the bend.

*The opera starts. Emma is on stage standing behind the two conspirators. "I want to kill him," one of them says. "I shall sink the knife into his side."*

*She looks at the man. He is Bruno Gentile.*

*It is the second act and the king and Amelia are singing a heartbreaking duet under the gallows. Suddenly there is a splintering sound and the wooden structure topples over on top of Marcantonio Speranza. Blood spurts from his head and drips off the stage into the orchestra pit.*

Emma shook, even though she was submerged in warm water. This was another warning, she knew it.

But what could she do when she could barely see? No one believed her. Speranza had discounted her warning. She decided to inch as close to Gentile as possible in the last act, even though she was supposed to be at the rear of the stage with the crowd of guests at the ball. He wouldn't recognize her; she would be masked, like everyone else. No one would pay attention to her, except Nate, and she wasn't sure what to do about him, yet.

Emma arrived at the Center for the Performing Arts about one-thirty to find Nate waiting for her at the entrance.

"Hi," he said taking her arm, "I see you made it all right."

"As long as I can wear my sunglasses, I'm okay. It's when I take them off that I'll be in trouble." She gave him a reassuring hug.

"Got your purse?"

"Right here, with all the IDs and cards that we don't seem to be able to live without these days." She held up her handbag triumphantly.

"Let's get some tea," he said, maintaining a firm grip on her arm.

"All right, but I want to watch the second act."

"Any particular reason?"

"I like the music." She gave him an innocent smile.

"Why don't I believe you?"

"Just keep an eye on Gentile."

He nodded as they walked into the community room and headed for the back table where coffee, hot water, and tea bags were always available.

They could hear the music and muted singing as

the opera began. The first act concluded without a glitch. Oscar the page, always played by a woman, had a beautiful coloratura voice that did justice to the difficult role. Speranza was superb and the audience applauded wildly. The stage director sat back nodding with approval at the success of the production.

As the curtain went up on the second act, Emma inched her way to the wings making sure to stay clear of the stagehands and singers. She still wore her prescription sunglasses so her vision was fairly acute. Nate followed right behind her.

They listened as Amelia and Riccardo sang their lovely duet, Speranza's voice a delight to the ear.

With those words, as they declared their love for one another, Emma heard a cracking sound from the gallows. She looked up in horror as the crossbeam of the wooden structure toppled off the base and fell onto the stage narrowly missing the two singers. Just like my dream!

Finelli screamed as Speranza grabbed her and pulled her away. The curtain came down to shouting and gasps from the audience. Stagehands rushed to the scene and pulled the singers to safety. Emma looked for Gentile. Was that him at the rear of the stage? She wasn't sure.

Emma and Nate moved out of the way but stayed in the wings watching the melee.

"Who is responsible for this?" Speranza yelled, his face livid with rage. "I could have been killed!"

"You," shouted the diva. "It fell inches away from me! All you think about is yourself, you miserable selfish creature."

"And who would support your weak voice, if not for me?" he asked.

"Oh!" She shouted in frustration. "I'll get even with you yet!" She stomped off the stage muttering obscenities in Italian.

Emma's eyes widened as she understood the words. Was she planning to do harm to the tenor? Nate simply rolled his eyes and shrugged his shoulders. The stagehands scurried about examining the structure to try and figure out what had happened.

The stage manager went out in front of the curtain and held up his hands to quiet the audience. "Ladies and gentlemen, if you will bear with us for a time, the performance will resume shortly. No one was injured in this unfortunate incident. We will continue without the gallows onstage." The audience applauded and sat back eagerly awaiting the next scene.

When Nate and Emma returned to the community room, she told him about her dream. "Do you call that coincidence?"

"As a matter of fact, I do. Do you think for one minute you were given a warning by some supernatural power?"

"Yes!" She was furious that no one would believe her.

"Go tell that to the stage manager and see what he thinks," Nate said.

Emma sat quietly without saying another word. When it was time to get into her costume, she stood up and walked to the dressing room without looking at Nate.

When the curtain went up on the last act, Emma stood in her place beside Nate. The setting was a sumptuous ballroom with crystal chandeliers hanging from the ceiling and a ballet troupe ready to dance. The women wore the opulent gowns of the eighteenth century. The guests all wore masks. Emma's vision, without her glasses, was poor, and the mask further limited her field of vision. She had no choice but to let Nate lead her onstage. She tried to make out Gentile, but the scene around her was nothing but a blur.

In the last scene, when Renato stabs the king, she strained to see anyone else close to him. The dancers were a few feet away and she could just make out two shadowy figures upstage, but nothing more.

When the curtain came down to riotous applause and "Bravos," Emma breathed a sigh of relief. Maybe this was all her wild imagination. But then—maybe it wasn't. There was still opening night.

# Chapter 42

In the apartment on Taylor Street, Bruno paced from one end of the tiny room to the other. What if someone saw him? What if he was caught and sent to jail? What would happen to his mother and Angelo? They depended on him. No, he must not be seen, and, most important, he must not be caught.

But what about the *strega* he had seen at the Lyric? He didn't believe in that superstitious nonsense, but he made the sign of the cross anyway. How did she know so much about him? Is it a sign? Am I doing the right thing? Maybe I should go home and marry Francesca. He pondered that for a long time. No, family honor must come first.

He put all thoughts of the witch out of his mind and went over his plan, but there was no way he could get close enough to Speranza in the last act without being noticed. A diversion of some kind, that's what he needed.

He thought about it for a long time, discarding one idea after another. Suddenly he smiled. It was so simple. He knew exactly what he could use and where to find it.

Bruno took his prize from the closet; carefully unpacked it and gazed at the sparkling object. He held it up to the light. The glassmaker's art was indeed masterful, the blade so thin that the light shone right through it. All he had to do was plunge it into Speranza and twist off the hilt. The sharp glass would slide into his belly and shatter—no blood, no mess, only the screaming while Bruno quietly slipped away, unobserved.

Oh *Dio*, I know You are guiding my hand to avenge my sister, he silently prayed. It will work, it has to. He wrapped the weapon in a sock and placed it under the clothes he intended to wear to the performance. Then he made his way downstairs into the dark, damp basement.

# Chapter 43

Crowds of people milled about at the entrance to the Performing Arts Center, chattering and laughing, eagerly waiting for the doors to open. The house had been sold out weeks ago, but some hopefuls begged at the box office for any returned tickets.

Sylvia had to pull several strings to get one for Maria. The wife of one of the VIPs was ill and Jim Greene had wheedled the ticket out of him with a promise to introduce him to Marcantonio Speranza.

Sylvia picked up Emma and Maria and drove them downtown. Maria wore a new black a-line dress that complimented her generous figure. Around her neck hung a long gold chain with an antique locket nestling between her ample breasts. She even had her luxurious gray hair done at the local beauty salon in a very becoming style.

Before they left, Sylvia skillfully applied a little blush and eye shadow. "Maria, you look lovely," she said.

The woman admired her reflection in the full-length mirror, turning three hundred and sixty degrees. "Not too bad, huh? Maybe I find a boyfriend, too."

Emma smiled but found it impossible to feel festive. Her gut told her something would happen tonight.

After she parked the car, Sylvia escorted Maria to her seat with the promise that she would come and get her after the performance.

Emma waved to them both and went backstage. An air of excitement permeated the place. She heard singers vocalizing as well as members of the orchestra tuning their instruments. Stagehands ran about calling to each other and adjusting the props for the first act.

Off to one side Emma saw the gallows. She could see reinforcing strips across the top and down the middle. There was no way it was going to fall at this performance.

She went to the community room looking for Nate. She had been cool toward him ever since the dress rehearsal and wanted to make amends.

A group of singers from the chorus came in and headed for a table filled with individual bottles of spring water kept at room temperature. One man stood apart from the others. He was in costume and full makeup. He took a generous gulp of water, swished it around, and swallowed. As if feeling her gaze, he turned and stared at Emma suspiciously. His eyes narrowed and seemed to say, *keep your distance.*

With a shiver, Emma met Bruno Gentile's stare. Did he recognize her? No, he couldn't see her eyes through the dark glasses. Even though he couldn't see it, she was also sending *him* a message.

"Emma," Nate called.

She turned toward the voice, and when she looked back, Gentile was gone.

"How are you tonight, Sparrow?"

"Nervous."

He nodded. "Your eyes?"

"Much better, but I still can't wear my contacts." She wanted to remind him of his promise, but thought better of it.

"Was that Gentile who just walked out of here?" Nate asked.

"Yes. He certainly sends out bad vibes."

"Don't worry, I'll watch him, just like I promised." He slipped his arm around her and kissed her cheek.

"You're a dear man, Nate," she said. "Thanks for humoring me. I see they fixed the gallows," she said pouring hot water over tea bags.

"I talked with one of the stagehands," Nate said, stirring in three spoonfuls of sugar. "He said the screws holding the top piece came loose."

Emma nodded. "I saw the reinforcing bars. How do they think that happened?"

"Probably in transit. It didn't appear to be tampered with. They're calling it an unfortunate accident."

"Too many unfortunate accidents," she muttered.

Nate sipped the tea with a loud slurp. Emma frowned.

"It's hot," he said, tweaking her under the chin.

They heard the muted sound of applause as the conductor stepped to the podium and the opera began.

Emma squeezed Nate's hand as she listened to Verdi's powerful music.

"You're interrupting my circulation," he said.

"Sorry. I'm just nervous."

"About going on stage?"

"Uh huh. I'm afraid I'll trip." She tried to laugh.

"You still think Gentile will try something, don't you?" He shook his head.

"I can't help it, Nate. I can feel it. It's so real to me." She felt goose bumps rise on her arms as she got up from her chair and paced back and forth. A few other supers trickled in as well as a number of the chorus members.

"Boy, the place is packed," one of the supers said. "Did you see the article in today's paper about the near miss at yesterday's rehearsal?"

Emma shook her head.

"Well, the reporter somehow heard about the tiff between Speranza and Finelli. Everyone who read it will be watching them during the love duet in the second act." She took a bottle of water and walked away.

"Opera singers are always quarreling," Nate said. "It doesn't mean anything."

"I hope they can at least pretend to care about each other," Emma said. "I remember a performance of *Manon Lescaut* where the tenor and the soprano hated each other. They weren't good enough actors to hide it from the audience. Reviews of that performance were poor. Come to think of it, I don't think those two ever sang together again."

She got up from her chair. "I can't sit here another minute. I'm going to watch from the wings until they shoo me away."

Reluctantly Nate followed her. He would keep his promise to watch Gentile, but, at the same time, keep his eye on Emma; he wasn't sure what to expect from her.

*In scene two of act one, the fortune teller, Ulrica, is making predictions. The king, disguised as a fisherman, goes to her den where he decides to have his fortune told. She tells him he is in danger, but he laughs it off. It is a dark scene filled with fore-*

*boding and foreshadows the tragic outcome.*

Emma watched as the conspirators mingled with the chorus. She watched Gentile, but he remained aloof. The scene ended without incident.

Act Two began. The reinforced gallows stayed in place. Speranza and the diva sang extremely well together, no apparent signs of animosity. Finelli was a superb actress as well as a fine singer. She hid her dislike of the tenor very well.

At the end of the act, Emma and Nate went to the dressing rooms to get into their costumes for act three, scene two. Emma kept her glasses on until the last minute.

"You're going to have to take those off," the makeup artist said. "They didn't wear specs at the masked ball."

"I know." Emma removed her glasses and put them carefully into the case. The world became a blurred haze. She squeezed her eyes shut for a minute, then opened them. It was a little better.

"Let's get started," the makeup woman said as she smeared foundation over Emma's face and neck. Then she proceeded with powder and blush and put a little star on Emma's chin.

"Go easy on the eye makeup," Emma said. "I'm just getting over conjunctivitis."

"Since you'll be wearing a mask, we'll skip the eyes," the woman said. "There, a little lipstick and you're done. Next . . ."

Emma vacated her seat and groped her way to the dressing room. One of the other supers graciously helped her into her costume. It had been taken in to fit Emma's sparse figure. The stays in the tight blue bodice gave her a somewhat busty look, enhancing the effect of her padded bra.

A number of petticoats held the heavy brocade away from her feet, but, for some reason, there was a petticoat missing tonight and the skirt was not as puffy as it should be. Emma fluffed it out, but didn't notice that the back dragged on the floor.

"Oh Guardian Angel," she whispered walking out of the dressing room, "please help me. You know as well as I that something is amiss. Since no one else will believe me, it will be up to you and me to prevent a disaster."

"Who are you talking to?" Nate asked coming up behind her.

"No one. Just muttering to myself like an old fool."

"Well you certainly look like a beautiful one."

"You look pretty good yourself," she said, getting up close and squinting.

"You're just saying that because you can't see me." He laughed as he took her arm. "You're trembling, Sparrow. Are you all right?"

"I'm fine, just stage fright."

Before the curtain went up on scene two of the last act, the chorus and supers took their places onstage. Crystal chandeliers sparkled with electric candles. A rich-looking sideboard draped with lace sported a candelabra at each end. Along the center stood sparkling goblets and decanters filled with colored liquids. Marble-like columns lined the back wall.

"Can you see Gentile?" Emma asked Nate as they took their places.

He looked around, but everyone was masked. "I don't see him, but I can't be sure. I think he comes on later."

Enthusiastic applause for the conductor and the orchestra — the music began — the curtain went up.

"Guardian Angel, don't neglect your job," Emma muttered. She couldn't stop trembling as she and Nate moved slowly across the stage exchanging nods with other players.

"There he is now," Nate whispered as two figures dressed in black and wearing red neckerchiefs stepped onstage partially concealed by one of the pillars. Renato, dressed in similar attire, came toward them.

*Renato says he doesn't think the king will show himself.*

Gentile furiously sings:
*Once more he has escaped.*

To Emma he seemed to spit out the words more vehemently than necessary.

*In an exchange with the page, Renato discovers what costume the king is wearing and recognizes him.*

*The dancers waltz around in a short ballet. Downstage, the king and Amelia meet and she tells him he is in danger. Again he says he is sending her and Renato away so she will be free of their illicit love. As long as she is near, he will be tormented.*

Emma inched forward, watching the panorama around her; everyone seemed to be moving in slow motion; they almost looked mechanical.

"Where are you going?" Nate whispered. "We're supposed to stay back here."

She paid no attention to him but kept inching as close to Speranza as she dared. The blood pounded in her ears; her limbs felt heavy; the entire scene took on a surreal look. Emma couldn't get near enough to see either the king or Gentile.

Off to one side two dancers did a Harlequin pantomime; jesters walked along playing lutes, followed by a group of dancers dressed as peasants. The music filled the auditorium growing toward the final crescendo. Emma crept closer attempting to orient herself. It was now or never.

As Renato began to approach the king and Amelia, Gentile reached into his pocket and removed a brown furry creature. Unobserved he placed it on the floor and shoved it with his foot.

The mouse squeaked and ran under the skirt of one of the singers. She gasped and ran toward center stage bumping into Emma and knocking her mask askew. Now Emma was completely blind. She tried to straighten the mask, but had difficulty maintaining her balance. She reached out, grasping at thin air, but was knocked from one chorister to another. One of them stepped on the hem of her gown throwing her further off balance. As she tried to right herself, Emma pushed her mask to the side. She saw a figure in black inching up behind Renato.

As Renato stabbed the king, Gentile reached out. Emma saw a glint of light and, with all the strength she could muster, threw herself against the bass.

"*Figlia de Putana*!" he swore as the dagger slashed across his arm and fell to the floor shattering, the sound muted by the orchestra. He shoved Emma so hard she fell across the prostrate body of the king who was valiantly attempting to sing over the commotion.

"Ugh," Speranza muttered. "What the hell?"

Oscar, the page, came running to the king and knelt behind his head as Speranza sang:

*"Do not fear, I am still your ruler."*

"Don't move," he told Emma under his breath, glaring at her. She knelt beside him opposite the page, her hands covering her face in shame. Oh God, she had ruined the performance and no one would ever believe what really happened.

*"Tutti assolve il mio perdono* . . . Speranza sang, granting pardon to all.

As the page lifted Speranza's left shoulder, she signaled to Emma to lift the right side.

*"Addio per sempre, o figli miei . . . per sempre addio,"* the king sang his goodbye with his dying breath.

The curtain descended to thunderous applause.

"Oh Signore Speranza, I'm so sorry," Emma said. "I tried to warn you. Someone was trying to kill you! He had a dagger!"

"You!" Speranza spat. "The crazy woman, backstage. Of course he was trying to kill me. That's part of the opera." The tenor sputtered and fumed.

As the principals went out and took their bows, Emma slowly retreated to the wings where Nate took her in his arms.

"Oh Nate—I ruined the last scene." She sobbed uncontrollably.

"Sh," he said. "It's all right. Those things happen. A mouse ran onstage from somewhere throwing everyone off kilter, and besides, you couldn't see." He tried to rationalize her erratic behavior without success.

"No," she said sobbing. "It was Gentile. He had a glass dagger. Didn't anyone see it?"

Nate looked down at her, slowly shaking his head.

The singers retired to their dressing rooms to take off their costumes and makeup animatedly discussing the strange circumstances surrounding the last act.

The stagehands swept debris off the floor. One of them noticed glass fragments, puzzled for a moment, then seeing that one of the goblets had fallen from the table and broken, he shrugged. He ignored the droplets of a dark liquid that stained the floor as he swept up the glass fragments and dumped them in the dustbin along with half-eaten sandwiches, orange peels, and one trampled mouse.

# Chapter 44

Emma sat in James' office groaning, her head in her hands. Nate stood beside her uttering consoling words.

"It's not as bad as you think, Emma," James said trying to ease her discomfort. "From the audience's perspective, the mouse wasn't even seen, just some commotion upstage." He leaned back in his chair and took a large gulp from the glass in his hand that held more than water.

"And as for what happened next, well, that was an unfortunate chain of events. People bumped into one another and you lost your balance and fell over Speranza's body."

She winced at his words. She knew he was just trying to make her feel better. "James," she said, "that's not what happened."

"I know," he said. "You claim Bruno Gentile had a glass dagger, or something."

"He did! I saw it!" Emma knew how ridiculous that sounded. "And I think he cut himself, but I couldn't see well."

James frowned. "When the stage manager examined the stage he did find some stains on the floor, but they could be anything." He leaned forward and took Emma's hand. "Look, I'm sure you *thought* you saw something. Didn't you tell me that you had an eye infection and weren't wearing your contact lenses?"

Emma nodded. She took a deep breath. She was beginning to have doubts herself. Maybe it *was* her imagination. Could it have been a reflection off the paste jewelry everyone wore?

"But," James continued taking another generous swallow from his glass, "just to be on the safe side, we have called in the police. They'll be here shortly to take your statement."

Emma knew that he was covering all bases. He couldn't let even a questionable attempt on Speranza's life go undocumented. It did make her feel a little better.

"I suppose my days as a supernumerary are over," she whispered staring at her hands.

"Not at all," James said. "You know, the whole thing looked staged. If anything, it added a bit of drama. Let's see what the critics have to say."

At that moment Sylvia, with Maria in tow, came into the office. "Mom, what in the world happened? Are you all right?"

"I'll explain everything later," Emma said. "Right now, I have to talk to this policeman."

An officer and a plainclothes man had walked into the office. "I'm Detective Schmidt and this is Officer Simmons. Who's in charge here?"

"I'm James Greene and this is Emma Winberry, the super who was involved in the—disturbance," James said draining his glass.

"Okay, what happened?" the detective asked Emma, scowling.

She took a deep breath and slowly recapped the events of the last scene. The detective scribbled a few notes and shook his head. He sent the officer to examine the stage and interview Speranza.

When the officer returned, Emma saw him raise his eyebrows and shake his head. "The singer didn't see anything but there are stains on the floor. We'll call in a forensics team to test them for blood."

"Mrs. Winberry," Detective Schmidt said, "I know what you *thought* you saw, but unless the stains are blood, there is no other evidence to corroborate your testimony." He gave a sigh of frustration.

"Look," Emma said, "I know what I saw, but since nobody believes me, I'm sorry I wasted your time." With her head held high, she got up from her chair and began walking toward the door.

"Just a minute," the detective said, "don't be in such a hurry. Since Mr. Speranza is such a high profile entertainer we'll send someone over to ask this Gentile a few questions and see if he's been injured. That way, if anything should happen in the future, our report will be on file."

At that moment a knock at the door heralded the entrance of Rosa Finelli. She walked in, head held high, her demeanor that of royalty.

"Signora," James said, "May I help you?"

"I came to tell you that I saw something suspicious onstage in the last act. The director didn't believe me, so I came straight to you."

All eyes turned to the soprano. She stood for a moment as if she were at a performance.

She looked at Emma and grinned. "I did enjoy watching you pounce on Speranza. I only wish you were heavier." She turned her attention to James. "One of the conspirators had something in his hand — something shiny, and I saw what looked like blood on his sleeve."

Emma held her breath. She wasn't the only one; it wasn't her imagination. Her eyes met Finelli's and the soprano nodded.

"Where were you standing?" the detective asked.

She turned to him with a disdainful look. "I was with the crowd of fools who let a mouse upset the performance." She gave him a look that said, don't you dare doubt my words.

"Thank you, Signora," James said. "That verifies what Mrs. Winberry saw. We're grateful to you for reporting it."

"I dislike Signor Speranza as a person," she continued, "but I wish him no harm. His voice is a God-given gift and it must be protected."

"We'll need statements from both you ladies," the detective said.

Finelli nodded and walked out of the office.

"Thank you," Emma said. "When can I go home?"

"Give this officer your statement and then you're free to go."

A figure in a long coat with a hat pulled down over his eyes and clutching his left arm, mingled with the crowd at the stage door.

"Dad, I can't see. Pick me up, please."

Bruno saw a man lift his son in his arms to enable him to see the famous singer. The boy reminded him of Angelo. He shook his head as he watched the father hold the boy lovingly in his arms. What am I trying to do? I must be mad. Am I willing to ruin my life and Angelo's, too? *Dio,* I asked for guidance and this is where You brought me? I could have done it if it hadn't been for that woman. Maybe it's better this way. Did Your hand direct her? He was filled with self-doubt and confusion.

The crowd cheered and jostled attempting to get closer as the renowned tenor came through the door flanked by two policemen and his manager. The officers made a path through the shouting fans as Speranza waved and was pushed into the waiting limousine. Bruno frowned. Police. So a report *had* been made. They would surely want to talk to him. He shook his head, turned and disappeared into the night.

# Chapter 45

"Bruno, what are you doing?" Gerard asked, staring at his friend in alarm. "What is that bandage on your arm?"

"What does it look like? I'm packing, getting out of here." He hastily threw his clothing into the old suitcases.

"I saw what you had in your hand," Gerard said moving in front of him, his arms folded across his chest. "You cut yourself, didn't you? Are you crazy?"

"No, just a man who wanted to avenge his family," he said with less assurance in his voice. "It would have worked, too, except for that clumsy woman." He snapped the suitcase closed with a loud pop.

"And you would have gone to jail. No way you could have got away with that. That woman was your savior. Maybe she was sent from *Dio* to keep you from making a terrible mistake. But I don't think anybody else saw," Gerard said. "Otherwise the police would be here by now."

"That *strega* said something. I saw police escorting Speranza to his car." Bruno stared at his friend. "Soon they will come here."

"Bruno, why are you ruining your life like this?" Gerard paced, his hands clasped behind his back. "Hate will destroy you. Let it go." He put his hands on Bruno's shoulders. "I've know you for a long time, my friend. You are a good man. Promise me you won't do anything else that might get you in trouble." He looked deep into Bruno's troubled eyes.

"I don't know, maybe you're right. I'm all mixed up. I have to go back home where I belong. Everything goes too fast here. Sometimes I feel like I can't breathe." He sat down and took his head in his hands. His shoulders shook, but he made no sound.

Gerard sat next to his friend, and for a long while, neither one of them spoke.

"Do me a favor," Bruno said.

"Anything."

"If the police come asking questions, tell them you don't know where I am."

Gerard nodded.

A soft knock at the door. "Gerard, Bruno," called Amalia, "I bring you food."

Gerard opened the door to his cousin's wife laden with a tray of bread and cheese. "*Grazie,* Amalia."

"Eh, are you going away?" she asked looking at the suitcases, a pained expression on her face.

"Bruno must leave. His mother is very ill," Gerard said. Amalia made the sign of the cross and put her hands on Bruno's shoulders. "You two are like brothers to us. You were here when we needed you. We will miss you. *Buona fortuna.*" She kissed him on both cheeks and left the room, pressing the end of her apron to her eyes.

Bruno quietly finished packing, then placed some bills on the dresser.

"And what about the other performances?" Gerard asked. "Who is going to sing Tommaso?"

"They have plenty of singers in the chorus who

can sing that role. I'll send a telegram from the airport saying my mother is sick and I had to leave." He put his hand on Gerard's shoulder. "This is the way it must be, my friend. Tell your cousin goodbye for me."

"Will I see you again?" Gerard asked.

"Who knows. Maybe someday."

The two men embraced. Bruno winced as he slipped on his jacket, picked up the suitcases, turned to his friend, and, with a wry smile said, "God bless America." He ran down the stairs and out to the waiting taxi.

# Chapter 46

After a restless night Emma sat sipping her coffee, and eagerly scanned the morning paper. She smiled as she read the critic's review.

*Last night's performance of A Masked Ball by the Midwest Opera Company ended with a bit of excitement onstage. A mouse ran out among the ladies of the chorus causing a commotion.*

*But the drama of the last scene was enhanced by one of the supernumeraries falling over the prostrate body of the king. This added quite an impact as the woman wept over Marcantonio Speranza's dying words. The performance was enthusiastically received by the audience. Kudos to the stage director.*

Later that day, Emma received a call from George Ross.

"Mrs. Winberry, we've decided to incorporate your — extraordinary performance into the production, with a few modifications."

"Why is that?" Emma asked, feigning ignorance.

"Well, the critics thought it was a new twist to the usual predictable ending, you know, more dramatic. They characterized it as extremely moving. Signor Speranza has agreed, as long as you don't fall on top of him." He laughed nervously. "Can you be here an hour before the curtain so we can go over it?"

"Yes," Emma said. "I believe I can."

When she hung up the phone Emma threw her arms wide and danced around the room. All eyes would be on her and Speranza.

Then panic set in. What if I flub it? What if I lose my balance and fall on top of him again? She would certainly be laughed off the stage. No! She could do it right, and she would. "But tonight I *will* wear my contacts!"

She looked in the mirror. The redness was almost gone and her eyes no longer itched. Unable to contain her excitement, she grabbed the phone and dialed.

"Nate, guess what?"

"I wouldn't even venture to try," he answered.

"George Ross wants me to repeat my act for the rest of the performances. The critics loved it! What do you think?"

"I think it's fantastic. I saw the reviews in the newspapers and I talked to a few people in the audience. They thought it was staged that way, even brought tears to their eyes."

She heard the pride in his voice. "Oh Nate, I'm so happy. But what about Bruno Gentile?"

"I don't think you'll have to worry about him any more. He wouldn't be fool enough to try again."

"Then you do believe me."

"Well, let's just say, it's possible. And after you raised doubts in everyone's mind, he'll be closely watched."

"Is that crow you're eating?" she asked with a snicker.

"You might say that, and it doesn't taste very good. What time are you supposed to be at the Performing Arts Center?"

"An hour before the curtain goes up."

"I'll be there to cheer you on."

James called her into his office a soon as she entered the opera house. "I got a call from Detective Schmidt," he said smiling at her.

"And?"

"That was blood on the floor. When an officer went to the address where Gentile was staying, he wasn't there. The occupants claimed they had no idea where he was. That was obviously a lie, because later we received a telegram from Gentile. He was at the airport about to board a plane for Italy. Said he had a family emergency and wouldn't be returning."

Emma looked at him, an innocent expression on her face, enjoying the moment.

"So, you may have been right. I just wanted to tell you that if he should ever return to the United States, he will be held for questioning." He smiled and took her hand in his.

"Thanks James, that means a lot to me."

A few minutes later she was onstage with Speranza. Emma was surprised at how calm she felt repeating the instructions the stage manager gave. What a difference contact lenses make, she thought. When I can see, I can even think more clearly.

Marcantonio Speranza looked at her with some misgivings, a forced smile, a nod of his head.

Emma felt confident. "I won't let you down," she told him and George Ross. She had been right and she knew she could do this.

Before the curtain went up, the stage manager announced to the audience that Bruno Gentile was indisposed and Albert Marshall would sing the part of Tommaso.

As the time drew closer to the final scene, Emma grew more nervous. She began to hyperventilate; her head spun; her vision blurred.

"Stop it!" she commanded. She took three deep breaths holding them as long as she could, then slowly exhaled. In a few moments her head cleared and she was in control.

*Guardian Angel, are you here?* She felt a slight pressure on her shoulders. When she looked up, she saw no visible person. She smiled, secure in the knowledge that she would be watched over and helped, if necessary.

As the final scene approached, Emma and Nate took their places upstage with the chorus and dancers. As the drama progressed, Emma calmly made her way downstage, always keeping a reasonable distance from the king. She found herself studying the crowd of performers, looking for Gentile, even though she knew he wasn't there.

When Renato stabbed the king, she moaned and fell to her knees beside Speranza, weeping. As Oscar, the page, knelt beside him and raised one shoulder, Emma raised the other.

He sang his goodbye, pardoning everyone:

*"Tutti Assolve il mio perdono . . . ."*

As he raised his arm in farewell, he slowly let his hand drop into Emma's.

The curtain fell, the cheers and bravos deafening.

The curtain rose again as the principals took their bows. Speranza grabbed Emma's hand and led her to the front of the stage. Rosa Finelli joined them for another bow. She looked at Emma and smiled.

Emma looked over the sea of faces applauding and cheering. She curtsied and smiled at Speranza and Finelli.

Nate stood in the wings, a huge bouquet of roses in his arms. He pressed them to Emma with an embrace as she walked off stage.

"I'm so proud of you, Sparrow. You were wonderful."

"Was I, really? Oh, Nate, my lifelong dream has come true. Tonight I truly performed in the opera, something I've fantasized about as long as I can remember." All those daydreams about singing the leading roles, the audience cheering and shouting, 'Brava.' Kneeling at the footlights, catching bouquets of flowers. Tonight, even though she didn't sing, it all came true. She stood for a moment still feeling as if she were in a dream. She felt a warmth encircle her and a whisper in her ear, 'Brava.'

"Come on," Nate said pulling her back to reality, "Sylvia and James are waiting for us. We're going out to celebrate."

# Chapter 47

"All right, Nate, I have three pages written on the role of the supernumerary in opera to put in the book." Emma was excited and proud of herself as she led him into the study. He sat down at the computer and looked at the screen.

"It's coming along nicely," he said scrolling down and reading. He turned and looked at her, a grin on his face. "You know, even though I've been writing articles for investment journals for years, I've always wanted to write a book. I know we can do this together. It'll be fun."

Emma felt a huge burden lifted from her shoulders. "I knew you came into my life for a reason," she said, laughing.

"I hope that's not the only reason," he said winking at her. He looked at what she had written, pecked at a few keys, and began adding more text.

"Let's get the outline polished," Nate said, "and then we can e-mail it to Cornell."

Emma smiled and sighed. This might just work after all.

# Chapter 48
# Late May

Emma and Nate again sat in the Church of the Trinity. Flowers surrounded the plain altar. An arch covered with carnations and roses spanned the aisle where the bride and groom would exchange their wedding vows. The scent of incense filled the air mingling with the fragrance of the flowers. Refracted light shining through the stained glass windows shed a surreal look on the scene.

Next to Emma, Maria sat sniffling softly, her blue dress bulging across her bosom with each intake of breath, one hand clutching her rosary, the other, her handkerchief. Next to her sat Pat with little Susan jumping on her mother's knee, just old enough to be inquisitive about everything. Sylvia and James sat next to them, their three month old son, James Jr., sleeping peacefully in his mother's arms.

As the organ intoned the opening chords of the wedding march, Emma whispered a prayer, "Frank, I wish you were here to see your youngest son. He's made a good choice." But she knew he was there, could almost see him standing next to Martin who was nervously twitching at the altar.

Emma had worked for weeks making the two

bridesmaids dresses, a soft lavender colored silk with a hint of a sleeve, gracefully curved in at the waist, the skirts flowing softly around the ankles.

Bertie, who had become like a daughter to her, wore Emma's mother's gown of cream colored satin altered to fit her, the bodice covered with tiny beads, the skirt simple and straight. On her head Emma had fashioned a crown of baby's breath with a diaphanous veil falling to her shoulders. She carried a bouquet of yellow roses and baby's breath.

Tears sneaked down Emma's face as she looked at her lovely soon to be daughter-in-law. Nate took a tissue and gently wiped them away.

The priest intoned the wedding mass; Bertie and Martin exchanged their vows; the bridal party marched happily out of the church; and the crowd threw birdseed, wishing them well.

Outside the church relatives and friends surrounded the bridal party, talking and laughing. A robust woman came barreling toward Emma followed by a small retiring man. She held her arms wide, her bright flowered dress billowing out around her. A huge saucer shaped hat almost obscured her face.

"Emma," she crooned, making smacking sounds in the air.

"Nate, this is my sister, Clara," Emma said escaping from the smothering embrace. Nate stepped back and held out his hand. The woman's grasp made him wince.

"Hello, I'm Nolan, Clara's husband." The little man stepped out from behind his wife.

Nate shook his hand and Emma gave him a peck on the cheek.

"I'm working on a new play," Clara said. "This one

will far surpass the other." She stopped for dramatic effect. "The plot is a total surprise."

"Hm," Emma said. "I can hardly wait."

"And this time," Clara said poking her finger at Nate's chest, "you must come, too. I insist!"

Nate tried to smile and simply nodded.

"Now, to the bride and groom." Clara grabbed her husband and whisked him off.

"She certainly is a formidable woman," Nate said.

Emma nodded. "I told you she was weird."

After a simple brunch at a neighboring restaurant, Bertie tossed her bouquet. Her sister deftly caught it as the two women exchanged a wink and a smile.

Later that evening Emma felt exhausted but satisfied. Her children were happily establishing families of their own and she had Nate. She picked up the phone and called Gladys.

"I'm so sorry you couldn't make it to the wedding," Emma said. "It was simple, but beautiful."

"I'm sure it was. Everything is in a state of confusion here. Mattie, my oldest, is due any day. She's gone into false labor twice already. And Cornell is having problems with one of his writers. The man is not getting his revisions in on time. This business is all about deadlines." She let out a sigh and a groan.

"So where did the newlyweds go on their honeymoon?"

"A Hawaiian cruise," Emma said.

"And you and Nate are off to Italy?" Gladys asked, an envious note in her voice.

"Yes, next week. We're touring the northern part. He wants to show me the eternal city in all its grandeur."

"Have a great time and call me when you get back. And, by the way, Cornell loved the manuscript you sent. He'll be sending you the copy-edits soon. It was a great idea for you and Nate to collaborate. I can't wait to meet him. Let me know when you two will be coming for a visit. Bye for now, and have a great time."

A few months earlier Nate had handed Emma a brochure describing a tour to Italy. He said, "I'm going to take you to see the antiquities of Rome, the Sistine Chapel, the Vatican Museum and St. Peter's Basilica. Then we'll take a tour through Venice, Florence and Milan, where we'll hear *La Traviata* at the opera house, a stop in Verona with a concert in the outdoor arena, and . . ."

"Wait," Emma said feeling breathless. "How do we do all that in ten days?"

"Non-stop. We can stay as long as we wish. Those places I mentioned are part of the tour package. We don't have to return with the rest if we don't want to." He smiled, a mischievous gleam in his eye.

"This feels like a—honeymoon," Emma said.

"It could be, if you want it to." Nate looked at her, his eyes asking the question.

She turned away, unsure of herself. "I do love you, Nate, but I'm not sure if I'm ready to get married. Give me a little more time, one more holiday season in my home; then, I think I'll be ready for a change. And I want it to be with you." She gave him a beautific smile.

"I understand. Take your time, Emma, but just remember, it's an open invitation. Anytime you want to say yes, I'll be here." He took her hand in his. "Just to let you know, the building I live in has a sixth floor. The management is planning to redo the entire area into two condos. Each will have six rooms with an atrium and access to the roof. You can still grow as many plants as you like." He raised his eyebrows in a question.

"You make it sound very inviting," she said. "One more season here and then . . . ."

The next few days went by in a blur, the long plane ride, changing money into Euros, being whisked from one hotel to another, viewing church after church. Emma was glad to be settled in the massive open-air amphitheater in Verona, a light breeze blowing over the crowds of people. She looked up at the stars just beginning to show themselves in the approaching twilight.

At that moment the audience began to applaud as the conductor took his place on the podium. A boy's choir was first on the program. Their voices soared in a lovely hymn. Then one of the boys stepped forward. He was tall and thin with a head of dark curly hair, his face cherubic, beautiful and unblemished.

He began singing Gounod's "*Ave Maria.*" The only sound in the vast arena was that of a bird flying high overhead. Its call seemed to complement the child's voice, rising pure and strong straight to heaven.

The last Amen shimmered on the air, clear and ethereal. Not a sound. Then the entire audience rose to their feet shouting and applauding. The boy stepped forward, slowly took his bow, and stepped back to his place in the choir. But the audience would not let him go. They kept cheering until the concertmaster consented to an encore.

A chill ran through Emma as she looked at the program.

Solo: Angelo Gentile. She nudged Nate and pointed to the name, a question in her eye.

"It's a common name," he whispered.

As the boy began to sing again, Emma looked at the front row. She saw a man sitting between two women, one young and obviously pregnant, the other older. At the intermission while it was still light enough to see, she lifted her binoculars and scanned their faces. Bruno Gentile looked up and seemed to stare back at her.

So it *was* him. But why had Gentile harbored a vendetta against Marcantonio Speranza? Was he, perhaps, the boy's father? She would never know.

*"Let it go,"* her inner voice said. *"It has played out as it was meant to."*

Emma put down the glasses and shrugged.

# Epilogue

Emma opened the daily newspaper, his eyes resting on an article on the front page below the fold. The heading read:

*The famous tenor, Marcantonio Speranza underwent surgery for a tumor on one of his vocal chords. The doctors fear there is irreparable damage and his beautiful tenor voice may never return.*

*The divo was not available for an interview, but his manager said he will retire to his villa in Tuscany with his family.*

What a shame, that beautiful voice, so much promise. But, there certainly will be others to take his place.

Across the Atlantic Ocean Bruno Gentile also read the article. "*O Dio*, I have waited a long time for this, but in Your infinite wisdom, You have seen justice done."

He was a happy man. Francesca had presented him with a son, a healthy boy with a lusty cry. He smiled and thought about his future; he was in demand in both Naples and Milan. And Angelo's voice surpassed even Bruno's expectations. He could see crowds cheering and hailing the greatest tenor since Caruso—Angelo Gentile.

# About the Author

Helen Osterman lives in Homer Glen, a suburb of Chicago. She has five children and nine grandchildren.

She received a Bachelor of Nursing degree from Mercy Hospital-St. Xavier College and later earned a Master's Degree from Northern Illinois University. Throughout her forty-five year nursing career, she wrote articles for both nursing and medical journals.

She is the author of the Emma Winberry Mystery Series.

Helen has had a life-long love of opera and always wanted to be a supernumerary, an extra in the opera, but the demands of her profession and family left this dream unfulfilled. She has done this vicariously though her character, Emma Winberry.

*Emma Winberry and The Evil Eye* is the prequel to the Emma Winberry Mystery series published by Five Star.

*Notes in a Mirror,* a paranormal/historical, also published in 2009 by Weaving Dreams Publishing.

*Song of the Rails, a love story,* also by Weaving Dreams, came out in June, 2011.

Helen is a member of American Association of University Women, Mystery Writers of America, Sisters in Crime, and The Authors Guild.

Website: www.helenosterman.com

CPSIA information can be obtained at www.ICGtesting.com
Printed in the USA
BVOW04s0639211113

336841BV00010B/996/P

9 781937 148140